CW01551334

The Return

Angela Hartley

This book is a work of fiction. Names, places, characters and events are all based on the author's imagination or are used fictitiously. Any resemblance to actual persons, living or dead, or actual events is purely coincidental.

April 2025

Text copyright © Angela Hartley 2025
All rights reserved.

ISBN: 9798309774883

Acknowledgements

Special thanks to all those who have supported me throughout the process of writing and publishing The Return, and to Sophie Hartley for the design of the cover.

Also to Carol Marriott-Clayton, Roisin Robertson and Melanie Sibborn Kay for their invaluable support in the editing process.

This book is dedicated to all my friends in Tenerife, with thanks for all the happy times we have shared there, and the wonderful memories we have made. I hope my story does justice to the island we love.

Also by Angela Hartley

Finding Home	Published June 2022
Forever Home	Published October 2022
After the Rain	Published March 2023
The Godmothers	Published October 2023
The Dishonourable Groom	Published October 2024

Available to purchase or download from Amazon

The Return

Angela Hartley

Chapter 1

As Antonio said goodbye and hung up the phone, he struggled to keep the emotion from his voice. Silent tears began rolling down his cheeks. He sat on his side of the bed, his back to the bathroom door, and waited for the enormity of what he had just heard to fully hit him. The shock would kick in eventually. For now, though, he just felt numb.

"You were on the phone a long time." The admonishment in his wife's voice did not go unnoticed. "Anyway, I've finished now. You can use the bathroom, if you want." Charlotte walked back into their bedroom, fresh from her morning shower. Her shoulder length blonde hair was neatly tied up in a headwrap, with the fluffy white towelling dressing gown making her look as if she had just emerged from a luxury spa after a pampering session. Her skin was glowing, the application of a range of expensive cleansers, moisturisers and skin lotions having all done their job.

After the phone had rung and woken her, Charlotte had gone directly into their en suite, closing the door firmly shut behind her. She had no idea who the call was from, or what it was about. Worse still, she'd had absolutely no interest in hanging around to find out.

The Return

"It was a bit early for a work call, wasn't it?" she chided, as she continued to massage hand cream into the palms of her hands, admiring her latest manicure as she did. "Can't you tell them to wait until after eight o'clock, at least?" She was clearly unhappy to have been woken before her alarm had gone off.

It was still only six o'clock in the morning yet it was already light outside, with the birds merrily chirping away in the distance. The sun was steadily rising and it promised to be a beautiful summer's day, with temperatures forecast to rise into the mid 20s. London would be warm, and without any breeze it would become unbearable.

The alarm had been set for six-fifteen. So, as someone who liked her bed, the phone call had just cost her a good half hour's beauty sleep. Getting up this early did not come naturally to Charlotte. Nine o'clock was more her usual routine, followed by a leisurely breakfast and a trip to the gym, the hairdressers, or lunch with friends. As a stay at home wife, she did not like to tax herself too much. And she certainly did not want to put herself out, or get her hands dirty doing anything her daily would do for her! After all, that's what she was paid to do, was it not?

Anyway, she had decided she might as well get up and get a head start on the day. She had a busy one planned. A taxi was booked for ten o'clock to take her to Paddington railway station, to enable her to catch the train. It was no use wasting time in bed now that she was awake, and no use lying there trying to get back to sleep, especially with Antonio on the phone next to her, chatting away to one of his colleagues about some trivia, or other. She believed the call could have waited, blaming her husband for always making himself too available. The number of times she'd heard him say, "don't worry, just phone me any time, day or night if you need to," believing himself to be indispensable. It grated on her, with each time he said it, or each time they called, she seethed that bit more.

Charlotte approached her dressing table and began opening and slamming drawers shut, looking for suitable clothes for the day, plus a selection of underwear and other knickknacks to pack into her overnight bag. As she would be away for two nights, so needed to plan ahead, and as someone who normally didn't travel light, had to think carefully about what she packed.

"I was thinking of wearing my blue linen dress, although what it'll look like after nearly two hours on the train, in this heat, isn't worth thinking about. No, I'll wear the red one instead, as I'd originally thought. That always looks good on me. I'll pack the linen one for tomorrow daytime, or the day after, perhaps. What do you think?" she asked rhetorically, having already decided. Anyway, what did it matter to her husband what she wore? He rarely noticed, and as he would not be accompanying her this weekend, he probably cared even less. He had not even noticed the receipt for the evening gown she had bought for tomorrow's function, or the shoes that she could not resist to accompany it. It was almost a shame he would not be there when she was all glammed up, to witness the effect of all his money well spent.

"Antonio, are you listening to me? You've not said a single word since you put that phone down. I'm going away today. You have remembered, haven't you?" Charlotte was heading off for the weekend to meet friends in Bath. It was a reunion of sorts from her school days. The private girls' boarding school she had attended from the ages of eight to eighteen was having a black-tie centenary celebration on Saturday evening and some of the Old Girls had been invited to attend, along with their partners.

Charlotte was not particularly bothered by the school itself, nor the fact it was a hundred years since it had been established. She had quite fancied being holed up in a fancy hotel though, with the handful of girlfriends with whom she still kept in contact, and more so, since they had all decided to go without partners. They'd planned meeting up at lunchtime later that day for a boozy lunch and a girly catch up, followed by some retail therapy. Then on Saturday a visit to the hotel's spa had been planned for some treatments, before the main event that evening. She would then head home Sunday afternoon, after a brunch or potentially another spa treatment at the hotel, depending on her mood. It was certainly not coming cheap, but she believed she was worth it.

"Sorry, what did you say?" Antonio replied distractedly, as he became aware Charlotte's voice was droning on in the background.

"Have you not been listening to a single word I've said? For pity's sake, Antonio. What can be so important at the restaurant, at this ungodly hour, that they need to wake us up to tell you? If it's Philippe again, he seriously needs to get a life." Philippe, Antonio's business associate and one of his oldest friends, was a bit of an old woman in Charlotte's opinion. Not someone she had ever warmed to.

"No, it wasn't Philippe or the restaurant. It was my sister, Sofía. She was sorry to ring so early," he added, quietly.

Charlotte also didn't have a lot of time for either of Antonio's sisters. They were too provincial and frankly too plain for her liking. Over the six years she had known them, she had found no common ground between them and herself, whatsoever. Their lives differed on every conceivable level. Of the two sisters, Sofía, the eldest, was perhaps the lesser of the two evils. She was more easy going and largely kept herself to herself. Now approaching forty and still unmarried, she remained at home, helping her parents out on their finca, the rural farmland from where they operated their small business. The prospect of marriage, or her ever finding someone to love, appeared to be something the family had long since given up on.

Whereas Carmen, at thirty-seven and two years older than Antonio, was a different kettle of fish entirely. She was someone she really could not take to. Carmen, living in the middle of nowhere, surrounded by pigs and geese, with two screaming kids could be high maintenance. She was fiery, opinionated and hot tempered. There were endless problems between her and her husband, Juan. Problems that she repeatedly brought to Antonio's door, as she laid out all her woes to him. She was usually looking for his sympathetic ear, or more likely his money, both of which he provided, without question. Charlotte had seen enough evidence of money being wired over, something she presumed he thought she knew nothing about. No, theirs was not her idea of life.

"So, what did Sofía want? I presume everything's okay," she asked, this time more gently, in an attempt to get him to open up, as from his body language she could tell something in the call had upset him and the fact he had still not said a word was starting to worry her. After all, she had a train to catch, so could do with him getting straight to the point.

"No, not really. She phoned so say that my father slipped off the roof of one of the outbuildings yesterday evening, whilst repairing some storm damage. He landed badly and damaged his skull when he fell. They managed to get him to the hospital, but he didn't survive it. It appeared his heart wasn't strong enough to deal with the trauma. She was phoning to tell me he had died, and asked if I could come over." His response was factual, almost as if he was speaking on autopilot, as he tried to contain his emotions.

"Oh, Antonio, I'm so sorry." As Charlotte spoke there was a degree of sincerity evident in her voice. She walked over to her husband and sat down on the bed beside him, gently putting her arms around him as he sobbed into her shoulder. "Do you want me to come with you? I could cancel my weekend. I'm sure people will understand." The sharpness of her earlier remarks now toned down, as she cradled her husband.

"No, thank you, I should be fine. There's nothing you could do anyway. I'll go. I'll just need to sort a few things out at the restaurant first, then look for some flights.   And I'll need to let Yaya Theresa know. She's going to be devastated."

The reality of what had happened was just beginning to sink in, and he had real concern for how his grandmother would react once he broke the news to her. Theresa was his maternal grandmother, so whilst it was not her son who had died, he was the son of her oldest friend, his yaya Rosa, and there was no doubt she had loved him like a son too.

As he sat there in his wife's arms, Antonio could not get his mind straight. His father had only been in his late fifties. A fit and athletic man, with no history of heart problems or serious illness. He had only spoken to him the previous week, discussing repairs on the farmhouse that were planned for the coming weeks. For Antonio the shock was unimaginable, so what would Yaya think at the prospect of burying her son-in-law, or how would she feel about consoling Rosa, the friend she had once been so close to, as she buried her son? The youth they had watched grow into a strong young man, a handsome man, who had fallen in love with his mother, Lucía, and then married in the small village church. How would she react to the news?

"I'll probably look to fly over tomorrow, or Sunday. It all depends on what's available. I imagine once I get there it will be straightforward, so I should be home in a few days. If I'm not here when you get back from Bath, at least you'll know where I am."

With that he made his way into the bathroom, to prepare himself for the day he'd hoped would never come, leaving Charlotte to consider her options as she turned her attentions back to packing for her planned weekend away. Her thoughts continued to vacillate between whether to continue, or whether she should accompany her husband to Tenerife. Twenty minutes later, the sound of Antonio slamming the front door shut, as he left the house without a further word to her, effectively made up her mind.

Chapter 2

As the flight made its final approach into Tenerife's south airport, Antonio, from his window seat, surveyed the scene below him. It was late Saturday evening and the twinkling lights allowed him to pick out landmarks, and to identify some of the smaller towns and villages nestled high in the hills. It was some years since he had last come home, but the landscape was as recognisable to him today as it had been as a small boy growing up on the island. With the Atlantic Ocean to his right and the rugged mountainous terrain to his left, that view would be something he could never forget, no matter what life threw at him.

As they passed Mount Teide, the majestic volcano responsible for the structure and formation of the island, he felt a strange pull on his heartstrings. The memories it evoked brought a small smile to his face. Why had it taken him so long to return, to come home, he wondered, and why had the catalyst for his journey needed to be his father's death?

Tenerife was the largest of the seven islands that formed the Canaries archipelago. It was situated off the coast of North Africa in the Atlantic Ocean. With flight times less than five hours from Heathrow, it was not inaccessible. In fact, it was a holiday island, with over five million tourists making the trip annually. The temperate climate and all year round sunshine made it a magnet for young and old alike, with the island offering enough attractions to keep most people entertained. So why hadn't Antonio been one of them? What had kept him away from the place of his birth, or distanced him from the family and friends he had grown up with?

London had been his home now for over half his lifetime. He had left Tenerife as a young boy, just about to turn seventeen. Now at thirty-five he was a grown man. A married man, with a successful business. With a lifestyle that was incomparable to anything he could ever have imagined or achieved had he stayed on the island. He had made a life for himself. A comfortable life, and one that if he was totally honest, his family struggled to fully comprehend, or grasp the significance of. His parents had never shown any real appreciation of all the hard work that had gone into achieving it, nor if he remembered correctly, ever commented on how proud they had been of him, or what he had built for himself.

As the cabin crew busied themselves before landing, Antonio allowed his mind to recall the time his mother and sisters had visited him in London, even dined at his restaurant. That was five years ago. Where had that time gone? He had invited his parents and sisters for the opening night of his first restaurant, keen to share his success with them. He also wanted to show off his city, his home, believing they would be as awed by the sights and sounds of London as he had been all those years ago.

Whilst his father argued he was unable to leave the farm, his mother and sisters had eventually agreed to visit. However, from the moment they reached his apartment it was clear they felt like fish out of water, and over the following three days that sense of unease never fully abated. The noise and commotion of the capital was somewhere they struggled to feel relaxed. And rather than showing any pride, his mother's overriding feeling was concern, forever worrying about what her son had taken on. In her eyes he would always be a small boy, from a remote village, not a young man, who was making a success of his life.

His mother sadly had little experience or appreciation of life off the island. Travelling was something she had rarely done, and other than a brief trip to one of the other islands for her honeymoon as a young bride, she had never travelled for pleasure. Holidays were not something she and her husband had ever had the luxury of taking. Then, once the babies arrived, they and the finca took up all their time, their energies, and above all else what little money they had left after the bills had been paid. So the extravagance Antonio was showing was something she could never appreciate. She did not feel at all at home in his new surroundings.

Language also proved to be a barrier, because whilst his mother and sisters had a general appreciation of English, none of them was sufficiently fluent to feel comfortable speaking it aloud. Antonio recalled how disappointed he had felt that they had been unable to make the effort, and how he had reverted to speaking Spanish to help them out. A language that to his shame no longer rolled off his tongue as comfortably as it once had. Spanish had almost become an alien tongue to him, realising how reliant he now was on speaking English; also how much he'd allowed his heritage to fade. He would always be a proud Spaniard, but with each passing day he felt he was losing that identify to the cultural pulls of his new homeland.

He also recalled how speaking Spanish had not gone down at all well, especially with Charlotte, his fiancée at the time. She found herself excluded from the conversations he was having with his family, a feeling she was not at all comfortable with. Charlotte loved to be the centre of attention, loved to have the limelight shone on her at all times, and from that initial meeting with her future in-laws, it soon became apparent she would not be getting that from Antonio's family. Antonio had been astute enough to realise that no close relationships would ever be developed between his family and future wife, either on that trip or once they were married.

Whilst he loved his fiancée and appreciated she had many attributes, he was wise to the fact that tolerance was not one of them. She displayed little patience with people on the best of days, and his family was not her type of people; a point that became evident from the moment they had first walked into his apartment after returning from the airport. Charlotte was waiting to greet them. Her cursory glance at the luggage they were carrying, and the clothes they were wearing, spoke volumes. Clean, functional, but not a designer label between them.

Whilst Charlotte remained polite to her future in-laws, as her own upbringing dictated, Antonio was not blind to the fact that she soon found whatever excuse she could to avoid being left alone with them during their visit, with her behaviour for the rest of the trip remaining distant, detached and somewhat aloof. He recalled how his mother and sisters proved to be needy, demanding of both his time and his company. But given it had been some time since he had last seen them, and after all they were his guests, that was understandable and he was happy to play out his role as host. Charlotte however, as his sparkling new fiancée, did not appreciate having to play second fiddle, or to be made to feel like she was pushed into the shadows whilst Antonio amused his family.

He also recalled how anxious his mother had become as she walked around the crowded streets, how completely outside her comfort zone she felt. As she'd grasped hold of his arm, almost afraid to let go, her normal confidence appeared to have deserted her. It was something that had really surprised him, given his memories were always of her being such a confident woman.

His sisters meanwhile were bemused at the breadth of fashions on display and the variety of people they saw. The obvious trappings of wealth, alongside increasing signs of poverty, also the vast range of nationalities and languages being spoken. To them London was more cosmopolitan and more multicultural than they had ever imagined and they did not know what to think about that, or what their friends would say when they attempted to describe it to them, once they returned home. Their friends came from similar backgrounds to theirs, shared similar pastimes and similarly had limited experience of life outside their village. So, whilst Antonio marvelled at his sisters' reactions, to him it was normal. This was his life.

He also remembered being disappointed that the sights and tourist attractions did little to hold their interest either, or the realisation that the shops were so far beyond their affordability they became somewhere they feared to tread. He hated the sense of embarrassment it created in him; an embarrassment that he had never had the sensitivity to appreciate before.

Then, when it came to the opening night itself, seeing the opulence of the restaurant, with all the finery his customers paid handsomely for, it did nothing at all to ease their nerves. Other, that is, than further highlighting the chasm that existed between their lifestyles and Antonio's, as they looked at one another, before deciding which piece of cutlery to use as each new course was presented to them.

For Antonio it was a real-life lesson, and a hard one at that. Until that point, he had never fully comprehended how much his upbringing, particularly the life he had made for himself since leaving the island, differed from theirs. This new sophistication only served to emphasise the unsophisticated nature of his family's rural lifestyle.

At the time, it had left a discomfort they had all struggled to deal with; a feeling that had never fully gone away. As Antonio drove them back to the airport, for their journey home, a small part of him was relieved. The larger part of him, though, was sad because as he watched his mother as she walked towards the departure gates, he knew in his heart that would be the last time she would ever venture to England.

That was five years ago. Five years since he had last seen his mother and sisters in person, and even longer since he had seen his father, or felt the warmth of his strong arms around him. As a family they remained close. Antonio still spoke to them often and helped them out financially wherever he could, however neither side had made any real effort to meet up again since that trip. Telephone calls, or more recently video calls, were all they had to keep their family connections going.

Antonio had always sensed the conflict between the two sides of his family, and over the intervening years had struggled with balancing the pull each side exerted. He knew Charlotte was someone who needed careful handling, and from the point they had married, he had fast learned how temperamental she could become, especially if she did not get her own way. So, whilst it was never spoken aloud, it was obvious from his parents' behaviour, and the fact that they were unable to make the journey over to London to celebrate his wedding, that Charlotte would never be made to feel like family. The two halves of his life were destined to remain that. Two halves, that under no circumstances would ever meet to make a whole.

As the plane taxied to a standstill, Antonio was forced to focus his thoughts back onto today. He was under no illusion that the next few days were going to be an easy ride. In addition, he was unsure of the welcome he would receive. Certainly not that of the returning hero. Yes, he was returning home, but not for the right reasons. That was going to be hard for him and his family to deal with.

"Are you okay, Antonio?" Theresa asked. "You look very pensive."

"Yes, thanks. It's just that it's bringing back memories, some good and some not so. It seems so long since I was last home. Seventeen years is a long time and I'm not sure what to expect, which I have to admit is quite frightening." Antonio continued to stare out of the window. "I don't think I've ever fully appreciated what you did for me all those years ago, Yaya. How you've shaped me into the man I've become, or what happened to that small boy I once was." He squeezed her arm affectionately as he spoke.

"You've become what you were destined to become, Antonio, I'm sure of that. Nothing more and nothing less. And what no one knows, is what life still has in store for anyone. Even you, my dear. Anyway, in terms of what will greet us when we get home, we'll need to face that together. I'm as guilty as you on that score, surely? So, whatever's lying in store for us, we'll deal with it. Don't you worry."

Chapter 3

The Past

Lucía was sitting at the kitchen table, with silent tears streaming from her eyes. Her husband, Mateo, had just left the room, slamming the door firmly behind him as he made his way outside to the yard. Some excuse about dealing with the pigs had been muttered as he'd left, but it was just that, an excuse to get out of the room before he too broke down in tears. He had always worn his heart on his sleeve and today there was no hiding what he really felt about what had just been suggested.

Whilst Lucía knew her mother's proposal made perfect sense, that did not make it any easier to digest. And even if she did eventually agree, it would never be something she would be fully comfortable with. Antonio was her son, her only son and she wanted him around her, not thousands of miles away in some foreign land. Now sixteen, and a strapping young man, he was roughly the same age as his father had been when they had first met over twenty years ago. So many of the qualities she had seen in Mateo she could see in Antonio, and that made her heart ache even more at the thought of him moving away.

Lucía remembered the first time she had seen Mateo, almost as if it had been yesterday. Where had those years gone? Time that had passed in a mere moment.

24

She recalled how Mateo and his mother, Rosa, had recently moved to live in their small village of Alto Verde, high in the hills of Tenerife, from the neighbouring island of Lanzarote. She had finished school the previous summer and at sixteen had started working on a local farm, helping the farmer's wife with the livestock and the upkeep on the finca whenever she needed extra hands. Whilst Lucía's family had its own small farm, which her mother and father operated between them, there was little for her to do there, so she was grateful for whatever extra money she could earn doing casual work for neighbours. Back then she had been a slightly built young girl, tall with thick dark hair, a pretty smile and an unassuming manner. Her strength belied her appearance and even though she had a tendency towards shyness with people she did not know, she had an inner confidence and could hold her own with any of the young lads in the village.

Mateo's father, Paco, had recently died in a freak boating accident. Following his untimely death, Rosa, with no direct family left on the island of Lanzarote, decided to return home to the village of her birth. His grandmother, Rosa's mother, who by then was in her mid-sixties, apparently needed her support, she had told her in-laws. Rosa's mother had missed her only daughter deeply when she had married and left the island, and the sudden and unexpected death of the man, who in her view had never been good enough for her daughter anyway, was the perfect excuse to call her and her grandson Mateo back home.

Rosa's in-laws had never welcomed the union of her and their son either. They had always looked down on their daughter-in-law, belittling her peasant background and openly accusing her of trapping their son into marriage by becoming pregnant. They had even at one stage suggested the child was not their son's, begging Paco to have nothing to do with her. Paco repeatedly tried to defend his wife and win his parents over, but the weight of his family's continued distrust made their life difficult. Paco, as the only son, worked alongside his father on a daily basis, managing the fishing fleet and dealing with the commercial side of their business. He felt like he was under constant pressure to do something to resolve the situation, from both sides, as with each passing year his wife became as distrustful as his parents, her attempts to win them over long since having dried up.

Now that Paco was dead, and the buffer between them and Rosa had effectively been removed, it was clear neither she nor Mateo would ever be accepted by the family, and life would only become more difficult if she stayed. So, rather than remain at the mercy of her husband's parents, she saw that coming back to Tenerife was the sensible option. It was her chance to rebuild her life and that of her only son, among family and friends she had pined for over the years, albeit, in the clear knowledge that life would not be easy on her return.

As a young widow, still only in her mid-thirties, with little if any financial security behind her, and aging parents that needed her support, there would undoubtedly be difficult days ahead. Picking up the threads of her previous life, a life she had reluctantly left seventeen years previously, would always be a challenge. She had left as a young bride, already pregnant and fearful of a life away from her family. Would people accept her and her son back, and what would she be able to do to earn the money she needed to support her family?

Mateo, with his striking looks and mysterious background, was an instant pull for the young village girls who immediately fell under the newcomer's spell, as well as being a popular lad with the local boys. He was strong, with the type of muscular physique that showed he was no stranger to hard labour, and the deepest of brown eyes that simply drew you in. Lucía, recalled with a smile that moment he'd walked into the farmyard at the finca early one morning, where she was already hard at work. He was looking for work himself, knowing that he needed to earn whatever he could to support his family's income. The look he gave her as he politely asked if she could direct him towards the farmer made her almost drop the bale of hay she had been lifting. She was mesmerised by him and whilst she could not hear the words he later spoke, her eyes remained curiously locked onto him as he enquired about labouring work.

Over the following weeks Lucía got to know Mateo a little more each day. He opened up about his life in Lanzarote, the loss of his father and the struggles his mother was continually faced with. They would sit and chat, shaded under the trees from the heat of the midday sun as they took their breaks, greedily drinking the cold water and munching on the freshly baked bread they had been given by the farmer's wife. They were among a small group of youngsters from the village, all helping with the harvest, collecting in the crops of tomatoes or bananas, as well as the potatoes that needed to be dug from the harsh dry soil. It was hard and unceasing work, but the days passed happily as they worked closely together.

Whilst Mateo, still only sixteen, was one of the youngest of the boys, his strength and his ability to drive and operate machinery, skills he'd acquired whilst working at his grandparents' fishing port in Lanzarote, made him a useful and popular member of the gang. "Many hands make for light work," he would often say as they wound their way back to the village at the end of each day.

Friendship between Lucía and Mateo soon developed into something much deeper, and before long into love. Lucía's mother, Theresa, and Mateo's mother, Rosa, had been best friends from schooldays. They had missed each other when Rosa had been forced to live in Lanzarote, so happily encouraged their relationship, in the knowledge that the two, once married, would settle in the village and build their family there. Neither was prepared to let their child leave the village, or be separated from their families again. Rosa had learnt the hard way, when she had married Mateo's father, of the difficulties that brought, and had no intention of allowing her son to befall a similar fate. Living far away, with in-laws who at best were tolerant of her, was not a life she wanted for Mateo. No, keeping them close and surrounded by love was what was important to both Rosa and Theresa, glad also that their children's union would cement their friendship once again.

Those close family values had been instilled in Lucía all her life. So now to sit and listen to her own mother discussing the possibility of taking her only son, Antonio, to live in England with her and her husband was something she struggled with. Yet, however much it pained her to accept it, she knew for Antonio it was the right thing to do. As with any mother, she wanted the best for her children. Sofía and Carmen, her two older daughters, were not cut from the same cloth as Antonio. They had both been anxious to leave school and marry, neither wanting more than what they could see in front of them. Their sights firmly set on babies and being pandered to by their husbands.

Antonio however was bright, with an intelligence that was far beyond that of his peers, or his years. Unlike Sofía and Carmen he had shone at school, with a thirst for knowledge that needed constant fuelling. Lucía had been forced to accept that a life on the farm would neither suit nor challenge him, and had lain awake many a night worrying what would happen once he left school, no longer having the structure or purpose that institution provided.

She and Mateo had long since been unable to answer the questions he asked, or understand the type of answers his enquiring mind sought. They were simple, uneducated folk, happy with the lot they had been dealt; earning an income that barely covered the costs of bringing up their family, let alone enough to fund any further education their son may want. Having such a bright child put pressures on them, pressures they did not know how to deal with.

What Lucía did know, though, was that if she failed to recognise his abilities she not only ran the risk of losing any potential he was showing, but there was a good chance of alienating her son into the bargain. He needed the mental stimulation that as parents they could no longer provide, nor the village could ever offer by way of profession. Love alone was no longer enough to keep their son close. So, whilst she had a heavy heart, her mother's offer to fund his education in England was something she and Mateo could no longer fight or ignore.

Lucía sighed. "Mama, I will speak to Mateo. I know how difficult he is finding it to consider letting Antonio go. He lost his own father at an early age, so understands a little of what this will mean to him. However, like me, he has accepted for some time that Antonio is not destined to follow him into the farm, or work alongside him, as Mateo did with Papa. He also wants what's best for our son, which I know is what you want too. I also know that you will take good care of him, so yes Mama, he can go to England, to live with you and get the education he deserves. As much as it pains me to say it, we will not stand in his way. We will simply pray that one day he will be returned to us."

With that she too headed to the yard to join her husband and to consider the implications of what she had just agreed to.

Chapter 4

The Present

Arriving late into Tenerife South airport, Antonio and his grandmother, Theresa, made their way to the car rental office to collect the keys for the car he had hired for the duration of their short stay. With all their arrangements having been made at the last moment, and it being the height of the holiday season, his choice of vehicles had been limited. Nevertheless, it was only for a few days, so he would have to manage with the small Seat Ibiza, if that was all they had left.

Travelling with only a small hand luggage bag each, they had swiftly made their way through the airport's security and out into the night air to locate their hire car. It was a mid-summer's evening, with thousands of stars twinkling in the clear skies above their heads. As Antonio breathed in the warm night air and raised his head to see the skyline, memories came flooding back of the countless times he had lain on his back as a young boy, gazing up and pondering the universe. How inquisitive had he been about the stars and planets in those days, he now recalled, ashamed to admit he could no longer remember the names of even the most basic of the constellations or planets above his head.

He realised his fascination with the vastness of the universe was one of the first things that had waned when he arrived in London all those years ago, replaced as it was by so many new and varied subjects to pique his interests. In those early days he recalled how he had wistfully looked out of his bedroom window, thinking of home and feeling homesick for his family and friends. He had sought out his favourite stars in the night sky, but the London skyline was so different from Tenerife's. Light pollution within the city, with its skyscrapers and fumes, to say nothing of the frequent cloudy skies and persistent bad weather, made star gazing almost impossible. Over time Antonio was forced to accept that no amount of stargazing or wishful thinking would change the here and now. He had been sent to England for a clear purpose, and that was what he now needed to concentrate on. Whilst he missed home, he could not afford to have regrets or doubts about what had taken place, or the motivations that had driven his parents' decision to send him away.

He recalled the day his parents had called him into the kitchen and sat him down, to tell him he was leaving Tenerife. It was the first he had heard of it and as such it came as a complete surprise. They had planned for him to travel back to England with Yaya Theresa in two days' time, to go to college at the beginning of September when the new term started. He was being enrolled to take a series of A Levels at the local sixth form college. Antonio's opinion had not been sought. The emotion in their voices as they explained what had been agreed was palpable. However, it was a done deal, as far as his parents were concerned at least, so even with the misgivings he'd had, there would have been no use voicing them. At sixteen he was not ready to leave home, to leave his family and friends and all he knew. He was still a boy, not yet a man, with the concept of what had been arranged daunting.

Equally he had known that village life was not his destiny either, with the thought that he would be expected to follow in his father's footsteps into the farm, perhaps then going on to marry the daughter of one of the locals, something he'd really struggled to get his head around. He had no interest in the farm and did not feel at home in the farmyard, nor out on the land driving the tractors around or working with the harvest. Antonio was always happier in the house studying, or preferably in the kitchen helping his mother with the endless cooking or baking she was expected to produce, some of which was sold at the local market to supplement their meagre income.

He had known from an early age that he was different from his sisters and the other boys in the village, and had sensed for quite some time that he did not fit in. Many a time he recalled feeling excluded from their games or discussions, yet when he was included how bored they made him feel, their lack of aspiration for anything beyond what they knew something he could not fathom. How he yearned for so much more than what they appeared to be prepared to settle for. Their quiet mapped out lives, doing hard and heavy labour, to earn the paltry income they would need, to support whatever families they eventually had.

So, perhaps now, looking at how his life had panned out, his parents had been wise to make the decision they had, even if at the time it had felt like the cruellest decision on earth to the young boy whose life they were upturning.

"Yaya, look, the car's over here," Antonio declared as he spotted the parking bay where the Seat Ibiza had been left. "Come on, let's get on our way. It's already dark and we've still got around an hour or so's drive ahead of us before we get there."

Looking at the car he had been allocated, Antonio wondered whether it was up to the drive, or whether the uphill and somewhat treacherous roads to the village might prove too much for it.

As Antonio started the car and headed towards the TF1, the main motorway around the island, Theresa sat back and relaxed into the journey. Like her grandson, it had been more years than she cared to remember since she had last returned to Tenerife, to the place of her birth. As such, arriving back had equally raised memories for her that had long since been buried. Emotions she was still struggling to process, regardless of all the years that had passed.

Looking across at the profile of her grandson, not for the first time she felt a great deal of pride in the man he had become; the man she had nurtured and encouraged to blossom. She had watched him grow from a beautiful baby, into a young and inquisitive boy, and then into someone who had often felt at odds with his surroundings and the life into which he had been born. It had pained her at times to see how uncomfortable he felt among his family, how different he believed himself to be, from his parents and his older siblings.

In those early days Antonio needed to fit in with everything, to feel a sense of belonging. At times Theresa could see how difficult it became for him when he was rejected or excluded from what the others were doing, the games they were playing. Taking him away from her daughter and son-in-law and all he knew was not an easy decision, although hindsight allowed Theresa to feel some pride in the part that decision had played in allowing Antonio to find himself. To find his own niche in life, away from the confines or limitations of the village of his birth.

As Antonio continued to drive, Theresa allowed her mind to wander back to Ramos, Lucía's father, her first husband. Ramos had died at the age of fifty, a couple of years before Antonio's birth. He and Theresa had been married for over twenty-five years. It could never have been described as a happy marriage, she recalled, with Ramos providing both a firm hand and a cruel tongue whenever, in his view, his wife stepped out of line. Life was difficult working on the farm and Ramos had a tendency towards drink, with whatever spare income they made often being drunk away in the small bar in the village piazza at the end of the week. He would return home late, his drunken state too often resulting in him becoming violent towards Theresa, and on occasion Lucía.

Theresa did her best to avoid him and to keep Lucía as safe as she could, a situation that was eased as soon as Mateo came onto the scene and showed an interest in their daughter. Theresa encouraged the couple's relationship. She could see Mateo made Lucía happy, but more importantly he provided a strong deterrent to Ramos' behaviour. Ramos, above all, was a coward. He would think twice before raising his hand to wife or daughter once Mateo was around.

Following the marriage of Lucía and Mateo, Mateo left his mother's house in the village and moved into the small farmhouse with Theresa and Ramos. Lucía had already been five months pregnant when they married, and moving in with his own mother and grandparents was not an option. Rosa, as much as she loved Mateo and Lucía, had neither the room nor the inclination to take on the responsibility for a newborn, alongside the ever growing demands on her time from her own parents. They had aged more than she had realised and had become increasingly reliant on her since her return from Lanzarote. Mateo had been a great help with his grandparents, and she would miss him sorely when he moved out. Even so, allowing him to stay, with a wife and child on the way, was not an option.

Baby Sofía was born four months later. She was a beautiful baby and had the same dark skin and deep-brown eyes as her father. Lucía and Mateo doted on their newborn daughter, and delighted in each stage of her development. Every smile and gurgle brought a loving response from the parents as they stared down at her in awe. The couple, though, were still only teenagers themselves, each only seventeen years old, and at a loss to provide for themselves, let alone a baby. Theresa stepped in to help out with Sofía, leaving Mateo to help Ramos around the farm and Lucía to help her in the farmhouse.

Mateo could see the potential in the farm. He was also not blind to the behaviours of his father-in-law. His tendency towards alcohol was matched only by his tendency towards idleness, neither of which Mateo was prepared to follow. He was a hard worker and with a small family to provide for, with Sofía being joined by baby Carmen eighteen months later, he knew he needed to make a success of the farm, despite the best efforts of his father-in-law to drink it into the ground.

Ramos' death one evening, whilst staggering back from the bar and stumbling into a deep gully at the side of the road, falling heavily against the volcanic rock and rolling down the hillside, was a shock, although not an unpleasantness. Theresa was glad of the reprise his death gave her, and for the first time in many years felt safe in her own home. She no longer had to mind what she did or said, fearful of Ramos turning his hand to her, or to her daughter or granddaughters if they stepped out of line. He was gone from their lives and for that she was relieved.

Solely for the purposes of appearance, for a brief period she played the part of the grieving widow, if only to keep the village gossips at bay. Regardless of the fact most people knew the type of man he was, there were behaviours that were expected of her, norms of grieving that needed to be adhered to. As a young widow, though, she was not prepared to maintain the pretence for long. His death had given her an opportunity to get her own life back on track. After all, she was still only thirty-eight years old, which was far too young for her life to be over. She smiled now as she recalled that time, the point at which her life changed.

After around an hour of winding his way up the mountainous roads towards the family's finca, carefully steering his hire car to avoid the potholes and ruts created by the weather, and allowing the moonlight to provide what extra light it could to help supplement the narrow beams of the car's headlights, Antonio eventually saw the old rusty gates to his parents' property. He indicated out of habit and turned left. The gates were wedged open. They looked like they had been that way for some time, as weeds and wild grasses had wrapped themselves around the mechanisms and metalwork, untended and unloved.

As he slowly approached the two storey stone farmhouse, he noticed it looked tired and in need of maintenance, as did the crop of outbuildings that were scattered around the farmyard. The sight of each brought back its own memories, and as he stared at them he wondered which of the buildings his father had been working on when the tragedy struck.

Looking at the state of each, in the limited light that was available, it could easily have been any one of them, he thought ruefully.

Antonio did manage a wry smile as he recalled his days as a teenager, of hearing shouts from his parents seeking him out to ask for help around the farm. With no desire to muck out the pigs or carry the firewood, he would regularly be found sitting in one of his hiding places in the outbuildings, his head deep in a book. Whilst desperate to avoid his parents finding him, and roping him into whatever chores they needed doing, he knew he was no match for his mother. She always managed to sniff him out, no matter how good he thought his hiding place to be. No, he had known from an early age the farm was not for him.

As he brought the car to a final stop, he could just about see that the lights in the downstairs windows of the farmhouse were switched on, which was a good sign his mother had stayed up to await their arrival. He had told her it would be around midnight when they arrived, so not to wait up for them, although as the farmhouse was unfamiliar to both him and Theresa, he was glad she had. Other than that, there was total darkness, with the meagre glow from the windows doing little to help cheer up the dilapidated property.

"Yaya, wake up. We've arrived." Antonio spoke gently as he stroked his grandmother's arm, not wanting to shock her more than was necessary. He had noticed her drift off to sleep some time ago and had driven carefully to avoid disturbing her. She was understandably tired. Now in her mid-seventies, and especially given the shock of what had happened, it was not surprising. Nor was the fact she had insisted on joining him for the journey, as from the moment he had broken the news that his father had died there had been no alternative than to bring her along. Her first words, once the shock of what he had said had sunk in, had effectively been, "When are we flying out?"

As Antonio closed the car door the farmhouse door opened. In the doorway he could just about make out the silhouettes of his mother, with his sister, Sofía, standing beside her. Although it was dark, they appeared to both be dressed in the customary black of mourning. Theresa walked towards her daughter and enveloped her in her arms, the sobs of both women all that could be heard in the quiet of the night.

Picking up their bags, and walking towards the house, Antonio was simply left to follow in their wake.

Chapter 5

Sunday morning arrived and Charlotte was just beginning to stir in her luxurious bedroom as the glare of the summer sunshine broke through the balcony windows. She stretched out in her king-sized bed and carefully opened her eyes as she adjusted to her surroundings. It was too bright and her head felt a little delicate, perhaps from a glass or two too much champagne, she imagined. It had been a good night, though, and well worth attending, and looking around she was pleased she had paid that little extra to upgrade her room to a mini-suite, rather than the standard rooms her friends had booked.

It was just after nine o'clock in the morning when Charlotte's mobile began to ring. She reached over to the bedside table to see who was ringing, glancing at the small antique travel clock adjacent to it as she did so. She always brought it with her whenever she went away – regardless of the fact both her watch and phone were more than capable of telling her the time, should she need to know, or set an alarm, if one was needed. In fact, they were both considerably more accurate than the old travel clock, which was known for losing the odd minute or two every few weeks, and needed regular winding up to keep it going. It had been her grandfather's, though, and he had given it to her as a going away present when she had first gone to boarding school at the tender age of eight. It had been his and he'd wanted his only granddaughter to carry on the tradition.

At the time, Charlotte had been touched by the gesture and whilst she thought it was an odd tradition she loved her grandfather so had honoured his wishes. Over the years the quirky clock had travelled far and wide, and it seemed only fitting that it should accompany her on this trip too, especially as it was to that same school she had first travelled, nearly twenty-five years earlier.

Looking over, she saw that the call was from her husband, Antonio. His handsome face suddenly filled the screen in front of her, with a photo taken on their honeymoon three years earlier. It was only a casual photo, one she had taken herself, on a beach in the Caribbean, one evening as they strolled along the seashore after enjoying a couple of cocktails at the beachside bar. He had looked so happy and relaxed, so in love, and it remained one of her favourite photos of him.

Nowadays he rarely seemed happy or relaxed, and in terms of love those first flushes of romance were certainly starting to wear thin. Charlotte had been under no illusion that she was marrying an idle man, nor someone who would wait on her hand and foot, but she had expected him to lavish a little more of his time and attentions on her than he currently did. He was always busy; his time largely absorbed by his business, his restaurants or more recently his family, and whilst it was still early days it was not quite the marriage she had expected.

"Good morning, Antonio," she managed to say in as light a tone as she could muster, trying to appear more awake than she actually was, or should have been given the time. Her throat was dry, her head was hurting and breezy was the furthest from how she was feeling at that moment. She was just thankful she had organised a late check-out at the hotel. Then again, given the circumstances, she imagined he would not be calling for a whimsical chat either. "Is everything okay in Tenerife?" she asked.

"Yes, everything is as expected and there's nothing for you to worry about. I just wanted to let you know that we got here late yesterday evening, how things were going and what plans Mama has made so far."

"Right, thank you," she replied, suddenly remembering her manners. "How are your mother and sisters coping, and did you pass on my condolences to them?"

"Yes, I did, they said to say thank you. They all appear to still be in shock, well Mama and Sofía are at least. I haven't spoken to Carmen yet. She's calling in tomorrow lunchtime, with Juan and the children, I understand."

For a couple of minutes Charlotte listened as Antonio told her about his mother, the funeral arrangements and what he was planning on doing over the coming days to help his family out. She neither interrupted nor offered any input, as no questions were asked of her or comments sought. She felt no more a part of his Spanish family now than she had the day of their marriage.

"So, with the funeral on Wednesday, in three days' time, I will stay until that is over, then make my way home. I'll aim to book a flight later today and should be home by Friday morning latest, in plenty of time for the weekend's bookings at the restaurant. I've already phoned Philippe to let him know, and he's happy to take control until I get back. We have a couple of large parties booked in on Saturday, with some special clients, so I am anxious to get back for that."

"Well, thank you for letting me know," Charlotte replied, disgruntled yet unsurprised that Philippe, Antonio's second in command, and one of his oldest friends, had known about her husband's arrangements before she had.

"I should be home, so perhaps I'll see you before you need to rush into the restaurant?" The questioning tone of her voice was unable to hide her disappointment, or the fact she once again felt like she was playing second fiddle to his business.

Suddenly there was a knock on the door. "Oh Antonio, I'm sorry, but I need to go. My room service has just arrived with my breakfast tray and I need to make myself decent in order to answer the door. Phone me later, if you have time that is," she added, desperate to hide the barb in her voice, as well as slightly annoyed that he had not even bothered to enquire how her weekend had gone.

As Charlotte lounged in bed, enjoying the selection of fruits and pastries that had been delivered to her room, along with the freshly-squeezed orange juice and extra-roasted coffee she had ordered, she let out a relaxed and contented sigh and reflected on the last couple of days with her friends.   What a marvellous time they had had.

On Friday, she and her two best friends, Valarie and Stephanie, had met for lunch as planned in Bath, before spending the afternoon mooching around the shops in and around Milsom Street. On impulse Charlotte had tried on a dress she had seen in the shop window of one of the more upmarket and independent boutiques on the high street. It was a glamourous full length evening gown in midnight blue, in a soft tulle, with a sweetheart neckline that accentuated her small breasts and complimented her slender figure perfectly.   Even though she said it herself, it looked absolutely stunning and the length was perfect for her, wearing the heels the helpful assistant had provided to ensure she got the full effect.

"You could wear that tomorrow evening, for the ball. It fits perfectly and wouldn't need any alterations," Valarie had suggested as Charlotte had twirled in front of them to show it off.

"Yes, unless the one you've brought is alright?" Stephanie questioned.

It was the word "alright" and the tone of Stephanie's voice that had swung her decision. She already had a more than suitable gown for the event, one that had cost the earth, complete with matching accessories. However this one was much nicer, and the colour was amazing on her as it really emphasised the depth of blue in her eyes. The other dress would not be wasted though, as there would surely be another event she could wear it to. And anyway, her shoes and clutch bag would match with the new gown just as well, so by doubling up it had actually saved her money, she argued, as she eyed the price tag and convinced herself it was worth the investment.

On Saturday morning they had booked into the hotel spa and had treatments, facials and manicures, before attending the hotel's hair salon to have their hair and makeup done for the evening. Overall, it was a proper pampering session, with the odd glass of champagne thrown in for good measure. Their drinks were delivered on silver salvers by a series of good-looking and exceptionally fit young men. "Do you think they've been handpicked by the spa, as eye-candy for their female clientele?" Charlotte questioned mischievously, giggling as she sipped the champagne, her eyes still locked onto the waiter's pert backside as he left the room.

As Charlotte and her friends had made their eventual entrance into the hotel's bar for pre-dinner drinks later that evening, it was fair to say that more than the odd head was turned at their appearance. The looks and compliments they received, to say nothing of the attention they garnered as they chatted with some of their old school friends and the dignitaries that had been invited, more than made all the effort they had gone to worthwhile.

Once the three-course dinner, the speeches and all the gratuitous self-congratulation were completed, the entertainment began. A lively four-piece band, complete with its own jazz tribute singer, played a medley of popular music to mark the passing of the centenary since the school's inauguration.

Valarie, sitting between Charlotte and Stephanie, groaned as the band began to play the fourth consecutive song that appeared to have set the tone for the evening. They were nursing their drinks, beginning to feel like wallflowers as some of the older couples had started to take to the dancefloor. "I'm not sure jazz is my thing, and this is starting to get awfully painful. Do either of you fancy taking a bottle of that champagne and seeing if we can find anything a little less dull to do in this hotel? There's bound to be more entertainment going on somewhere, isn't there?"

"It's not that bad, Val," Stephanie replied, tapping her feet along to the rhythm. "In fact, I think he's got a good voice and I'd quite fancy a dance. What do you think, Char, shall we give it a go?"

Before Charlotte had time to reply, a man approached their table. He was around forty with closely cropped dark hair and was impeccably dressed, in a white dinner jacket, his bow tie now loosened around his neck, and the top button of his dress shirt slightly opened. All three women watched agog, noticing the obvious confidence in his swagger.

"I hope you don't mind me asking, but would any of you ladies care to join me on the dance floor?" His smile brightened up his face, with the faintest of wrinkles appearing around his mouth and eyes as he spoke.

Before Stephanie had the chance to jump in, the man held out his right hand in invitation to Charlotte, the look in his eyes making it painfully clear to whom his question had actually been directed.

"Oh, thank you," Charlotte replied, a little embarrassed by the directness of his approach. "I'm not the best of dancers, though, as I'm afraid I've got two left feet. I'd no doubt stand on your toes and ruin those beautiful shoes. Perhaps Stephanie might make a better partner," she offered, looking over at her friend.

"I'm sure you're not that bad, and please don't worry about my shoes. I can always get another pair," he replied, his gaze never leaving her face and his persistence clearly showing that he had no intention of taking no for an answer. "I'm Miles, by the way. Miles Davenport. I'm one of the sponsors of this evening, so I can assure you you're in safe hands."

As Charlotte was reluctantly led to the dance floor by the tall dark stranger, Stephanie and Valarie were left to watch on in awe. He was absolutely stunning and after ten minutes of watching as their friend was confidently twirled around the dance floor, showing no signs of returning to them soon, they were forced to consider their own fate.

"Do you think we've been abandoned, Val?" Stephanie enquired, starting to feel even more like a wallflower and annoyed no one had approached her for a dance. After all the effort she had gone to, she knew she looked equally as stunning as Charlotte, so could not understand why she had not attracted any attention herself. Having left her husband at home to watch both their toddler and three-year-old, she was desperate for some fun.

"I don't know, Steph. Although my suggestion to take a bottle and do a runner is still an option. I've just noticed the waiters refilling the drinks station, so there's plenty of drink around." She smiled over, equally concerned where the night was going. The music had started to grow on her, yet even she was beginning to feel a little disgruntled at the fact Charlotte had been asked to dance and they hadn't. Valarie was currently between men, after a recent broken engagement, and would have loved to have had the opportunity of getting back in the saddle, as her mother kept telling her she needed to do. "Let's give her a few more minutes before we decide. Although, looking at the way those two guys are approaching, we could be about to be in for some luck of our own. Bagsy the one on the right, Steph!"

Charlotte vaguely recalled Valarie and Stephanie joining her and Miles on the dance floor, eventually having secured partners of their own, and vaguely recalled them leaving at some stage too, although she was not entirely sure of the facts or the timings, or even who they had left with. She just recalled having an amazing night, most of it spent dancing with Miles as he'd effortlessly guided her around the dance floor. He had held her closely, gently singing along to the music, almost serenading her as he'd whispered in her ears or gazed into her eyes.

Whilst on occasion she'd laughed, generally whenever she'd failed to avoid standing on his toes, she also remembered feeling slightly uncomfortable at times with the effect his attentions were having on her body. The way he held her felt so natural, his arms gently caressing the back of her gown, or wrapping themselves around her waist. And the warmth of his body, along with the musk scent of his aftershave was so intoxicating it made her lightheaded.

That night was the most she had danced in years and it was a long time since she had danced with anyone other than her husband. It was just a bit of fun, though, she argued to herself, batting away those feelings. But there was no doubting that dancing with Miles had made her feel relaxed and happy, and she could not avoid being flattered by the obvious attentions he had showered on her. It had certainly worked wonders for her self-esteem.

She also remembered the way he had escorted her back to her room at the end of the evening. It was after two o'clock in the morning as they exited the lift, with the chaste kiss he placed on her cheek as he left her at her door leaving her wanting more. What a lovely man, she had thought dreamily as she watched him walk back down the corridor towards his own room, briefly turning and blowing her a kiss, before she closed her door.

Miles Davenport had been the perfect gentleman and meeting him had been the perfect end to a perfect weekend. She knew very little about him, and he knew even less about her, and Charlotte was okay with that, given the chances of them ever meeting each other again were miniscule. They were simply two strangers who had enjoyed an innocent evening together. That's all it had been, or would ever be, was the thought she chose to console herself with.

Although, as she regarded the business card he had handed her, with the suggestion that if she was ever in the area again she might want to get in touch, she had to recognise it certainly left a fluttery type of sensation in her stomach. The card simply read: *Miles Davenport, Consultant*, with his mobile number and email address printed in embossed gold lettering. Quite mysterious really.

"If ever I'm down this way again, now that sounds like a dangerous idea," Charlotte admitted to herself, with a silly grin on her face as she allowed her mind to wander back for a moment longer than was necessary. As much as she hated to admit it, or make comparisons with her husband, Miles was certainly more her usual type. Whilst Antonio was lovely in his own way, undoubtedly dark with his Mediterranean colouring and a handsome enough face, sadly that was as far as their similarities went.

Slotting the business card safely into her evening purse, Charlotte finished off her coffee before deciding it was time she should get up. Time to pack and head to the railway station and catch the first available train back into London. Although neither the thought of going back to an empty house, nor the prospect of an empty bed for the next few nights was something she was looking forward to, especially now that Antonio had informed her that he was planning to be away until Friday.

Once again, he was putting his family and their needs above hers, and she was getting very bored with that. Nevertheless, what was her alternative? After all, all good things had to come to an end.

Chapter 6

After Antonio had put the phone down to his wife, completely unaware of the fact he had annoyed her by not enquiring about her weekend, he had gone back into the main living area of the farmhouse. His grandmother and mother were sitting at the kitchen table, holding hands with their heads down, quietly talking. They stopped as soon as he entered the room and looked directly at him, unable to hide the worried expressions on their faces.

Sensing something was troubling them, and instinctively knowing it was not simply their grief that was being expressed, Antonio moved closer. He studied his mother's face and noticed how drawn it was, with more worry lines than was appropriate for a woman only in her mid-fifties. She had always had lovely olive coloured skin, fresh from the outdoors lifestyle she enjoyed and an ample figure that befitted a farmer's wife. Today she looked almost as old as his grandmother, her pallor drained of its usual colour, with the black dress she was wearing all but hanging off her.

Comparing her against his grandmother, though, was not fair, as he had to admit his grandmother neither acted nor looked like a woman in her mid-seventies. She was always well turned out and continued to dress fashionably, whatever the season, in clothes the quality of which was unquestioned. Additionally, any signs of aging were kept at bay by her weekly classes at the gym and frequent lunches out, along with regular visits to the hair salon and manicurist all contributing to keeping her looking and feeling young. No, there was no comparison between mother and daughter, and certainly not on a day like today.

The previous evening, after he and Theresa had arrived, countless tears had been shed around the kitchen table. They had all stayed up into the early hours talking and reminiscing about Mateo, and although they were tired when they had eventually retired to bed, this morning his grandmother looked as spritely as ever. She displayed no obvious signs of tiredness after their long journey the previous day, whereas his mother looked like she had not got any sleep whatsoever, the bags under her eyes looking even heavier than those of the previous day.

"Mama, what is it?" he asked, gently putting his arms around his mother. "Has something else happened?" Theresa and Lucía exchanged a glance, both women unsure what to say or how much to burden him with. Lucía knew it was not Antonio's problem; it was no longer his life, and she had no desire to worry him. Whereas Theresa knew of her grandson's kindness and knew that continuing to keep secrets from him was not how they should proceed. He had a right to know and a right to help, if that was what he chose to do.

"Antonio," Theresa began, looking over at Lucía. "We were just discussing the farm and what's going to happen to it, now that your papa isn't here to run things, as he has done for the last forty years." As she spoke, Theresa continued to look at her daughter, gauging how much she should say. Sensing a tacit approval, she continued. "Lucía has just been explaining to me that without Mateo, she will be unable to keep the farm running, potentially even keep the farmhouse. It is understandably adding further worry and distress to an already difficult situation."

"Mama, is this correct? I thought you had a few local men who came in to do the more manual work, and that you and Papa had stepped back from most of the heavy lifting these days. Can they not carry on, or can you not employ an additional pair of hands to pick up the slack?"

To Antonio it appeared a simple solution. Throw some extra resource at the problem and in time it will sort itself out. The farm was a reasonable size and whilst it was obviously rundown aesthetically, with most of the buildings in disrepair, if last night's memory was to be relied upon, it still managed to produce its crops, selling whatever produce it made at market, surely? Although as he thought this, Antonio had to concede he couldn't quite recall what his father's farm produced these days, or where the produce went. Whether he supplied wholesalers, or sold locally to markets, it was all a little distant to him.

"Well yes, there are a few farmhands who help out, so that's not the real problem. According to your mama, in recent years your papa got himself into some debt, largely buying new equipment for the farm. He took on a bank loan, secured against the farm and this has not yet been repaid. The farm has not yielded what it should, so money has been tight. The bank has recently been calling in the loan, and with it being secured against the farm itself, the farmhouse and your mama's home, as well as her livelihood, are all at risk."

Antonio looked at his mother, questioningly. "Why is this the first I have heard of this, Mama? If you needed money, why did you not mention that to me? I could have helped, you know that, don't you?"

Lucía cut him short. "Antonio, this is not your problem. The farm is not your life nor your responsibility, and your papa was a proud man. He did not want to trouble you on the rare occasions when you rang, especially when you had your own business and family to worry about. You have so many demands on your time that we did not want to become a burden to you, too." The mild rebuff in her voice did not go unnoticed.

"Mama…….." he began, wanting to add, "I have always been there for you," but he instinctively knew that had not been the case. He had fallen short as a son, and the full realisation of that was only now starting to dawn on him. To have not come home for all these years, nor to have witnessed first-hand the life his parents had been living, was unforgiveable. He had been so obsessed with his own life, his own success, that in his mind he had been guilty of trivialising theirs. That same life he had in fact been born into, then turned his back on as soon as a newer and shinier version had been offered to him in England. All he had wanted to do was show off that new life, to boast to his parents and make them proud of what he had made of himself. What sort of son did that actually make him? Certainly not one of whom they should have to feel proud.

Sensing the growing tension in the room between mother and son, Theresa continued. "Antonio, this is the first I have heard about this also, so please don't be too harsh on your mama. She has enough to deal with at the moment, without this. However, I have decided I will stay here with Lucía for a few weeks after the funeral, to see what I can do to help. Apart from anything else, it will do us good to have some time together, and for me to spend some time with my grandchildren, and great-grandchildren, won't it mi hija, my daughter?" Lucía gave a wan smile to her mother, no longer feeling so alone.

"And, with your permission Mama, I will speak to the lawyers and the bank tomorrow morning and see what needs to be done to deal with the loan, if that is something you'd be happy for me to do? I will not see you lose your home, or your livelihood, though, I can assure you of that. Please do not worry on that account, Mama."

Lucía smiled at Antonio, grateful for his support and no longer able to offer any argument to change his mind. "Thank you. I am happy for you to speak to whoever you can, and I will give you all the information you need. I'm just not sure what good it will do," she said, resigned to her fate.

With that Lucía left the room, shut her bedroom door firmly behind her and remained there for the rest of the day.

The following day, shortly after lunchtime, Carmen arrived with her husband, Juan, and their two young daughters, Maya and Anya. They had walked the short distance to the farm from their small house located nearer to the centre of the village. As the children charged through the door Sofía and Theresa were in the kitchen, tidying away the remains of their mid-day meal.

Lucía had returned to her bedroom, the door once again shut firmly behind her, with the intention of seeking the peace and solace she needed. It was a small house and recently the walls seemed to be closing in on her. Dealing with her own grief was bad enough, without having to contend with that of other peoples', and since her mama and Antonio had arrived, with their questions and desires to help, it had all become too overwhelming for her. She appreciated their presence, and was glad they had flown over to be with her, yet she needed time alone to process her thoughts and feelings, and knowing the imminent arrival of her younger daughter, Carmen, with her boisterous family, would only add to the chaos, Lucía had sought to get away. As much as she loved her young granddaughters, today was not the day to be entertaining them.

Antonio had witnessed their arrival and had even heard Carmen and Juan bickering as they approached the house. He had seen his two young nieces running ahead of their parents, presumably to get out of the firing line. At ten and eleven years old they were understandably full of life. Carmen was obviously unhappy about something and Juan appeared to be getting the brunt of whatever it was. Antonio knew better than most that his sister could be high maintenance, then again, her husband was no angel, so he judged it was best not to get involved. Some couples thrived on drama, unhappy unless they had something to moan about, and Carmen and Juan easily fell into that category. No doubt it would iron itself out over time, Antonio surmised, before the next trigger happened and it all started over again.

Antonio was sitting in the car talking to the bank, grateful of the privacy the small vehicle afforded him, also grateful of the fact he could get a phone reception in such a remote location. The farm, he now realised, had limited Wi-Fi, something he had never considered before. On the limited occasions he had phoned or video called his parents, he had got frustrated at their lack of reception, without ever questioning why. Now he knew. In fact, now he was realising more about his parents and their circumstances than he had ever imagined.

Antonio had earlier put the phone down to the solicitor, and had needed to take a few moments to absorb what he had been told. He had been shocked to discover that the previous summer his father had notified the solicitors that he, Antonio, would deal with his parents' affairs, should anything untoward happen to him or Lucía. Of his three children, Mateo had told them that only Antonio would have any grasp of business or legal matters, should the time ever come when he himself couldn't deal with things.

Mateo had accepted a long time ago that Antonio was clever, perhaps too clever for their family. He had always been aware that farm work was not for him, and that he would not be following in the family's farming tradition, as he and Lucía had. So when they had reluctantly allowed Theresa to take Antonio to England all those years ago, barely an adult, Mateo and Lucía had both known he was destined for greater things than they could provide.

Mateo was a relatively poorly-educated man, who'd largely managed to get by on his wits and his strong work ethic. He had left school at fifteen and had laboured all his life, with no formal education or qualifications to his name. He had mastered reading and writing and knew enough mathematics to ensure he was not cheated at market, but he'd known his limitations, and those of his wife who had no head for business either. Lucía was more than capable of managing the household accounts and eking what limited money came in to pay for the food and bills, but give her something complicated to deal with, or difficult questions to answer, and she would flounder and easily become flustered.

Sofía, as their eldest daughter and someone who despite all their best efforts to marry off was still living at home, should have been more than capable of dealing with their affairs. Being unmarried, though, Mateo did not trust what little he had being placed into the hands of a potential suitor.

Whereas Carmen, his youngest daughter, was flighty and unreliable, with her husband, Juan, someone who Mateo knew could not be trusted. Mateo had seen him in the bar too many evenings for his liking and occasionally in the company of other women. He feared there were many similarities between his son-in-law's behaviour and that of his deceased father-in-law, Ramos. At times he feared for his daughter and the life she had chosen, to say nothing of the two little girls they had brought into this world and the lives they were being forced to lead.

No, he had not wanted to trouble either of his daughters. Whereas Antonio, a successful businessman in England, with money of his own and someone who could speak fluently in English as well as Spanish, was the obvious choice.

The solicitor had drawn up the papers without any qualms, believing Mateo was being cautious, if perhaps a little pre-emptive with his actions. However, having just spoken to Antonio, and learning of his client's unfortunate and early demise, the solicitor admitted that sadly that would appear not to have been the case.

As Antonio had then sat and waited for his call to the bank to be answered, his mind had been spinning with all the permutations, based on what the solicitor had just told him. At least he now understood the dilemma with which Lucía was faced, clearly a lot more than his mother did. But did that make it any easier? He was at a loss to figure out what to think himself, let alone advise her on what the best options might be. Dealing with the immediate problem of the money that his father owed to the bank would be the easy part. The rest would take some time, and a great deal of thinking through.

"Gracias, Señor, I appreciate you taking the time to speak to me," Antonio said fifteen minutes later, after a lengthy discussion with the bank manager. "I will arrange the transfer of the outstanding money immediately. Hopefully that should be sufficient to deal with the bank's immediate concerns. In terms of the other matters, I will arrange a longer discussion, once I have spoken to my mother, that is."

With that he ended the phone call and remained in the car, quietly mulling over the enormity of what he had just learned.

Chapter 7

"Antonio, is everything alright?" Theresa enquired when he eventually returned to the house some thirty minutes later. She had watched from the window and had been worried as he appeared to be taking a long time on the phone. "You look like you've just seen a ghost. What did the solicitor say to you?" She was attuned to his looks and mannerisms, and from the way he wrung his hands and the frown lines on his face she could tell that something was clearly wrong. She was unsure what and did not want to hazard a guess.

"I'm fine, Yaya. Thank you," he replied a little distracted and unsure exactly what he wanted to share of the discussions that had just taken place. The small house was full and noisy, with both his sisters, as well as Carmen's husband and children there. Now was not the time to talk, apart from which he needed to speak to his mother first, once he had got his own mind around what the solicitor and bank manager had just told him. He also wanted to check out a few things, and for that he needed access to the internet.

"I think I'll just go through to my room for a moment, if you'll excuse me. Then I'm going to pop down to the town to pick up a few things. Do you need me to collect anything for dinner?" he asked, trying to deflect further discussion. He was aware there was a small pasteleria on the main road, somewhere he could sit and have a coffee and a pastry whilst making use of their Wi-Fi for his research.

"Give me a few moments and I will check with Lucía as I'm not sure what's in the larder. I'll also check who's staying for dinner and what the plans are. I don't know what Carmen and Juan are doing, or whether they are thinking of leaving the children here. They're in the middle of some argument and I'm not sure I want to interrupt them," Theresa whispered, looking over at her granddaughter in despair.

Carmen was certainly the hot-headed one of the family, and for once Theresa was unsure whether to side with her or Juan, who was looking increasingly uncomfortable with the way the discussion was going. Sofía was sitting in the corner of the room attempting to entertain the children as well as distract them whilst the argument played out between their parents. Her calm and unassuming manner led Antonio to believe this was not the first time she had acted as peacekeeper, or given the way the argument was playing out that it would be the last.

"Don't worry about dinner, leave it to me. I'll call into the shops when I'm out and get what we need. Then I'll cook enough for everyone." Antonio was happiest in the kitchen and for him to take charge of the food and the shopping was an easy way of helping the family out. He had to admit he was not dealing at all well with the emotional outpouring of grief by his mother, sisters or grandmother, and even though he had been back at home for less than forty-eight hours, a few hours break would be more than welcome.

In terms of his two nieces, Maya and Anya, they were proving quite scary. He and Charlotte were used to living in an adult world. With no children of their own, or none in their close circle of friends, they had surprisingly little experience of children in general. This was also the first time he had met either of his nieces in the flesh, so he had no idea what to do or say to them. He was certainly not a hands-on uncle, that was for sure. As he watched the way Sofía was dealing with them, her calming influence over the situation evident, he had to admit some mild admiration for his sister.

An hour and a half later and Antonio was still sitting in the café, with the tapas lunch he had ordered on a plate in front of him, still untouched and his coffee long since gone cold. Thankfully, it was a quiet afternoon and no one seemed to be bothering him for the table.

He had logged onto the café's Wi-Fi and was busily surfing pages, following links wherever they took him and trying to get whatever background information he could to support what the solicitor had already told him. It wasn't that he did not believe what he had been told, it just seemed incredible that his father had known some of what he was now reading, yet had chosen to not tell anyone about it, or deal with it in any material way, for over six months. Six months, and not a word to anyone! Antonio could not imagine how his father must have felt, unable to confide in anyone about the news he had been given, presumably not even his own wife. Or even himself, his son, who by this stage he had already made an executor of his estate. Should he at least not have been told? He was baffled by what must have been going through his father's mind at the time, and to think that he had died with all this whirling around his head simply compounded the tragedy further.

As Antonio sipped his cold coffee, continuing to delve into whatever information he could find, he questioned whether this knowledge his father had carried had even contributed to his death. Had he been so distracted that it had caused him to lose concentration, perhaps falling from the roof of the outbuilding after failing to take the usual care and consideration? Sadly no one would ever know the answer to that. Moreover, no one would ever learn what Mateo would have eventually done about the situation, had he survived his fall. Because one thing was for sure, he would not have succeeded in hiding it for another six months.

Confident he had found as much information as he could for the time being, Antonio logged off the internet and put his tablet back into its case. He still had the shopping to do for the ingredients for dinner and the concept of siesta time had passed him by. He needed to hurry or all the shops would be shut.

As he walked out of the café, he mumbled "hasta luego," to the young girl behind the counter.

The Return

"See you later," seemed the appropriate thing to say, given he was certain this would not be the last time he would need to use the café's internet.

Chapter 8

Dinner later that evening proved to be a relatively sombre affair.

Whilst Antonio had been down to the town, some of the local villagers had wandered up to the finca, offering their condolences and bringing along food and prayer offerings. A small mound of cards and candles was slowly forming, almost as a shrine, outside the outbuilding where the accident had happened. News of Mateo's sudden death the previous Thursday had shocked the whole village, and people had been taking it in their turns to call in on Lucía, to show their support and sit with her whilst she wept. It was a close and highly religious community and this was their tradition, and as Mateo and his family were well respected members of that community, for them there was no alternative other than to come and pay their respects.

Carrying his provisions into the house, Antonio had made his way to the kitchen in order to prepare a simple chicken casserole. It was a wholesome meal that could be made in sufficient quantity to feed the family, plus anyone else who was still loitering around at dinner time. He had not recognised any of the faces of the people who had called in so far, and once the introductions had been made, he had left them to their discussions. He was sure they were all well-meaning, but he had too much going on in his own mind to engage in their chatter and frankly he was embarrassed to admit he was still struggling with the language, particularly some of the local dialect spoken by the elders of the village. Whilst Spanish was his native tongue, English had become his first language, and over the years he had become more than a little rusty.

After dinner, Carmen and Juan left with their children, and Sofía went upstairs to her room to read, leaving Antonio downstairs with Lucía and Theresa. It was around nine o'clock and the two women looked exhausted after the long hot day, wanting nothing more than to simply relax on the veranda in the cooler air of the evening. Antonio could see the strain on his mother's face through the kitchen window, and the anxious looks his grandmother kept giving her whenever she thought no one was watching. It was clear Theresa was worried about her daughter.

Whilst Antonio did not want to add to her concerns, he knew that sooner or later he needed to sit his mother down and explain the situation to her. Keeping the information to himself was not something he felt comfortable with, but presumably like his father he did not know where to start. Was today the right moment, before his father's funeral on Wednesday, or would it be worth waiting another day or so, he pondered to himself as he stared out of the window.   There were obvious pros and cons of each approach, although the only thing Antonio knew for certain was delaying it indefinitely was not helping anyone.

Joining them on the veranda, carrying them each a cup of tea, Antonio spoke gently to his mother. "Mama, I need to speak to you, about what the solicitor told me, and following my discussions with the bank manager. Would now be a good time?"

"You're a good boy, Antonio," his mother replied, gently patting his leg as he sat beside her. "I'm sure you can deal with it by yourself, can't you? Is there any need for my involvement? If I need to sell the farm, then just let me know and I will look at renting a smaller house in the village. It's only me now, so I don't need anything big, just a couple of rooms to see my days out!"

"Lucía, I will not have you talking like that," Theresa replied as calmly as she could, albeit unable to hide the sternness in her voice. Allowing her daughter the space to grieve was one thing, encouraging her into a fit of depression was something else entirely. "You are still a relatively young woman, not yet sixty. Your life is far from over so there is plenty of time for you to rebuild it, whether that's on the farm or somewhere else. Mateo would not have wanted to hear you talk like this. Please don't be so despondent, we will get through this, together."

Theresa knew she had to be careful in what she said. It was far too early to suggest Lucía could perhaps love again, as she had, or even remarry should the right man come along. No, her daughter was far from that stage, and the suddenness and shock of Mateo's death had hit her hard and gone deep into her core. Theirs had been a loving relationship, a happy marriage and one that was far from the role model she and Ramos had provided their daughter.

When Ramos had died, Theresa had wanted to party. She was glad to see the back of him and only sorry it had not happened sooner. If it had they could perhaps have avoided some of the hurt he had inflicted on both her and Lucía. The finca would also have been in a stronger position financially, had he not drunk all their money away. Mateo was cut from a completely different cloth. He had been as honest as the day was long, and as trustworthy as any man could be. He was a good father, a good husband, a good friend and a good employer. The constant stream of well-wishers over recent days was a testament to that alone. Theresa recognised that even if Lucía did ever get herself to the stage where she was ready to love again, she would have to go a long way to find any man as worthy of her love as her husband had been.

"Mama, it will not come to that. For one thing, I would not allow it, and for another after my discussions with the bank and the solicitor there is no question of you having to leave the finca." Antonio waited to judge the look on his mother's face before he continued. She raised her eyes slightly and gave him an enquiring glance, almost inviting him to say more.

Seeing this as a positive, Antonio continued. "It would appear Papa only owed a few thousand euro, which was, as you'd said, a bank loan secured against the property. According to the bank manager he took it out around two years ago to buy the new tractor. It was only these last few months that he didn't make the repayments. The bank manager, when I spoke to him, apologised on behalf of the bank for writing the letters in the way they had, explaining it was an administrative error to send them out, without speaking directly to you or Papa first. Anyway, I have already repaid the outstanding amount, so there is no further discussion to be had with the bank on that matter. I can also assure you, speaking to the solicitor, that the deeds on the finca are secure too. These will be transferred into your name now, as Papa's sole beneficiary. Nothing or no one can change that."

The relief on Lucía's face was palpable.

"So, did Mateo leave a will, Antonio?" Theresa enquired, glancing across at her daughter. "Lucía was unsure, weren't you, mi hija?" Lucía nodded.

"Yes there is a will, Yaya. It is very simple, really. Papa left everything to Mama, with him nominating me to be his executor. I had no idea of that, until Señor Levi told me earlier when he read the will out to me. Papa apparently asked him to arrange the paperwork last summer, which was why I was able to talk to the bank so freely."

"That is good then. Thank you, Antonio, for doing that. Rest assured I will repay you the money, when I have the chance," Lucía said, her face displaying a wan smile, unsure where she would ever get the money from, at the same time knowing she did not want to be indebted. "At least that is the end of it, then," she continued, almost talking to herself. "I'll need to speak to some of the men to understand what needs to be done around the finca and perhaps even get someone in to help me manage it, if there's any spare money, once the bills have been paid." She sighed and looked over at Antonio. "I know very little about what Papa did on a day to day basis, or the financial side of running the farm. He never felt the need to trouble me with his business, and I never took the time to ask," she admitted sadly.

Now, resigned to running the finca herself, albeit with help and support, Lucía could at least relax in the knowledge her home was not going to be taken away from her, as she had previously feared. That alone was a huge relief. Over the days since Mateo's death, it had been a living nightmare for her, unsure which way to turn, or what to do for the best. She had wanted nothing more than to lock herself in her bedroom and weep. The loyal farm hands had simply continued without any direction, doing whatever they felt was either their routine or tasks they knew needed to be carried out. No one had bothered her, and for that she had been truly grateful.

Lucía however recognised that situation was only temporary. Over time they would need direction and decisions would need to be taken, neither of which she felt at all armed to do. It was going to be a steep learning curve for her, but as her mother kept reminding her, she was still a relatively young woman, so what was her alternative? She knew no other life.

"Mama, please don't worry about the money. It was nothing, and there is absolutely no need to repay it," Antonio began, feeling he should continue now that he had the momentum. At least after that first bit of positive news his mother was in a much better place than she had been only half an hour earlier. He just hoped she would be able to maintain it.

Theresa smiled, knowing that would be Antonio's response. He had a kind heart and was generous to a fault, with a wise head on his young shoulders. Learning he was Mateo's executor had also been a comfort for her. She was reassured he would do whatever was necessary to ensure Lucía was well provided for. Of that she had no doubt.

Antonio took a deep breath before continuing. "Mama, whilst the loan and the position with the finca and the property has been dealt with, there was something else that I learned that we do need to discuss. It is something that's going to have much wider implications. It's something Papa had known for some months, and for whatever reason did not choose to share with you. Are you happy for me to discuss it with you now, or shall we wait until the morning?"

With a puzzled expression, Lucía and Theresa exchanged a worried glance. What else had Antonio learned that Mateo had kept from them? More importantly, was something in their past perhaps coming back to haunt them, in a way that they were unprepared for?

"Your Mama is tired, Antonio," Theresa responded in an attempt to buy them some more time. "I think perhaps there's been enough said tonight already, don't you, Lucía? Why don't we wait until the morning, when we'll all be feeling more refreshed after a good night's sleep?"

"No problem, Yaya. I'll bid you both good night then," he said, rising from the chair and giving them both a kiss on the cheek as he left. He was disappointed, although he knew that the way his mother was feeling it was inappropriate to push her too hard. Of more concern to Antonio, though, was the exchange of glances he had witnessed between the two women. Did they have knowledge already of what he was about to tell them, or was there something more, of which even he was unaware?

"I'm just going to pop outside first and ring Philippe and Charlotte before I turn in, so I'll see you in the morning. I'll need to let them know my travel arrangements, and I find the reception is much better outside. I'll speak to you both tomorrow, buenas noches."

As Antonio left the room mother and daughter simply stared at each other, certain neither of them would have a good night's sleep after what Antonio had just said. The unspoken question became almost like the elephant in the room, with neither able to say the first word to begin the conversation that was long overdue. What on earth had he learned, and what possibly could the wider implications be to which he'd alluded?

Chapter 9

Later that evening, around ten o'clock, Charlotte's mobile phone rang. She was at home relaxing in bed and watching the television, after a leisurely day of doing very little. Real Housewives of Cheshire was playing out in the background and the call was disturbing her viewing. In truth, though, she wasn't really concentrating on the television, as her mind was miles away. Thankfully it was not a programme that demanded her concentration.

The weekend away in Bath had exhausted her, and having eventually arrived back into London Paddington the previous evening, much later than she had originally planned, she had not felt like doing too much today. In truth, she did not have much to do any day. At least not since she and Antonio had married and she had opted to become a kept woman. Giving up her job as a production assistant at one of the local TV stations was no hardship, although she did miss some of the gossip and the occasional brush with celebrity it had afforded her.

Nowadays the daily came in to clean twice a week, the laundry was collected each Tuesday morning and returned pressed and ironed, ready for hanging straight back into the closet and the shopping was managed by an internet order each Friday, delivered directly to the kitchen. All Charlotte had to do was empty the bags, restock the fridge and put the wine and champagne into the chiller. Other than that what else did she have to fill her time? Make a meal if she was hungry, go out for a walk or visit the gym if she wanted exercise, or arrange a catch up with a friend if she fancied a gossip. Not the most fulfilling of lives she had to admit.

Antonio's picture appeared once again on her screen. "Oh God, what is it this time?" she questioned herself as she picked up the handset. Each time he rang it was to feed her another snippet of news from his travels, and frankly it was starting to get tiresome. She had as much sympathy as the next man, but he was certainly testing her tolerance with his continual ringing.

"Darling, how are things going today?" she enquired, trying to inject a lightness into her voice that she was simply not feeling. "Is your flight all booked now, and what time do you land on Friday morning? I presume you'll get a taxi to pick you up from Heathrow to bring you home, or will you be heading directly to the restaurant?"

"Charlotte, hi. In fact, that's what I'm ringing about. There's been a slight change in the plans and I won't be home on Friday, as I'd thought. I've just got off the phone to Philippe and he's happy to manage everything for a few more days, as well as pass on my apologies to those clients we have booked in. It's unavoidable, unfortunately."

"Sorry, what's unavoidable? You said you'd be home Friday morning, latest. The funeral is on

Wednesday, so what on earth is keeping you in Tenerife any later than that? Surely, you've not booked a few nights out, or planning on catching up with old friends, are you? It's not turning into a little holiday, is it?" She was beginning to wonder if she should have gone too.

"No, of course not. I've not even thought about that, although now you come to mention it, it's possible some of my old friends may turn up for the funeral. I'm not sure they will recognise me, though, or me them. It's been such a long time. We've all aged and moved on."

Charlotte was becoming exasperated. She was annoyed and her sarcasm had obviously gone way over his head. Antonio and she were rarely on the same wavelength when it came to their sense of humour, in fact increasingly they were not on the same wavelength for most things.

"So, what's keeping you then? I thought you'd said it was such a big weekend for you at the restaurant, you couldn't afford to miss it." Another attempt at sarcasm.

"It is, it's just that something's come up that I didn't expect, so I'm having to fly out to Lanzarote on Thursday or Friday, depending on when I can get flights and a hotel booked. I'll have to look tomorrow at what's available."

"Hang on, did you say Lanzarote? I'm totally confused now. What on earth's going on over there?" Charlotte, convinced this was the first time she had heard Antonio mention Lanzarote, realised she had better start concentrating, so she lowered the volume on the television. "Do you want to tell me what all this is about?"

"If I'm honest, Charlotte, I'm not sure I know what it's all about myself yet. That's why I need to get over there. It was something the solicitor told me yesterday, to do with my father's estate, and I need to look into it. I told you he'd made me the executor, didn't I?"

"Yes, you did, although you also said your father's estate amounted to a small finca in the remote hills of Tenerife, and a handful of pigs. In the middle of nowhere, away from civilization. A few ramshackle buildings with some livestock and produce, the exact nature of which you weren't sure, if I recall correctly?"

"Well, yes, although not quite the description I used that was basically what I'd thought. However, there's another dimension that I previously wasn't aware of, and that's what I need to look into. Anyway, given it's getting late, why don't I ring you back tomorrow and let you get some sleep now? You could then tell me about your weekend away. You haven't mentioned it yet. I hope you all had a nice time and that your friends were well." Antonio couldn't remember their names exactly and didn't want to hazard a guess. Just a couple of old school friends, Charlotte had said.

"Yes, we had a lovely time, thank you. Other than that, there's not much really to report," she offered, unprepared to be drawn further on her weekend away. "Okay, good night then, Antonio. We'll speak tomorrow, and perhaps by then you'll be able to update me on the next gripping episode of your travels!"

With that, she hung up the phone. Something was going on with her husband, and for once Charlotte had absolutely no idea what that might be. He was being mysterious, which was so unlike him. He was normally an open book, what you saw was what you got. Perhaps the mystery might make him a little more interesting, she pondered, because as things currently stood, she was starting to get extremely bored by the whole situation.

The weekend hadn't helped in that context either, and her chance meeting with Miles on Sunday morning had not made it any easier. After checking out in reception, around eleven o'clock, she had casually bumped into him. He was relaxing in the coffee lounge with the Sunday papers. He had looked up as she passed, with a cheeky grin on his face. It was almost as if he had planned it and had been awaiting her arrival.

Dressed casually in beige chinos and a button down pale-blue shirt he looked just as handsome as he had suited and booted in his dinner jacket the previous evening. He looked relaxed, with an air of confidence that just bordered on being cocky.

"Good morning, Mrs Pérez. I was hoping I might catch you," he had said casually, maintaining that smile on his face. "Would you like me to help you with your bags and drive you to the railway station, or could I perhaps tempt you into a spot of lunch? Assuming you're not meeting anyone or have anything important to rush home for, that is?"

"Actually, no. My friends had an earlier check-out, and my husband is away for a few nights, so I'm a completely free agent," Charlotte replied, wondering why she had added that last comment. "In fact, I've absolutely nothing to rush anywhere for and lunch sounds like a wonderful idea, so thank you," she answered displaying more confidence than she actually felt.

As Charlotte watched his expression, his eyebrows lifting at the mention of her husband being away, she could feel a certain frisson between them. She had felt something the previous evening too, when they had danced together, and had simply put it down to the champagne and the occasion. She'd believed it would pass as soon as she had sobered up and life returned to normal. Once the glamourous ballgown was off and the jeans were back on, she would just revert to being plain Mrs Pérez again; almost like Cinderella's encounter with Prince Charming at the ball. Although seeing Miles again this morning, and noting the reaction it was having on her stomach, to say nothing of her inability to form coherent thoughts as he continued to stare at her, that was obviously not the case.

"Well, let me take your case from you, madam," he joked, offering a small bow. "Then I suggest we drive to a little country pub I know, where the food is excellent and the views are spectacular.

Follow me," and taking her case in one hand and her hand in the other he led her outside to the carpark.

Charlotte went along with Miles' suggestion, without question. She was completely sober yet felt as giddy as a schoolgirl. Then, as he opened the passenger door of his Porsche to her and smiled across, he simply said, "buckle up, we're in for an interesting ride!"

Chapter 10

The following lunchtime and Antonio was back in the café, using their internet again. This time it was an elderly lady behind the counter who'd smiled and nodded as he'd politely asked if it was alright for him to sit for a while. He was feeling more like a local each day, even recognising the occasional face and stopping to pass a few words with someone who knew him or the family, or to accept their condolences on the loss of his father.

He was surprised so many people took the time to chat, or even enquire about the restaurant and his life in England. He was equally surprised most appeared relatively up to date on his comings and goings, meaning it was obvious his mother or sisters spoke of him often. Antonio smiled, in an attempt to disguise a misplaced feeling of pride, alongside his growing feelings of shame. In England few people even knew Antonio came from Tenerife, let alone that his family still lived there. He realised he rarely spoke of them, their finca or the type of lifestyle they enjoyed, other than to those close friends or family he knew he could trust. He preferred to live in the moment and focus on building up his image as a renowned chef, a successful restauranteur, a businessman of note, rather than harp back to his peasant upbringing. No one would be interested in that.

Drinking the large cup of coffee he had ordered, he logged onto the internet and started searching for flights to Lanzarote and accommodation in and around the area he needed to be. There appeared to be a regular schedule, and as he was only looking to book one night in a hotel, he didn't anticipate any problems. His father's solicitor had also provided him with the name of the solicitor in Lanzarote he should contact to confirm his journey, and he had just spoken to her. She was happy to support his visit and would make herself available for whenever he arrived. So now he just needed to finalise the details.

Whilst Antonio still struggled to believe what he had been told, it was starting to feel worryingly real. And after the discussion with Lucía and Theresa earlier that morning he at least felt he was making the journey with their full knowledge, if not their scepticism of what the outcome might be.

"Antonio, what you've heard cannot be true. I'm sure there is a misunderstanding somewhere. Your great-grandfather had no time for his grandson, Mateo, or Mateo's mama, Rosa, for that matter." Theresa reacted quite strongly to the news Antonio was sharing with her and Lucía. "In fact, when Mateo's own papa died, his parents did little to help Rosa or Mateo out, financially or otherwise. She came back to Tenerife, almost penniless. Back to the mercy of her home village and the family and friends she had been forced to leave. Staying with her in-laws was not an option she could ever consider, without Paco there to support her. Rosa even told me many years later about the time they'd had a paternity test done on Mateo, without hers or Paco's knowledge, because they suspected she had tricked them into marrying their son, hence I can't believe it's true."

"Yaya, I can only tell you and Mama what I have been told, and what I have researched over the last couple of days. I have found quite a lot of information on the internet, about the Pérez's family interests in Lanzarote, and the death of José Pérez, my great-grandfather, last year. He was quite an old man when he died, yet from the reports he was still very much active in terms of running his business interests. He'd managed to outlive his wife and his daughter, who according to the reports had never married. There were also reports of his son's death, in the boating accident all those years ago, with the reports suggesting there was no remaining family, which left a massive question mark over the old man's estate."

"And what you're saying, Antonio, is that Mateo had been contacted – and had been told he was their only surviving family, is that correct?" Lucía was still struggling to take all this in.

"Basically, Mama, yes. When Señor Pérez' solicitors read his will, which had apparently been updated about ten years ago, shortly after his daughter's death, he named his grandson Mateo Pérez as his sole beneficiary. According to Papa's solicitor, Señor Pérez had kept tabs on Rosa and

Mateo following their return to Tenerife, and whilst it's true neither side ever got in direct contact again, he did formally recognise him as his bloodline, eventually." Antonio noticed the look on his grandmother's face, one of utter disbelief. "Presumably the DNA test you spoke of Yaya, put paid to any suspicions he might have once had, and in old age he presumably mellowed, especially with no other children or grandchildren on the scene to inherit."

"So why did Mateo never tell me?" Lucía questioned. "Why did he keep this information to himself for so long. Did he not trust me enough to tell me?"

"No, Mama, I don't believe that's the situation at all. I imagine he just didn't want to trouble you. According to Papa's solicitor, Papa did not want to believe it, and thought if he ignored it, it would probably go away. He felt like he knew nothing about his family in Lanzarote, other than the little he could remember growing up, and none of that was positive. Yaya Rosa had never spoken of them in a good light, so I imagine he didn't want to think about them either, or bother you or her about it. Yaya Rosa is an old woman now, and he probably did not want to add to her worries. So he told his solicitor he already had enough on his plate, looking after the finca and the family, to go and worry about a fishing boat in Lanzarote."

"So is that what we're talking about, Antonio? Mateo has inherited an old fishing boat, that's in Lanzarote? Because if that's the case, it won't do him any good now, or us for that matter, will it? I suggest we should ignore it, just as your papa was doing."

"No Mama, it's not that simple." Lucía's naivety in dealing with the situation was endearing, if not a little misplaced. "I'm not just talking about an old fishing boat. I'm led to believe we're talking about a fishing industry, as well as investments and property, that when taken into consideration amount to a significant amount of money, as well as responsibilities that need to be dealt with. By all accounts, José Pérez was a very successful business man, who had multiple interests that currently are all held in abeyance, awaiting someone to deal with them. And as Papa is no longer here to do that, then I, as his executor, need to. This is not something that can be ignored any longer."

He waited a moment, allowing the shock of what he had just said to sink in with both his mother and grandmother. "Hence why I am planning on going over to Lanzarote to meet with Señor Pérez's solicitor as soon as the funeral is over. I want to understand the full picture, and the implications for myself. Although, if what I've gleaned so far is true, then Mama, you will never need to worry about money, ever again."

"Oh….." Lucía was speechless with the look on her face indescribable as this latest part of the picture began to sink in.

"Mama, let me go to Lanzarote and meet with the solicitor first, then I'll come back here and we can talk more. At least then we will have the full picture and I can help you decide what needs to be done."

So now with the flights booked, the appointment made to meet the solicitor and his diary free for the next few days to make the trip, all Antonio had to do was think about what questions he needed to ask, and what options he might need to present to his mother on his return.

This trip to Tenerife was certainly not turning out to be anywhere near as straightforward as he had anticipated, and what the future held for him and his family was now a complete mystery.

Chapter 11

Sitting in the cold dark church, surrounded by family and friends, Theresa allowed her memories to distract her from the solemnity of the funeral service and the full requiem mass her daughter had chosen for her husband. The church was packed to the rafters, with more mourners gathered outside, unable to get into the building and rest their weary legs. It was midday and the sun was at its hottest, with people taking whatever shelter they could in the shade of the sprawling trees smattered around the old village plaza. They were prepared to weather whatever conditions, provided they felt part of the service.

Theresa had been touched by how many of the villagers had joined them along the way as they had walked to the church from their finca, processing up the cobbled streets of the village, almost as if it were a pilgrimage. They had stopped at Rosa's house along the route, where Antonio had gently taken his grandmother's frail hand and escorted her the remaining distance, his strong arms providing the support she needed as her legs almost buckled as she struggled to contain her emotions.

Theresa had visited her old friend the previous day to offer her own condolences and provide whatever support she could. They had so many shared memories and experiences, with Mateo being an important part of both of their lives. As she had left Rosa's small house Theresa had noticed a mound of flowers and cards stacked outside, similar to the ones at the finca. Religious mementoes and prayer cards expressing the shared grief felt by the villagers.

Theresa had spent a few moments reading some of the cards, sad to realise that since her move to England some thirty years ago the strict Catholic religion in which she had been raised had fallen by the wayside. It no longer formed part of her everyday life, whereas here among the villagers it appeared central to their existence. She tried to recall the last time she had actually been inside a church, and imagined it was perhaps her second husband's funeral nearly four years ago. Where had that time gone, in fact where had all those years gone since she and Rosa had been young girls? Those careless years, before the strains and stresses of married life and all that had brought to their doors.

In truth, neither of them had married well, had they? She to Ramos, with all the trials of being married to a brutish man, or Rosa to Paco, married into a family that would never accept her, or her son. Had neither of them been pregnant at the time, she imagined both would have made much different choices, led such different lives.

She recalled the day they had first met Paco, and how in awe of him she and Rosa had both been, with his fine clothes and the lifestyle he appeared to enjoy. It was 1962 and they were working in a hotel in the south of the island, waitressing or acting as chamber maids, depending on what jobs needed to be done. The tourist trade was just starting to flourish on the island and casual labour was in high demand.

With little else to do in the village, many of the youngsters got involved. It was good money, but hard work. They were bused down from their village to the resort early each morning and returned at the end of the day, exhausted. Occasionally if there were functions on, they were put up in basic accommodation nearby, as it was too late to risk driving up the winding and precarious roads back to their remote villages.

Ramos also worked at the hotel, in the kitchens peeling vegetables, or helping to keep the bars stocked. In those days, he was broad-shouldered and strong, and his good looks made him an instant attraction with the young girls, especially when he produced a bottle of something he had stolen from the bar and shared it around at the end of the shift.

This particular night, the hotel was hosting a wedding reception. She and Rosa were waitressing and Ramos was working behind the bar and serving drinks. The main dining hall was full of guests and the meal was a formal four-course dinner, with traditional Canarian dancing following the speeches. After serving dinner, the waitresses were expected to clear away the dirty crockery, before waiting around until after midnight in order to clean the function room once the event had finished.

It had already been a long day and at eleven o'clock Rosa and Theresa were taking their break near the hotel's service entrance. It was a balmy evening and as it was hot inside the hotel several of the guests had similarly wandered outside. It was a full moon and the views were spectacular. The stars could be seen twinkling in the clear night sky with the lights of the other hotels shining brightly in the distance.

Paco was leaning against a tree in the hotel's gardens - about twenty feet away, casually smoking a cigarette and taking in the fresh night air. He looked very sophisticated in his suit, with his dark wavy hair just teasing the collar of his jacket. Rosa had noticed him in the main dining room, and had even caught his eye as she had placed his soup down, careful to avoid spilling it down him as her hand slightly quivered. The smile he had given her had made her blush, and throughout the evening he had continued to look at her whenever she was in the room, ferrying in course after course or removing the dirty plates.

As they were standing having a cigarette of their own, quietly chatting to avoid disturbing the guests, Paco called them over. They knew they shouldn't, however Rosa encouraged Theresa to go with her. After all, they were only sixteen, naïve and had no fear of the consequences.

"Come on, what harm can it do?" Rosa had argued, a mischievous glint in her eyes. "We've only got ten minutes anyway, and then we'll have to get back inside and start the clear up."

Theresa had gone along with her, equally interested as she too had seen him in the dining room. Before long, it was obvious Paco was flirting with her friend, and Rosa was lapping it up, charmed by the mysterious stranger.

Then Ramos appeared, carrying a couple of bottles of wine in his hand that he had taken from the bar, with a cheeky grin on his face.

"Rosa, Theresa, do you want to come back to my room as soon as we finish and help me with these?" he'd suggested, initially unaware Paco was there, or that he was one of the guests at the wedding.

However, Paco had overheard him and instantly asked, "Can I come too? I could do with some fun." Rosa had simply smiled and nodded, before giving him the directions to the apartment block in which the hotel staff were being put up overnight.

By the time the evening was over all four were drunk. They had sat on the floor laughing and joking, and as Rosa had fallen for Paco's charms, so too had Theresa fallen for Ramos'. As two o'clock in the morning approached, each couple collapsed onto one of the single beds in the small room they had been allocated, a small privacy curtain all that separated them.

The following month sadly the girls found that the boys were not all they had fallen for, when they realised they had both become pregnant. Ramos and Theresa were promptly marched down the aisle as soon as her parents realised what had happened. Their shame otherwise would have been too much to consider.

Rosa's parents had more trouble tracking Paco and his family down, given he was from Lanzarote, although once he was found the same fate befell him and Rosa. None of the parents were pleased with the outcome – least of all Paco's parents who remained convinced Rosa had trapped their son.   As far as they were concerned, he was an eligible bachelor, who could have had his choice of girls. Why did he need saddling with the daughter of a peasant farmer?

The day Rosa moved to Lanzarote, to live with the Pérez family, was a sad day for Theresa. Losing her friend and confidante was one thing, but then to learn that Rosa was unhappy living away from home with Paco's family further added to Theresa's sadness. And even though over the years Rosa had grown to love Paco, that feeling had never extended to his family, so it was with mixed feelings when she arrived home following his death. Sad to lose her husband, concerned about her son, but contented to be back on the island of Tenerife, with Theresa and the rest of her family again.

In time, Rosa was the only one who truly understood how unhappy Theresa was with Ramos, how difficult he made her life and how his bouts of drunkenness often turned to violence. It was Rosa who was there to support her when he died, and Rosa who stayed with her through the years that followed, as the two of them watched their children, Lucía and Mateo grow close and eventually bring up a family of their own. And it was Rosa who was there at the end, when the difficult decisions had needed to be made. They had certainly been there for each other over the years.

So now to see her friend burying her son, she wondered how she would feel in similar circumstances. Rosa had not had the easiest of lives, nor had had the same breaks as Theresa, and that had taken its toll on her health. She had aged far more than Theresa and looked much frailer than her years would suggest. As she watched Rosa, her head bowed as the final prayers were being said, she wondered what the implications of the fortune that had recently befallen the family would mean to her. Lucía would ensure her mother-in-law benefitted in some way from whatever it was that Paco's father had left to his grandson Mateo, surely?

It would be a discussion she perhaps needed to have with Antonio, she mused, once the picture was clearer; once they knew more about what the legacy they had been left actually meant.

For now, they just needed to get through the remainder of the day and pray that the rest would sort itself out, one way or another.

Chapter 12

What Antonio believed would be a short forty-eight hour trip to Lanzarote, where he intended to fly in, deal with what needed to be done and get straight back on a return flight, turned out not to be the case. It had taken a full week, seven long days and nights.

As he buckled himself into his aircraft seat ready for the short return flight, he was surprised at where that time had gone, or how relaxed he was feeling after what had been a surprisingly busy few days. To him, used to living life against a tight schedule, with little time to do anything other than manage his business interests, and being surrounded by people who were constantly looking to him for decisions, spending time by himself and outside of his normal routine had come as a bit of a culture shock.

Now, as he reflected on his time away, he had to admit that at points it had almost felt like a holiday. It was certainly a long time since he had stayed in a hotel for pleasure, or been waited on by people who were not on his payroll. It was even longer since he'd enjoyed so much free time, or just his own company to contend with. He'd had time to amble along the promenade on an evening, to stop for a snack or a cold beer during the daytime, even time to appreciate the views and engage in a spot of people watching, if he chose to; certainly time to appreciate the gentler side of life.

Whilst London had a lot to commend it as a capital city, and it was after all his home and where his businesses were located, it was not somewhere he'd ever felt truly at peace. There was never any real sense of tranquillity in the lifestyle he had built for himself. The hustle and bustle was something that had become the norm, with the adrenaline it gave him simply the buzz he needed to keep operating at the level to which he continued to push himself.

Lanzarote had certainly given him both thinking time and breathing space. Space to grieve his father in a way that until then he had not even realised he'd needed.

Charlotte had not been at all happy as his plans continued to slip to the right, or the fact, as she saw it, he was holidaying without her. It had certainly not helped when he had inadvertently described the five star hotel he had checked into, or the spa facilities it had, with its infinity swimming pool and its close proximity to the coastline and the golden beaches. She had argued she should fly over and join him for a few days, adding that she could enjoy the hotel whilst he did whatever he needed to do. Antonio, realising Charlotte was a distraction he did not need, did not allow himself to bite at her suggestion. He had enough to contend with without having to deal with her demands too.

On the Friday morning, he had met with José Pérez's solicitor as planned at her plush office in

Arrecife, the island's capital. Whilst he had spoken to Señorita Camila García on the phone and found her pleasant and helpful, he was completely unprepared for the vision that met him in the flesh. She was of a similar age to himself, somewhere early to mid-thirties, striking in appearance and with a figure that was shown off to its best in an expensively tailored suit, with alarmingly high heeled shoes that even Charlotte would have struggled to balance on, let alone walk in. Antonio found her smile alluring and her voice almost hypnotic as he endeavoured to concentrate on what she was saying. She was certainly very attractive and he wondered if he needed to be on his guard, particularly if her plans had them spending any length of time together.

Seated behind her glass desk, with her long legs crossed under the table top, Camila had outlined more detail about his great-grandfather's estate, answering some of the questions Antonio had been unsure of after reading what information he could find on the internet about the family's business. He attempted to focus on her face as she began to describe how *Pesca Pérez* had started as a local business, founded in Lanzarote over a hundred years previously by José's father and grandfather. At its inception it involved a single small fishing boat that would go out on a daily basis into the Atlantic waters and catch whatever it could.

At the time José's grandfather was happy to continue as he was, catching enough to eat and feed his family, with a little left over that he could sell at market to provide a basic income. His son, though, was ambitious. He had recently married and had a family to feed, with a new baby on the way. He wanted more and after buying a second boat he took on extra fishermen and started expanding his horizons.

Over the following ten years their fleet continued to grow and their harvest increased, with their fortunes eventually turning when they began to fish for the lucrative tuna. They also had luck on their side, with their hard work eventually paying off when they struck business deals to provide the growing local hospitality industries with the fresh fish they needed.

From there the business continued to flourish, the number of vessels in the fleet increased and with profits ploughed back into the business, by way of investment in machinery and facilities, they created a thriving and profitable business, ultimately exporting a large proportion of their catch, once the local markets had been saturated.

When José joined the business, he took it to another level. Unlike his father and grandfather before him, he had enjoyed a good education and saw the wider commercial benefits his forefathers had never considered. In time he began investing the profits in property, as well as in stocks and shares and other tax efficient schemes he discovered.

Over the following years they became a very prominent and wealthy family, as well as a major employer on the island, and as such they began to enjoy the lifestyle that wealth provided.

José was the only son of an only son, so when he and his wife had Paco, he became destined to take over the family business. Their elder daughter sadly enjoyed ill health and they had accepted she would never marry or have children, so all their hopes were pinned on Paco making a good match and producing the dynasty the family so desperately needed.

Paco's untimely death in a freak boating accident, with his widow then taking their son Mateo back to Tenerife, meant any hopes they may have had were soon diminished. His widow was a Pérez by name only, and with no interest in the business or their lifestyle, even if they had wanted to keep her or their grandson close, it would never have succeeded.

Over the years José and his wife had kept a watchful, if distant, eye over their grandson, praying one day for his return, although in reality they had long since recognised the probability of that happening was futile. So, after his wife and daughter's early deaths, José finally accepted, other than Mateo, there was no remaining bloodline. He was by then a very old man and his fortunes had to go somewhere, whether he liked it or not. If not to his grandson, then the government would take it, and that was not something José was prepared to contemplate.

Antonio had quietly listened to the story, taking in whatever Camila told him at face value. He struggled to summon up any emotion for his great-grandfather's plight and felt distant from what he was being told. Over the years the little he had heard about his father's side of the family had been tarnished by the stories Rosa, Theresa, or even his own father had told. He could not recall anything good ever having been said about his paternal great-grandparents, so there were simply no good memories on which to cling.

"So, Señor Pérez," Camila had broken into his reverie, her tone suggesting it was time to concentrate on the business to hand. "Now I have outlined the background, what I would suggest is that tomorrow I take you to the factory and introduce you to Señor Días. He and his team has managed the business for some time now, effectively since Señor Pérez stepped down from operational control, over twenty years ago. Naturally they continued to run it, once Señor Pérez died. He was very loyal to your family and I believe you will like him.

"I will then take you to the house in which your great-grandfather lived, and where he subsequently died. As you will appreciate, he was a very old man when that happened, only a matter of weeks short of his one-hundredth birthday. His carer lived in the house too, for the last ten years of his life at least, once he became physically less independent, that is. Although I understand, according to some of my colleagues who have dealt with his affairs over the years, he was still quite astute and clear thinking, right until the end.

"As you will see when we visit the property, there have been many adaptations, for his comfort I imagine. Also, as it has sat unoccupied since his death last year, sadly it is not currently in the best of repair.

I will then arrange for a meeting with the estate agents, to understand the position regarding the other properties too, if you would like? There is a mix of commercial and rental units, I understand.

"Finally, on Monday afternoon, I will take you to the bank to introduce you to the manager there who dealt with the stocks and shares portfolio, and the other investments Señor Pérez had. They will no doubt advise you on those matters better than I can."

"Thank you, Señorita García, you have been most helpful," Antonio said, rising from his seat as he realised their session was over. She had certainly given him a lot to think about, as well as a reason to stay for more than the forty-eight hours he had originally intended. Realising he now had time on his hands, and with no idea what he would do to fill it, he enquired, without really thinking, "Would you care to join me for dinner this evening?"

Taken aback, Camila was momentarily lost for words. "Oh, thank you, but no, Señor," she stuttered. "I have other plans this evening. I will collect you at your hotel at ten-thirty in the morning, though. Until then, good day Mr Pérez," her tone indicating the meeting was now definitely over.

Antonio was left feeling more than a little embarrassed by the way he had uncharacteristically invited her out to dinner, to say nothing of the sheer shock it had engendered on her face as she had declined.

The following day, their relationship was purely professional with any embarrassment either party may have felt well and truly parked. The visit to the factory and the meeting with the management team went well. It was clear the business was being run efficiently and there was a great deal of pride in what they did. Antonio even recognised the brand, and acknowledged the high quality of the fish it produced. It was a brand he had used in his own restaurants over the years.

The viewing of the house itself was emotionless, as was the drive past the other properties in which his great-grandfather had interests. They all appeared to be fine properties, just nothing that held any interest for him. He could not see his mother having any interests in them either.

After speaking with a local estate agent on the Tuesday afternoon, Antonio arranged for valuations of the various properties to be carried out. He discussed the process, should they decide to put them on the market, as whilst it was clearly his mother's decision, he wanted to at least be armed with the details. He had also learned that a fair offer had been made to buy *Pesca Pérez* as a going concern, should they decide to sell the business, and on the Thursday morning he had made a couple of calls to understand the offer in a little more detail. Whilst everyone had impatiently been waiting to deal with Mateo, no one had balked at the idea of dealing with his son, Antonio. He had a good head on his shoulders and to his credit he was dealing with the issues, some of which in their view had dragged on for far too long.

As Antonio left the island, tired but satisfied he had made good progress, with the promise to deal with whatever else needed to be dealt with efficiently once he got back, in reality, he knew he had barely touched the surface. There was still a lot more to be done and top of the list was speaking to his mother. After all, it was her inheritance and the decisions were hers to make. Although he feared the size and value of what was involved would blow her mind, with the complexity something she could never be expected to grasp. Ironically, Antonio sensed that was probably why his father had chosen not to engage her, especially if everything had been presented to him, or discussed in such a legal manner that he had simply not understood it fully himself either.

It was certainly a tangled web of interests and instinctively Antonio knew the process of sorting everything out would take time, as well as it having the potential to become complicated the deeper they went into the details. So, as much as he had his own interests back in England, he was faced with a dilemma. He could not contemplate walking away, nor abandoning his mother, expecting her to deal with whatever legal dramas eventually played out. As his father's executor he had a duty to see it through. How he best discharged that duty, whilst at the same time balancing the business and personal demands of his own, became a conundrum that had kept him awake as he'd lain alone in his plush hotel room.

The Return

As he bid goodbye to Camila, with the further promise of being in touch in the coming days, he wondered what would become of life on Lanzarote, should his family's affairs there come to an end. It was clear the Pérez family name had been held in high esteem for well over a century, with buildings and businesses proudly carrying that name, but was that enough for Antonio, or any of the family for that matter, to ever consider wanting to settle there? He somehow doubted it.

Chapter 13

"Oh, you're finally coming home this time, are you?" Charlotte had asked sceptically the following weekend, with what was becoming her usual sprinkling of sarcasm whenever she spoke to her husband these days. His short trip, which had only been expected to take a couple of days, had expanded into three weeks. It was clearly not the first time his plans had changed and frankly she'd had enough of his empty promises.

His week in Lanzarote without her hadn't helped her mood either, nor had the further week he had chosen to stay with his family after the trip. He was obviously in no rush to get home to see his wife, so why should she care? In fact, she was actually managing to cope quite nicely without him.

"Yes, my flight's booked for tomorrow afternoon, meaning I should arrive back into Heathrow around seven o'clock tomorrow evening, provided there are no delays. I'll arrange a taxi, so don't worry about picking me up." She listened quite dispassionately to his arrangements, having never given a second thought to the concept of driving to the airport to collect him.

"Okay, and will you be coming home, or going directly to the restaurant?" Before she asked the question, she sensed the answer that would be forthcoming. She was aware Antonio had been in regular contact with Philippe, and knowing they would have already discussed what would be happening, as usual she would be the last to know.

"I'll come home as I'll need to have a quick shower and change my clothes first. I'll then pop into the restaurant for a couple of hours to check what's happening. Philippe's more than happy to continue to manage things, but I'd like to show my face and reassure myself everything's okay. I won't be late, and I can bring dinner back later with me, if you'd like?"

"Whatever!" Charlotte was beginning to lose her patience. It was obvious from the fact he had not even enquired how she was that he had barely missed her, nor it appeared was he in any hurry for them to spend their evening together. All it did was reinforce her belief of where she now stood in her husband's pecking order.

It was something she'd had a lot of time to mull over during recent weeks, and the time she had spent with Miles over the last few days, if nothing else had helped focus her mind even further.

He had messaged the previous Tuesday evening, saying he was in town for a few days. His planned three-day business trip had been curtailed, due to his client needing to leave urgently, unforeseen personal circumstances had been blamed. So, at a loose end and finding himself with a clear diary for the remainder of the week, Miles faced the option of either returning home early, or staying in London for some downtime. He wondered if Charlotte was free to join him for dinner, or even the theatre if he could get tickets. "Although absolutely no pressure, given it's such short notice." He had however added a jokey emoji to the message, to demonstrate how hopeful he was that she'd take pity on him by accepting his invitation.

Charlotte had been sitting at home, feeling down and nursing a meal for one when the message beeped through and it had made her smile. Since Miles had driven her to the railway station in Bath the previous month, after spending an enjoyable Sunday afternoon together, they had messaged each other with increasing frequency. His messages had begun as funny, quirky almost, with a string of emojis that made her laugh. They occasionally bordered on the flirty side, but given she was at home alone, bored and feeling abandoned, Charlotte did not mind. She'd quite enjoyed his company and having him as a friend to message became an innocent distraction while Antonio was away.

She was however drawn into his humour and before long found herself responding in a similar vein, almost encouraging him with her own set of crazy emojis. After all, Miles knew she was married and had certainly never tried anything on, so what was the harm in a bit of meaningless banter, especially as she was unlikely to ever see him again?

Accepting his invitation to dinner, though, had the potential to take their friendship to a whole new level, particularly as at the back of her mind she knew he had a hotel suite at his disposal, in a rather plush

London hotel, if she recalled correctly the one he had mentioned.

Charlotte was also not naïve and had recognised the 'banter to flirting ratio' in their messaging had recently taken on a more suggestive turn - phrasing that perhaps came dangerously close on the innuendo scale to something that could no longer be classed as merely platonic. So, was his offer of dinner just that, or was there more on the menu, at least as far as Miles was concerned?

Charlotte was certainly attracted to Miles but until that point cheating on her husband had not been something she had ever contemplated. Close friends had had affairs, which largely had ended badly and it was not a road Charlotte had ever seen herself travelling. She recognised she had too much to lose. Deep down she may well be annoyed with her husband, but she did still love him.

Miles was dangerous though, particularly as his attentions towards her were just when she was feeling at her most vulnerable, most alone and almost abandoned. Could she fight him off, if that's what it came to – and if it did, would she want to? No, she was being paranoid and reading far too much into it. It was, after all, only dinner.

Eventually deciding to go, she'd texted back saying she would meet him in an hour's time, before promptly throwing her meal for one into the recycle bin and heading upstairs to get herself ready.

Sitting now, having just put the phone down to Antonio, Charlotte had mixed feelings about hearing he was finally coming home, especially as she recalled the last few days and the fun she'd had with Miles. The memories made her smile.

After their initial dinner, they had met up each day for lunch, or walks through the park, or had dinner in his hotel, followed by a couple of nightcaps in the bar. He had been attentive throughout, generous with his time and above all else provided a great distraction. He had also acted like the perfect gentleman, with any concerns she'd originally had proving unfounded. Each night she returned home in the taxi alone, a kiss on the cheek as intimate as they had become. Their time had remained almost platonic, although the closer they had got over those few days, the more she imagined otherwise, and lying in bed each night it was Miles' arms she pictured around her, not Antonio's. He had sparked a real desire in her, a longing she had not felt in a long time, and unless she was reading the signs completely wrong, she sensed a clear danger of that feeling being reciprocated.

So her husband's imminent return home was creating a real dilemma for Charlotte. Miles had gone back to Bath, back to his life and family there. She clearly needed to forget about him and snap out of whatever it was she was feeling – and quickly, before Antonio returned home and suspected her of doing something she was not actually guilty of, yet.

Chapter 14

A week after returning from Lanzarote, Antonio eventually returned to London, leaving Theresa at the finca to care for Lucía, Sofía and the rest of the family.

He and Theresa had discussed it and neither felt Lucía was ready to shoulder it all by herself, particularly given everything else that had happened since Mateo's death. The finca was demanding enough, without all the added complexities arising from the nature of the inheritance that had been unearthed during Antonio's trip to Lanzarote. Lucía was still grieving the death of her husband, her mind was far from thinking straight, and rightly so. Sofía and Carmen were having to deal with the death of their father too, as well as support their mother, whilst keeping going with their own lives. Clearly none of them was strong enough to deal with it without some support, and for Theresa remaining in Tenerife was not an issue. She was happy to stay and provide the proverbial shoulder to cry on, or that extra pair of hands should either be required.

Unlike the rest of the family, Theresa knew Antonio was strong and much more practically minded. He was grieving Mateo's death in his own way, but he did need to return to London for his own business interests, his own family. It was clear from his occasional comment that even though Philippe was coping, Charlotte was unhappy that his stay had been extended yet again. Continuing to extend it indefinitely, whilst things were sorted out, was no longer an option.

In truth, though, Theresa was happy to be staying around. She had nothing she was desperate to return home to anyway, especially not since her second husband's death.

Duncan had died over three years previously, having left her a very wealthy widow. Since then, she had begun to find herself rattling around in a house much larger than her needs, her life drifting along without any real purpose. It had become almost superficial with the monthly trips to the hair salon, the stores, the gym and the various restaurants she frequented taking up most of her free time. She had once been a vibrant and busy woman, supporting Duncan in his many business interests, so becoming a lady of leisure had started to wear thin. If she was honest, even with all the money and her many friends, she was becoming quite lonely. She needed a new distraction. After all, she was still only in her early seventies, and as someone who was healthy and took pride in herself, God willing she still had many years ahead of her.

When Antonio had returned from Lanzarote, after having met with the solicitors and estate agents on the island, he had talked them both through what he had discovered. Theresa had found it astounding the amount of money they were actually talking about, with the various aspects that were involved in the estate making it even more exciting. Duncan had been a businessman-cum-consultant, and among his many interests was somebody who loved to dabble in property. He would often buy up old properties or defunct businesses, then using his vivid imagination redevelop them, or reshape them into profitable operations for himself or his clients. As such, Theresa had a good appreciation of what was involved and smiled at the thought of how much Duncan would have relished the conundrum that was now facing them. He would have instinctively known what to do, or what best to advise, and would have been rubbing his hands with glee at the prospect of getting started. "Raising the phoenix from the ashes," had been one of his favourite phrases whenever his new plans began to come together.

As Theresa listened, she wondered what Rosa would think of Mateo's inheritance, especially how it had now all come to Lucía. It was true to say Rosa had always known when she married into the family that it was wealthy, but perhaps she had never appreciated quite how wealthy, or how far their business interests stretched - or importantly what would become of their money once their son, Paco, died.

Theresa also wondered, once Rosa learned of the situation, whether she would question why she'd not been left anything herself, although knowing how the family had felt about their daughter-in-law, perhaps she would not be too surprised. Hopefully she would be pleased for Lucía and her family. In fact, she imagined Rosa, would not welcome the complications the money would bring, particularly not at her time of life. No, it was clear from what Antonio had said, it would take some work and a great deal of patience to unravel the various strands.

The more Theresa thought about it, the more she questioned whether the Pérez family had ever offered to support their daughter-in-law or grandson in any way, once Rosa had returned to Tenerife. It was not something she and her friend had ever discussed, although she imagined not, noting the relatively impoverished lifestyle Rosa now lived. Lucía would no doubt look after her mother-in-law and see her comfortable in her old age.

Whilst Theresa nodded along as Antonio spoke, offering the occasional comment or question, Lucía was having a great deal of difficulty getting her mind around the figures, never mind the concept or the size of the inheritance Mateo had been left, from a family he did not really know, and which by a strange quirk of fate had suddenly fallen into her lap. She was more concerned about the day to day running of the finca. Putting food on the table for her family remained her priority, with her imagination having no desire to consider what life could be like beyond that, now that money was no longer a worry.

But what to do with the inheritance remained the big question, and one for which no one had any immediate answers. Antonio had been patient as he had outlined the different facets, even offering his initial thoughts on a way forward. The fishing business, *Pesca Pérez,* could easily be sold off and would make a handsome figure in its own right. There was no urgency as the business was being well managed. Equally as the fishing industry was one he imagined Lucía knew little if anything about, or wanted any involvement in, in his mind selling it would be the wisest option.

José Pérez's family house was grand and stately, as well as being situated in a prime residential location, but again not somewhere he imagined any of them would want to live. Selling that would be the easy option too. He would just need to arrange for someone to clear the property and recover any personal, or valuable items. It was not a major concern, although he suggested it perhaps needed to be attended to more as a priority, given the property was abandoned and in some state of disrepair.

Theresa and Antonio both noticed Lucía's expression. It clearly showed no interest in visiting or clearing out the house, or at the prospect of it containing anything of value. The house appeared to hold absolutely no interest to her, whatsoever.

The remaining properties were all commercial lets, with regular incomes coming in against each. Antonio had seen the accounts and was surprised by the number of bars, restaurants and office complexes in which the family's interests lay, and how well-maintained the properties all appeared to be. Putting them on the market was clearly an option, or in Antonio's mind continuing to let them was probably preferable, given the healthy returns they appeared to be making.

By far the easiest to deal with were the stocks and shares and the cash investments, with a quick discussion with the financial and legal advisors all that was needed to start the processes of transferring the documents into Lucía's name, as well as dealing with the probate and taxation issues from both Mateo's and José's estates.

Lucía had glazed over on more than one occasion, and the more she heard the easier it became to understand why Mateo had not told her about it earlier. If he could not get his own mind around it, how on earth had he expected his wife to?

Theresa had watched the discussion as it played out between her daughter and her son, with real sympathy in her eyes. Lucía was a simple soul, a hard-working farmer's wife, someone who had never been faced with anything of this enormity before. It was obvious she would need guidance and support, and Antonio would need to be extremely patient as he led her through the myriad of decisions that would be required from her over the coming months.

For now, though, it was sufficient that Antonio had given them his assurances there was more than enough money in the bank to guarantee Lucía had no problems or worries. She could continue with her life, comfortable in the knowledge he would do whatever needed to be done to sort everything out for her, one way or another.

So, all Theresa needed to do was simply be there for her daughter. The thought of simply kicking her heels waiting around in the heat of Tenerife, as opposed to pounding the pavements of London, did not appeal to her though. Staying around to offer whatever help and support was one thing, but she was more anxious to start to get involved in the shaping of the future, whatever that may be.

It was time to start imagining the future, something Duncan would be proud to hear her say. Time to look to their own particular phoenix, as it emerged from the ashes!

Chapter 15

September arrived and the autumnal nights began to draw in. The days were becoming shorter, the night-time temperatures were starting to fall and the prospect of an Indian Summer appeared to be a distant hope.

In the two months since Antonio had returned home to London, he had largely concentrated his efforts back into his business. He had three restaurants in and around the London area and all were doing well, with everything running like clockwork. The menus were regularly updated, featuring the best of the seasonal ingredients the markets had to offer. Staff at all of the premises were efficient and loyal to Antonio and Philippe, his second in command, and customer reviews continued to be positive, with bookings all the way up to Christmas looking healthy. Overall, there was nothing for Antonio to complain or worry about, at least not as far as that side of his life was concerned.

He had also spent a lot of his downtime dealing with his father's estate, regularly having discussions with his mother and Theresa as things needed to be done, or decisions needed to be taken. So far, with Antonio's guidance, Lucía had decided to sell José's main house, proceed with the sale of *Pesca Pérez* as a going concern and continue to rent out the commercial properties. There was still a considerable amount of legal work that needed to be undertaken to finalise everything, but at least the decisions had been taken, leaving Antonio clear to handle the negotiations.

He was finding the process interesting and frustrating in equal measure, the Spanish legal systems and the mañana attitude of the abogados, the lawyers he had employed, something he was struggling to get his mind around. In the restaurant industry everything was fast-paced, so at times their laid back approach was infuriating. It didn't help that being so far away meant that popping his head around their door to chivvy them along was not an option either. Nevertheless, at least things were moving in the right direction, with the removals company he had employed to clear the old house now set to arrive in the following week to start the clearance process.

"Charlotte, have you got a minute, please?" Antonio waved over to get his wife's attention as she entered the kitchen, dressed in her designer loungewear, her ear pods wedged into her ears clearly humming along to the music.

"Sorry, did you say something?" she asked, reluctantly removing one of the ear pods. Her sole purpose had been to refill her coffee cup before returning to the sitting room to continue reading the latest edition of Hello! and she had not expected any distraction.

She sidled towards the coffee machine. He had risen much earlier and having already had his breakfast, was now sitting at the kitchen table catching up on his emails. At the same time, he was looking on the internet for flights.

"It's just I've got to return to Lanzarote next week, to oversee the house clearance, and I was wondering if you wanted to join me. I know it's short notice, but what do you think to a few days in the sunshine? I'll book a room at the hotel I stayed last time. I'm then planning on going from there to Tenerife, which means, if you came with me, you could see the finca too before flying home. It's just, I imagine, I may have some personal items that will need dropping off, and I could do with catching up with Mama."

Charlotte was stopped in her tracks and with her back towards her husband, at least it meant he could not see the surprised look on her face. It was the first time he had directly asked her to accompany him to the Canaries, as well as the first time he had actually invited her to visit his mother's house. As such, she was in two minds about what to do. The chance of a few days in the sun certainly sounded appealing, and the hotel looked spectacular. That part of the trip would be fun and she could easily imagine herself in the spa, or the infinity pool, sipping cocktails. She'd even seen a few nice dresses in the shops that would be perfect to take with her.

However, flying on to Tenerife and spending time at the finca, where even by Antonio's admission everything was 'basic', made her think twice. Added to this, the fact she was no closer to Lucía or Antonio's sisters today than she had ever been, or Theresa for that matter, someone to whom she could never warm, the thought of bunking down with them was not at all appealing.

There was also the question of Miles. Their friendship was becoming more complicated by the day, as although she had tried desperately hard to steer clear of his charms, she sensed she was beginning to lose that particular battle.

Over the last couple of months, even with Antonio back in the country, they had continued to message each other, occasionally meeting up for the odd lunch date, if he was in the area and she could find a suitable excuse, one that wouldn't lead her husband to question. Thankfully Antonio was neither suspicious nor jealous, or someone who watched her movements close enough to notice any nuances in the changes to her behaviour. As such she felt confident he had not suspected anything. In fact, he barely noticed she was in the room most days, which made his request to accompany him even more surprising.

Having refilled her cup, she turned to face him. "When are you thinking of going, and for how long?" she replied in an attempt to buy herself some thinking time.

"I'm looking at flying out the day after tomorrow, as my meeting with the estate agent at José's house is in two days' time. In terms of returning home, well that depends on what I find, or what needs to be done when I get there. Maybe a week or two, max."

In Antonio's mind he'd effectively scheduled a week to ten days, although if it took longer then so be it. Sorting out his father's estate was certainly taking more time than he'd originally imagined, but perversely he was enjoying the challenge it was bringing. The opportunity to understand more about his Spanish heritage and refresh his language skills, as well as learning about different processes and businesses, was certainly exciting him and getting his juices flowing again.

He'd finally admitted to himself that simply running his restaurants had become stale and for the first time in his life it was no longer central to his existence. Philippe and the rest of his management team was coping admirably, even relishing the opportunity, which in turn allowed Antonio the space and confidence to step back. For once that felt really good.

"I think I'll give it a miss then, if that's ok?" Charlotte eventually replied, smiling over at her husband, after appearing to check the calendar on her phone. It was completely empty.

"Are you sure?"

"Yes. It's just I've got a lot on in the next week, with some appointments I don't really want to have to reschedule, and by the sounds of it you'll be busy anyway. I wouldn't want to be in the way. Perhaps next time, my love."

The little white lies flowed effortlessly off her tongue, and before Antonio found any inclination to question her about what was so important that she couldn't rearrange and agree to accompany him, she gave him a brief peck on the cheek, picked up her coffee cup and proceeded back to the settee to continue to read her magazine.

Rather than question his wife, Antonio was secretly relieved when she had declined his invitation. He had felt obliged to include her, especially after her complaint the previous time when he had failed to invite her. In truth, though, his offer was only half-hearted, with the thought of her in Tenerife, with his mother, sisters and Theresa something he was struggling to get his mind around. The atmosphere would have been strained and under no circumstances would he have wanted to act as referee between the women in his life. He had long since accepted those two worlds would never align, and if for some strange reason they did, he did not want to have to consider the consequences.

His family and wife were cut from entirely different cloths. His wife had become increasingly avaricious and materialistic, and for that reason alone he had been quite sparing with the amount of information he had been prepared to share with her about what he was doing with his father's estate. The basics certainly, but had she known the true extent of the sums of money involved, she would have been on the first flight over, demanding her share, or at least a say in how it was to be spent. That was a complication he did not need. It was his mother's inheritance, his mother's decision, not anyone else's.

He clicked to confirm his flight booking and as he sat there, looking over at Charlotte, he pondered their relationship; importantly what it appeared to have been reduced to. For the first time he realised how much it had waned over recent months, to a level where there was almost a sense of nonchalance between them. There seemed to be fewer things connecting them by the day, with any shared interests they'd once had appearing to have gone by the wayside. He realised they did little as a couple anymore, rarely socialising. These days spending time within the confines of their house was the only real time they spent together. Even then, like now, they were often in different rooms and seldom simply sat and chatted, as he imagined other couples did.

They had friends who were in happy relationships, then again where were they these days? Many of their friends had fallen away too, couples with whom they used to socialise had not been in contact with him for a while. Perhaps that was his fault, recognising his busy schedule and unsociable hours often proved difficult to organise or plan around. Then again, he couldn't recall any events or activities being discussed that he had struggled to accommodate, so perhaps it was not entirely his fault after all.

No, there was something not quite right, and whilst he could not articulate exactly what that was, it did leave him to wonder where that left Charlotte, and what her feelings were about their current situation. What did she do with her time during the day, or the evenings for that matter, and was she meeting their friends without him, perhaps? He had no idea, and worse still it apparently did not appear to be bothering him. He knew she had always been socially independent, so would happily get on with her life in his absence. Although, as independent as she was, he did admit she was high maintenance; traits he had become well accustomed to, even before their marriage. Traits that meant she needed regular distraction and entertainment.

Retail therapy had always been something Charlotte excelled at and where she turned whenever she was at a loose end. In fact, since giving up work shortly after getting married, and hence becoming less financially independent, she had still managed to rack up bills on his credit cards, without breaking a sweat. As each month's bill hit his account Antonio had not been particularly concerned. After all he could afford it, and he was more than capable of supporting a wife, even one who had no great desire to go out to work. No, she kept their home almost like a showhouse and whilst there were the occasional moans in those early days, she didn't appear to complain too much. Was she still happy and fulfilled with her life though, or more importantly with her husband, or had the magic gone for her too? Did she need something else, something other than what he was currently providing?

After only a few years as man and wife Antonio felt with every fibre of his body he should try harder to reconnect. To try to understand his wife more and above all try to rebuild the passion he had so obviously felt for her before their wedding. He recalled that day they had married, and how gorgeous and sexy his bride had looked as she entered the registry office on the arm of her father. The designer gown that fitted her so elegantly, emphasising the contours of her body in all the right places. She was absolutely stunning and he couldn't wait until he could be alone with her, until they were back in his apartment, in his bed.

He had always felt she was way out of his league, almost unattainable, yet there she was prepared to commit her life to him. They often say opposites attract, and with him and Charlotte that was clearly the case. With her stunning good looks and her model figure, what had she seen in him though? Whilst he didn't like to be too hard on himself, as he was handsome enough and had a certain charm about him, Antonio never pretended she couldn't have had the pick of the crop, if she had wanted. He was aware of a couple of her ex-boyfriends, and knew without doubt that the type of men she generally attracted had a lot more in common with her than he would ever have. A crop of men with similar social backgrounds, similar connections and importantly a crop of men of whom her parents would have more readily approved.

Looking back, he realised how guilty he was of not putting their relationship first. Demands on his time frequently meant compromises needed to be made, or arrangements cancelled at the last minute, all of which had a knock-on impact to their social life and resulted in them spending less time together, more time apart. Charlotte, as his new bride, had initially gone along with his needs, eager to please and perhaps fearful of upsetting his business, or his wider family commitments. However, over time, she had continued with her life, regardless.

He was also forced to accept most of the blame in terms of her spending habits, conscious he'd encouraged her to console herself with whatever took her interest, rather than ever attempting to rein her in. Her numerous shopping trips must have been a poor substitution for him not being there in person, his gold card perhaps tempering the pill somewhat.

Working long and unsociable hours had not helped their sex life either, with tiredness and familiarity replacing the desire they had once experienced. He recalled how they had always enjoyed a very passionate relationship, yet over recent months everyday life had somehow got in the way, resulting in it becoming almost routine, less spontaneous and certainly less frequent. That was normal, though, wasn't it? After all, passion could not be expected to last indefinitely, unlike love.

He reflected on how even in death the love his mother had for his father still shone brightly. Had his and Charlotte's love survived, or worse still had it ever truly been there in the first place? Once those layers of lust had worn away, the gilding gone, had there been anything deeper, anything capable of withstanding the obstacles life threw their way?

In fact, did he still look at her the way he once had, or she him for that matter? He forced himself to recall what she had been wearing only minutes earlier, and failed - admitting he'd barely noticed her as she'd walked into the kitchen, other than as a presence in the room. At the same time, she had hardly looked in his direction either, and had not made any effort to engage, even to say good morning.

No, it certainly didn't feel that way and watching her now, her head bent as she sat curled up on the settee, messaging away on her phone, it gave him plenty of food for thought. Especially as he realised the smile on her face was not one that he felt at all responsible for putting there.

Chapter 16

José Pérez' house clearance had gone smoothly and other than some letters, photographs and papers that were found in a secure box, Antonio had chosen to take nothing from the property. There were some nice pieces of furniture and some artwork that would be auctioned off at a later date, otherwise the contents had been donated to charity or taken by the removal firm for distribution. There were people on the island who would benefit from it, just not them. Under other circumstances his mother might have chosen some of the pieces for the finca, but nothing that warranted shipping home, and now with the huge inheritance there was nothing that she could not afford to buy from new, if she chose.

The box of papers that had been locked away in the old desk in the study appeared important, though, and given the solicitor had gone out of her way to hand over the keys to the box, it was clear that this was something he was being directed to take. The solicitor also handed over a hand written letter, addressed to his father, with her sincere apologies that it should have been given to him earlier, at the same time as the will had been read, but for some reason had become misplaced.

Now sitting in the kitchen at the finca, the sturdy box on the table before them, Antonio, Lucía and Theresa were sifting through its contents. The letter had not proven to say anything more than to reinforce the terms of the will, leaving everything to Mateo, with a suggestion that if Rosa was still around she should be taken care of. The tone and sentiment of it was surprising, as it appeared to express a degree of remorse over the actions that had taken place all those years ago. By his own admission José was a proud man, and although he admitted his wife had begged him to get in touch with Rosa and Mateo, and make their peace on numerous occasions, he had never been able to do so.

Whilst he acknowledged he had long accepted Mateo as his biological grandson and had even come to terms with the fact Rosa had not tricked his son into marriage, nevertheless he did not like to admit he had been wrong to have those feelings in the first place. He also referred to a series of notes, also included in the box, that he had found after his son's death. Notes that showed the depth of the love Paco had for Rosa, highly personal notes that he had read and wept at. Whilst he had never thought Rosa was good enough for his son, his son perversely believed himself unworthy of his wife's love.

It was a tangled mess and one to which José had been unable to reconcile himself. Leaving his estate to Mateo was his way of attempting to make amends, and although the wording of his letter never actually went as far as offering an actual apology, it was obvious that the years had softened his perspective.

"Oh look, Mama. Is this a photo of Yaya Rosa as a young girl? She looks pregnant, and that's presumably Paco by her side. Would she have been carrying Papa at the time? They look happy, don't they?"

"Let me look, Antonio," Theresa asked, taking the photo and studying it closely. It was indeed Rosa, looking beautiful in a blue and lemon floral dress, proudly showing off her bump and holding hands with Paco. They were standing on the side of a dock, with a series of small fishing vessels clearly visible in the background. She was so young, just seventeen years old and even though she had been forced into a marriage to avoid the scandal, in those early days she had been happy. Theresa smiled. She had seen few photos of her friend once she'd left Tenerife, or of Mateo as a young baby, and whilst they had written often and shared their news, photos were seldom included. "Yes, she does look happy, and initially she was. I think she loved him and he wasn't a bad man. In fact, he was a very good looking man, Antonio, and I believe he loved her in his own way. He perhaps just lacked backbone, particularly when up against his father."

Theresa smiled at the memory of Paco the night they had all met, casually smoking his cigarette and looking very sophisticated in his best suit; a wedding guest at the hotel at which she and Rosa had both been working. Who would have thought a few short months after that event, he and Rosa would be attending a wedding of their own.

"It didn't take long, though, before she became homesick and wanted to come back. Paco was working hard for his father, so there wasn't much time for family life. She soon became lonely, especially when another child never arrived. Rosa also missed her parents and yearned to bring Mateo to meet them, but Paco wouldn't come over and Rosa wasn't able to travel alone, not with a small child. I think her in-laws were very controlling, of Rosa and Paco. She didn't have an easy life, even though money was never an issue."

Lucía took the photo and smiled at it. She had never seen any photos of Rosa as a young woman, and certainly none of Mateo as a small child. When he and Rosa had come back to Tenerife after Paco's death, their possessions had hardly filled two suitcases. Rosa often said any mementos of their life in Lanzarote had been left there, where they belonged. All she needed were the memories in her heart and her son by her side. The rest she could well do without.

"Mama, just think, Yaya was pregnant with you at the same time, wasn't she? I'd love to see a photo of that too. See what your fashion sense was like in those days!" he laughed. "Plus, I'd love to see one of you pregnant with me. I know I've seen photos of you carrying Sofía and Carmen, but I don't recall ever seeing one of you carrying me, have I?"

Being back on the island and looking into his family's history these last few months had made Antonio more sentimental than he had ever been, as well as more relaxed around his family. He was getting to know them as people, and feeling comfortable being with them. It was a feeling he had struggled with when communications were limited to the occasional video call or messaging. Their discussions had felt strained and awkward, always rushed and never actually touching subjects of any significance. Now, rummaging through these old papers and photos was having a real effect on him, one that he was struggling to fully comprehend. Whether it was all part of the grieving process, with his father's death hitting him more than he'd realised, he wasn't quite sure. "Can we look through some of your old albums later?"

Theresa and Lucía exchanged a glance, a glance that spoke volumes between them, yet left Antonio completely baffled.

"Mama, what have I said? You've gone as white as a sheet, almost as if you've seen a ghost. Are you alright, do you want me to fetch you some water?"

"No, I'm fine, Antonio and thank you. It's just going through all this has been quite emotional for me. I think perhaps we've done enough for today, don't you Mama?"

"Yes," replied Theresa, sensing her daughter's discomfort. "Why don't I take this box and sort through what I think we need to keep. Then perhaps I'll walk down and see Rosa later. I think she'll be interested to read those notes, as well as to see some of the old photos. She'll also be pleased to learn that in the end José did mellow, a little, although I think she'll struggle to believe he ever had a kind word for her."

With that, Theresa picked up the box and Lucía retired to her bedroom, leaving Antonio left wondering what on earth had just taken place.

The following morning, when Antonio had driven down to the café to deal with his emails over a quiet coffee and pastry, Theresa and Lucía were once again sitting around the kitchen table, nursing their own drinks. Each was lost in their thoughts, unable to fully articulate to the other what they were thinking.

Eventually Lucía broke the silence. "Mama, we need to tell him. We should have done so a long time ago, whilst Mateo was still alive. I just hope we're not too late," she sighed. She'd had a sleepless night, her mind going over and over what Antonio had said the previous evening, and how she could possibly answer his question. A really innocuous question, however a problem she was at pains to find a solution to.

"I know, mi hija," Theresa replied, sensing her daughter's discomfort. She equally had tossed and turned all night, her mind similarly trying to identify the best way of dealing with the issue. The knowledge that this day was an eventuality, something that could not be avoided, had not sat easily with her either, for some time now if she was honest.

"He needs to know, and I by rights should tell him. It is I who took him away from here, from all this. So it is I who should explain why. Please don't worry, my love, I will try to find the right words to explain it, and trust he will understand."

"I pray that you are right, Mama, as I cannot afford to lose his love too." Losing Mateo was one thing, but the thought of losing Antonio's love was almost too hard to bear.

With that the two women simply sat and stared at each other.

Chapter 17

The Past

The night Mateo raced home to inform Lucía and Theresa that Ramos had died, having fallen down a deep gully in a drunken stupor on his stagger home from the bar, was a night Theresa had never been able to forget. He was her husband. By rights she should have been devastated by his death and the suddenness of her loss. She should have wailed and shrieked at the news, cried until her eyes held no more tears. She should have demonstrated the normal behaviours of a grieving widow. Instead, she quietly smiled to herself. The inner calm she was feeling, at no longer having to see his face, or feel his hands all over her body, was beyond belief. The relief that she no longer had to fear for her own life, let alone that of her daughter or granddaughters was even greater. He could no longer harm any of them.

To everyone else though, she had maintained the persona that was to be expected. The outside world would witness her pain, and within the small village and the surrounding areas she had put on the performance of her life.

However, having just turned thirty-nine Theresa was still only a relatively young woman and whilst Ramos had taken most of her good years from her, she still had a lot ahead of her. A lot of living to do and now that he wasn't there to control her, she could start to do that.

Rosa was the only one who truly understood how Theresa felt. She was the only one to whom Theresa had confided over the years, about the fears she'd faced or the pain she'd endured. Rosa was the only one she could trust with her innermost feelings. Her friend would not judge her and as such she felt free to act and speak openly in her presence.

They would go into the island's capital, Santa Cruz, on occasion, catching the bus down the long winding roads. When there they would mosey around the town or walk along the seafront, breathing in the fresh sea air and relaxing in the sunshine. As the capital of the island, Santa Cruz had become a relatively busy metropolis, full of holiday makers and people of different nationalities. It was the 1960s and the vibe was electric.

The two women would gaily amble around the city arm-in-arm, without fear of being spotted, or fear of being judged. Those outings most represented the times when Theresa could truly relax and be herself. She was no longer Ramos' widow, she was Theresa, a young woman who was looking for a good time. She would enjoy a drink, she would shed her widow's weeds and put on a pretty dress, with her hair and makeup done. As an attractive woman, she was also not against flirting with the local men as they enjoyed a beer or a glass of wine at the pavement cafes.

Rosa by comparison was happy to simply be away from the village for the day, enjoying the change in scenery and a break from her normal routine. Village life suited her and unlike her friend she had no interest in other men. She was contented with her quiet life and the knowledge that her son and granddaughters were close by. She'd had enough excitement and was not looking for anything else, whereas Theresa was different. She yearned for more. She yearned for the life she believed she had missed out on. The life Ramos had stolen from her.

Late one afternoon, whilst sitting outside a café drinking a glass of wine and waiting for the bus to arrive that would take them home, an extremely good-looking Englishman approached their table and asked if he could buy them a drink. He was perhaps in his late thirties or early forties and smartly dressed. He had been watching them for some time from across the road, appearing to read his newspaper and had eventually decided he would join them for some company. He told them he was travelling alone and in town for a couple of days on business.

Theresa immediately said yes and invited him to sit down with them, indicating to the waiter to bring him a glass of wine over. She liked the look of him, with his smart clothes and his quirky foreign accent, and as they had twenty minutes to spare before their bus was due to arrive, she could see no harm. He was quite talkative and although his Spanish was understandable, the accent and occasional confusion of words and verbs had them in hysterics. Theresa gently corrected him and before long they were laughing and joking like old friends.

When the bus eventually arrived, Rosa gathered up her bags and arose from her chair. "Come on Theresa, we need to go. We don't want to miss the bus, do we?"

"Oh, do you really need to go, ladies? It's still early, could I not buy you another drink, perhaps?" the stranger asked, smiling directly at Theresa as he posed his question.

"Thank you, but the next bus isn't for another two hours and we need to get back," Rosa replied, intent on leaving. The stranger's eyes pleaded at Theresa not to leave, even if her friend needed to go. Theresa read his unspoken words, as clearly as if they had been screamed from the top of the mountains or laid out in bright lights all along the promenade.

"Rosa, why don't you go home and I'll catch the next bus? I'll see you tomorrow morning. Hurry, it's going shortly, and as you said, you don't want to miss it." Theresa was suddenly eager to be left alone with the stranger. She was enjoying the attention he was giving her and it had been a long time since a man had actually invited her for a drink. "It's a lovely evening and as I've nothing to rush home for another drink won't hurt, will it?"

Thirty seven years later Theresa recalls how another drink had led to another drink, and then to dinner, followed by a late night stroll along the sea front. The last bus home was well and truly missed, and when she woke the following morning in the luxurious hotel bedroom, naked with the man's arms still wrapped around her, her dress flung over the bedroom chair with what little underwear she had been wearing on the floor beside it, she realised her life was far from over. She had enjoyed the most passionate night of her life, a night she would never forget, the memory of which would need to sustain her when she returned to the village and to the drab life she had carved out for herself there.

Although almost two months later, the happy memory turned into a horror story when she realised she was pregnant, by a man who's name she didn't even recall – Edward, or Edwin or Edgar? He was British, she knew that, otherwise what did she know about him? To her he was simply a stranger, someone who had made her feel good about herself and shown her a good time. To him, she was someone who had filled a lonely evening away from home, and now he'd be back playing happy families, probably with his wife and two point four children around him. There would be no tracking him down, or marching him up the aisle, as had happened when she had become pregnant by Ramos all those years ago, her parents adamant they would not face the shame of a pregnant unmarried daughter living under their roof.

For most of the world time had moved on. It was the swinging sixties and around the world youngsters were high on life, drugs and rock and roll, taking their pleasures wherever and whenever they chose.   The uptight post-war conventions their parents had endured in the nineteen forties and fifties were long gone. A new and vibrant world had been born, with opportunities there for the taking.

However, in their small Canarian village the old values were still very much evident. The outside world had largely passed them by, with the Catholic traditions still very much honoured by the townsfolk. An unmarried mother was still to be shunned, so a recently widowed woman, becoming pregnant by an unknown stranger, would certainly not go unchallenged. It would not be tolerated and people would look badly on the whole family. Theresa, Lucía and her daughters would no longer be able to hold their heads up in the town, and Mateo would be looked upon with pity, his mother-in-law a laughing stock. What's more, it could also threaten the meagre business the finca managed to make, as people sought to buy their produce elsewhere.

A solution had been needed and, as shocking as it was, between them one had been found. And surprisingly that solution had come from Rosa herself. With careful management, she believed Lucía could pass the child off as her own. The baby would simply be another to add to the two daughters she and Mateo already had. Everyone would be delighted with the newborn. "It will be a gift from God, they will declare," Rosa had said, thinking how the news would travel. A plan that would leave Theresa and Rosa free to play the role of doting grandmothers, and God willing, it would provide Mateo with the son he and his wife had struggled so long to conceive. A child who, for all intents and purposes, would be a Pérez, taking Mateo's name.

It was a simple plan that had been concocted and enacted with ease, leaving no one even the slightest bit suspicious. Lucía and Mateo not only treated Antonio as their own, but they loved him as such. Theresa reluctantly stood back, allowing them to take the lead in his upbringing, which in turn enabled her to continue her life with her dignity still intact.

However, being so close to her son, yet unable to love him as a mother should, proved more of a challenge than Theresa was prepared for. Watching him day by day as he developed from a baby into a little boy, with a mind of his own and a thirst for life was difficult. She yearned to steer his life, but knew she couldn't. She wanted to indulge him, yet had to step back and treat him like she did her other granddaughters. Showing him any favouritism was never an option if the façade was to be maintained.

In need of a distraction, but mainly an excuse to get away from the village for a few hours each day, Theresa applied for a role in a local hotel, working in their bar and restaurant. Food was one of her passions and dealing with people was something to which she found herself suited. The growing hospitality industry was desperate for people and the role matched her limited skill set perfectly. She had matured into a striking woman, with an olive complexion and luminous dark hair that shone when the sunlight caught it at the right angle, and with a little attention to her appearance she found she could become quite a glamorous woman. She made a very attractive and popular addition to the hotel's staff.

A chance meeting with Duncan Lomas one evening, whilst she was working behind the hotel's bar, led to a friendship developing between them. Each evening they would chat and occasionally after her shift she would stay behind enjoying a small night cap with him, before driving herself home. It began as purely platonic, although with each passing day she could see he was developing feelings for her. After dinner as he walked into the bar, she saw the smile on his face widen, with his eyes instantly lighting up at the sight of a friendly face.

Theresa knew she had to tread carefully, having learned Duncan was a recently widowed man and was taking his first holiday since losing his wife eighteen months earlier. He was a kind man, in his late fifties, but he was also very lonely. He loved to chat and spoke openly telling Theresa he was a business man, rattling around in a large house in central London, without any close family of his own, just an old mutt who followed him around aimlessly, now that his mistress had died. Regular walks around Hyde Park were fast becoming the highlight of his day. Theresa saw the sadness in his eyes, but also heard the hope he still had that his life was not over. He just needed to move on and find that someone special to help him fill his days.

The more they spoke and got to know each other, the more Theresa realised that she quite liked him. He was easy company, good looking in a rather distinguished way and relatively fit for his age, and with no men in her bed since Ernie, or Eric, or whatever he had called himself, Duncan made her realise she was missing some affection. There was certainly the potential of a physical attraction developing between them.

After his holiday and his return to England, they agreed to keep in touch and began writing to one another. Duncan would write long letters that revealed his quirky sense of humour and self-deprecating style. He would talk about his life in London, making light of his business interests, something at that stage Theresa neither understood nor cared about. He also started to hint at the nature of the feelings he was beginning to have for her.

Theresa's letters by comparison, whilst warm, would be short and to the point. She was more guarded about what she said or revealed about herself, and was always wary of inadvertently saying the wrong thing.

Nevertheless, an invitation to visit London soon followed, something that Theresa gave serious thought to before accepting, especially as by now she could see the writing on the wall, and was not oblivious to the hidden meaning between some of the things Duncan had suggested. It was clear that although he enjoyed their friendship, he was hoping for a more physical relationship between them, and whilst she was not averse to that in principle, she had to remain vigilant.

At the end of her visit, whilst walking the dog through Kensington Gardens and along the banks of the Serpentine, Duncan proposed marriage to her. They had stopped for a moment in the sunshine, watching a group of children playing in the distance. Theresa was completely taken by surprise, as he knelt down before her and presented her with a diamond ring, asking if she would do him the honour of becoming his wife, the next Mrs Lomas.

As far as Theresa was concerned the concept of marriage had never entered her head. She had simply enjoyed their ten days together, dining in some of the best restaurants in London and wandering the city, taking in the sights. He had been attentive throughout, and had shown her nothing but kindness. Even his dog, a beautiful golden retriever called Mollie, was adorable and would come to her for attention. And his home, a grand three-storey town house in Notting Hill, was beyond anything she had imagined. It had five bedrooms, and, although she had been given use of her own room and en suite, it was not long before they had slept together. Whilst she found him attractive, it was fair to say the earth had not moved for her that first time, but neither had she been put off by the experience. After all, with practice it was an area they could work on.

No, a proposal of marriage, after such a short period of time, had been totally unexpected. Yet the more she thought about it, the more she realised

Duncan's proposal did offer her an opportunity for a new life, one far away from Tenerife. She considered her position carefully. She too was widowed and looking to move on, and whilst they were culturally very different people, she believed that over time Duncan was someone she could grow to care for, even perhaps love. Moreover, from what she had experienced in London, she believed he would take good care of her, which above all else counted for something. Being a woman, alone in life, was not all it was cracked up to be, Theresa had realised to her cost.

However, there was that one thing she had not told him. That one thing she feared would put the proverbial spoke in the wheel if it were ever to come out. The secret that until then she had kept close to her heart, for fear of what Duncan or anyone else for that matter would say, or how they would treat her. So, while the idea of getting married was not unappealing, she was not prepared to enter into it on the basis of a lie.

Yet was the risk of asking Duncan to keep her secret a step too far and was it a risk she was prepared to take? There again, was it a chance she could afford to pass up on? The dilemma must have been evident on her face as after she did not respond Duncan carefully closed the box and got back to his feet.

"What's wrong, my love?" he asked, conscious he had probably read the situation all wrong, and jumped in too eagerly with his ill-thought-out proposal.

"Shall we sit down for a moment," she began, nervously leading him and Mollie to a nearby park bench. "Before I answer your question, Duncan, there's something I need to explain. Your response to what I am about to tell you will govern my answer, as well as the rest of our lives. So please think very carefully before you react."

Taking a deep breath she entrusted Duncan with her secret, speaking more openly and honestly to him than she had ever done in her life. She was choosing to trust him with her innermost feelings, feelings that had haunted her from the moment she had taken the decision to follow Rosa's suggestion.

As he sat and listened, occasionally prompting and questioning, Theresa watched his reactions, mindful that at any moment the life she had built for herself, and that of her son, could come tumbling down.

It was a secret she was thankful to say Duncan had not only respected for the duration of their happy marriage, but one that he had taken to his grave.

Now all she needed to do was work up the courage to tell Antonio the same thing. How to admit to keeping the most important part of his life from him, by allowing him to believe the lie that Lucía was his mother, not his sister. Or how Mateo, the man he was currently grieving, was not his biological father, but his brother-in-law, his sister's husband. How will he ever make sense of it?

It was not made any easier by the fact she could not even offer him the first name of the man with whom she'd conceived him, in a frivolous one night stand, let alone a surname. By rights he was not a Pérez, yet as his paternal parentage was unknown, other than the fact he was half British, she could not offer him any alternative. The fact they had even lied to the authorities in terms of his birth certificate, and in the eyes of the church when he was baptised, would not go down well either. She and Rosa had conspired in the worst way possible as they encouraged Mateo and Lucía to be recorded as his parents.

No amount of love that any of them had showered on him since would ever make up for the hurt he would feel once he understood the truth. It was a truth she feared could tear them all apart, and a truth that had the potential to almost kill her. Without Antonio in her life, what would be the point of going on?

At least the simplest question of all, in terms of why Lucía didn't have any photos of carrying him during the pregnancy, would at least now be an easy one to answer, Theresa admitted to herself wryly.

Chapter 18

The Present

Later the following afternoon, Antonio had driven himself down to the coast, unsure precisely where he was heading. He just pointed the car in the general direction of the sea, driving almost on autopilot. He needed to get as far away from the finca, and as far away from his mother as he could, both of them for that matter! He needed to think and he needed a stiff drink, and he couldn't do either with them around. Although he was a social drinker, serious alcohol was not something to which he'd ever felt the need to turn. He had seen too many people go down that particular slippery slope and he was not prepared to follow them. Nothing was ever that bad, in his view. Today though might just prove to be the exception to that rule.

He could barely believe what he had been told. He could barely believe he had been fed a lie for all of his thirty seven years, and worse still had never questioned or suspected anything. Was that a reflection on him, or a reflection on them? Had he been too naïve to see what was before him, to ever question the signs, or had those he'd loved just been too good at playing their parts? Because one thing was for sure, they had all pulled off the performances of their lives and he had been completely hoodwinked.

His whole life now took on a different perspective. His mother was his sister, his grandmother was his mother, his biological father was not even someone who could be traced, let alone named. Mateo, the man who had brought him up and loved him as a son, was his sister's husband. They shared no bloodline, whatsoever. Whatever had enticed him to get involved in such a deception, a crazy idea concocted by his own mother, Rosa? It was all one unholy mess and Antonio didn't have the first idea how he should respond, or what his thoughts and actions needed to be.

He parked the car and walked down to the beach, slipping off his sandals as he went, welcoming the feel of the coarse wet sand between his toes. He needed a walk to clear his head and contemplate what his life had descended to. Only six short months ago he had been managing his businesses, living in London, happily ignorant to all that was playing out around him. Simply devoting himself to his work and to his family. He was newly married to a beautiful woman, with two parents for whom he cared deeply, even though they did not see each other often, and sisters and grandmothers he doted on.

Knowledge of the Pérez family and Lanzarote was limited to nothing more than a casual comment made by his father many years previously. The place where he had grown up, where he had lived as a young child until the age of seventeen, before moving, following the untimely death of his father. There was never talk of any residual family there, or of wealth, and certainly no prospects of any inheritance. It was a story about a life that had a clear line drawn under it once they had left the island to return to Tenerife.

London had been his home for over half his lifetime, a place he had been brought to because he believed his grandmother wanted to provide him with a good education. She recognised he was bright and needed more than life on the finca could offer. That was true, and he would be forever grateful for that. However, her motivations, it now transpired, had not been entirely selfless. She had missed and wanted her son with her and Duncan, her new husband, had simply done whatever it took to enable that. With his connections he had ensured doors to the right schools were open to him, the right opportunities placed before him. Money had never been an issue. Even in death Duncan had continued to provide for him, leaving him property and a large sum of money, forever treating Antonio like the son he had never had.

Although the pieces of the jigsaw were beginning to fall into place, and making a strange sense of the life he had lived, the fundamental foundations on which that life had been built were all now in question. Why had he never been told any of this before, and if he had not found those stupid photographs, how long would he have been allowed to continue without the knowledge he now had? In fact, would he have ever learned the truth?

As the cold Atlantic Sea lapped against his toes, those foundations were sinking fast, almost like the sand under his feet. For once Antonio had absolutely no idea how to react, or what to think, or even who to talk to, to try to make any sense of how he was feeling.

Sitting in a bar, nursing a half empty glass of cold beer, Antonio realised it was time to go home. Drinking was not the answer after all. It was time to go back to his wife and to his business. Above all, it was time to put some reality and perspective back into his life.

Chapter 19

Antonio inserted his key into the lock and the front door opened quietly. He placed his bag on the floor and eased his coat off, hanging it on the newel post of the staircase. It was only six o'clock in the evening and yet the house was in total darkness, giving an eerie sensation to his homecoming. The autumnal nights had closed in noticeably since he had left, only a matter of weeks ago, and there was a dampness in the air. It all added to his general feeling of despondency. He had flown home at short notice, managing to get a late availability flight, totally distracted, and now realised he had forgotten to let either Philippe or Charlotte know of his change in plans.

He had not spoken to either of them for a couple of days, and when he had last spoken, he was still intending to be away for another week. Philippe appeared happy with his arrangements and Charlotte did not complain, so neither had given him any cause for concern. In fact, the business and his marriage appeared to be the only two things he could rely on at the moment, and that at least provided him with some degree of comfort.

Leaving Tenerife very early, the morning after receiving the bombshell news, he had driven to the airport, dumped his hire car and booked onto the first available flight into Heathrow. He had simply thrown his belongings into his bag and left the finca in a hurry, unable to face further discussions with either Theresa or Lucía. He needed space and if nothing else he needed time alone to think; time to decide on what his future course of action needed to be.

It was not an easy position to be in, because above all else, Antonio realised there was no way he could walk away from the obligations he had taken on. Mateo's and José's estates still needed to be managed, the questions around the inheritance still needed to be dealt with, and that was still his responsibility. So, whilst it was something he was unprepared to neglect, he judged a couple of thousand miles distance between them would not hurt - and it might in fact help, for a while at least. Nothing was that urgent.

As he started to climb the stairs in the darkness, a text message pinged into his phone; a simple message from Theresa.

"Antonio, we love you, please let us know you're okay. We're worried about you."

How on earth could he respond to that, after everything they had both said to him? Whilst their love for him was never in question, their motivation certainly was, along with the deception they had masterfully upheld for so many years. Had he been told years ago that Theresa was his mother, even at the time she had taken him to London, then no doubt he would have dealt with it. He would have eventually accepted the situation, too young at the time to perhaps question the drivers that had led to the need for the deception in the first place. Or too young to understand the perceived scandal they had felt would have played out, should the truth have ever come to light within the village. Fears that his mother would have become a laughing stock, the Merry Widow, a scarlet woman and the disrepute that would have brought on them all had, for them at least, been real.

It would also have made more sense as to why he had been taken from his supposed parents, at the tender age of seventeen, to live a life completely separate from them, in an alien country far from home. His need for an education on the surface appeared plausible, but it was far from the true reason he now realised. The number of nights he had lain in his new bedroom, wondering if he had done something wrong, imagining he was being punished by being sent away. The tears he had shed, and the homesickness he had felt, none of that would have happened, although he imagined there would have been a myriad of different feelings for him to contend with.

He would, though, have had time to adjust and importantly he would have had time to develop the relationships that he now realised he had missed out on. What would loving someone as a mother, compared to loving them as a grandmother have felt like, or as a sister rather than a mother? Part of him felt robbed. Also, knowing now that Sofía and Carmen were in fact his nieces, not his sisters, was equally difficult to take in. He presumed they were still in the dark, and wondered whether there was any plan to tell them too, or whether it would remain a dirty secret indefinitely.

As hurt as he was, he still had to acknowledge Theresa and Duncan had done so much for him over the years, and whilst he now understood more of the reasons behind that, was that justification in itself, or just a way for her to appease her earlier behaviour, with Duncan a willing collaborator? Today such behaviours would hardly raise an eyebrow, although forging official documents would still be illegal, and that was something Antonio did need to think carefully about. He did not know what he actually felt about that, or whether he would ever want anyone to be answerable in the eyes of the law for that particular deception. He might not like either of them at the moment, but there was no question about the depth of the love he still felt. Regardless of their questionable actions towards him, they were his family and that fact would never change.

As he got to the top of the stairs, he could hear muffled voices coming from his bedroom. Presuming Charlotte was in there watching one of her reality TV programmes, he quietly turned the handle, not wanting to startle her, particularly as she was not expecting him home. He still needed to think carefully about how much he was prepared to share with his wife about what he had learnt over recent days. Not just his parentage, but also the size and state of the family's inheritance. It was a big decision, especially as he had a growing sense that his feelings towards her were changing, and if he was honest had perhaps been on the slide for some time now. Time away from her had not affected him half as much as he had expected, and from their regular telephone conversations it didn't appear to have affected her that much either. He had the sense she had coped admirably in his absence, and just wondered whether the size of his next credit card statement would reflect the extent of the distraction she'd needed whilst he'd been away.

His most recent break had allowed him to see their relationship with a lot more clarity, and although any thought of divorce was still a long way off, in his mind at least, if their relationship was worth salvaging then they would both need to put a lot more effort into repairing it. The specifics of exactly how they would go about doing that for now would need some discussion, and Antonio realised that was another thing he needed to add to his growing to-do list of things to think about.

If only the rest of his life was as clear, he mused to himself as he stepped into his bedroom, putting a forced smile on his face so that she would not detect anything was wrong.

"I'm home, darling," he announced, pulling off his tie and moving his hand to switch on the bedside light. The room, like the rest of the house was in darkness, with the television, which he'd presumed was on, being switched off.

As the light came on, his wife's startled face turned towards him. She had not heard him enter and was lay on the bed, scantily clad in some lacy underwear, which Antonio didn't recognise, so presumed was new. It was obvious from her reaction her thoughts were elsewhere.

"Oh, Antonio, I wasn't expecting you home so soon," she replied, her eyes moving quickly from her husband to the en suite, where the outline of a man was just visible. He had not heard the door open either, and was emerging from the bathroom wearing nothing but a satisfied smile. That was at least until he came face to face with Antonio, at which point he did not know which way to look, or how best to hide his embarrassment.

"This isn't what you think," Charlotte began in a desperate attempt to recover a situation that was beyond recoverable.

"No, I'm sure it isn't," Antonio replied, a wry smile on his face and at a complete loss what else to say. In his mind there were no two ways to explain what he had just witnessed, and as surprised as he was at what he had walked into, there was a certain lack of shock or even anger at seeing his wife's body being flaunted in such a way. After the last few days, he was simply immune to any such feelings. "I'll go downstairs, and give your friend some time to find his trousers, shall I?" he questioned, staring directly at the man. "Then, Charlotte, I suggest, we should talk. And if I am wrong about what's actually going on here, you could perhaps enlighten me."

On which note, Antonio retraced his steps back downstairs, his tread this time nowhere near as quiet as he made his way into the kitchen. As he opened the fridge to get himself a drink, he wondered if his life had perhaps somehow just become more difficult, or alternatively, if by walking in on his wife and her lover, post coital, he had neatly addressed the one question, that until this point he had not even realised had made its way to the top of his to-do list.

Chapter 20

By the end of November, two weeks later, Charlotte had packed a small bag with all her essentials and had left the house she and Antonio shared, moving a couple of miles across London and into a small studio apartment. It was owned by one of her friends and ex-colleague at the television studio, Maddie Jones, who was working overseas for a couple of months, on assignment in some war zone or other, Charlotte seemed to recall, so she had kindly offered to let her use it when she was away.

Whilst the apartment was far from ideal, and even by London standards extremely on the pokey side, it was a far cheaper alternative than booking into a hotel, so would suit Charlotte for the time being. By moving out she felt it would give both her and Antonio a little breathing space; time apart whilst they worked out what they wanted from their relationship.

The last two weeks, living under the same roof, had been extremely difficult. They had tiptoed around each other, ate at different times, slept in separate bedrooms and both politely avoided the elephant in the room whenever their paths did cross. A screaming match, even a heated argument might have helped, however it was in neither of their temperaments to act that way. Antonio, particularly, felt able to bottle up his feelings, to the point where he became almost impenetrable, unable to be drawn on even the most innocuous of topics. In fact, they had hardly spoken on any subject throughout the whole period, with Miles' name never having been mentioned by either of them.

Charlotte, knowing she was the guilty party, believed it was not in her best interests to instigate an argument. Whilst it might have helped clear the air and add clarity, even at the risk of a few bowls or mugs becoming collateral damage as they were flung across the kitchen, she felt that approach was a high-risk strategy. A small part of her remained hopeful of a reconciliation between them, her every action an endeavour to show the remorse she was feeling. Although she feared a more permanent solution may be on the cards, at least as far as Antonio was concerned. So, whilst the word *divorce* had still not been directly voiced, the scent of it hung in the air, like the proverbial bad smell whenever they were in the same room.

Charlotte had been mortified to have been caught in the actual act of having an affair, and seeing the hurt and sense of betrayal in Antonio's eyes as she'd entered the kitchen, once she had shown Miles the door, was unbearable. She tried to explain she had never set out to hurt him, at pains to point out it had been the first and only time she had ever done anything remotely like that. She stressed she had never cheated on anyone before, let alone her husband.

Reading Antonio's body language, she sensed her argument sounded more like her lack of practice, or experience in the art of deception, was an attempt at excusing her behaviour, which for Charlotte it had clearly not been. As he sat motionless, drinking his beer and listening to her attempts to explain, her words jumbled among the sobs as she tried to speak, all that kept going around her head was the feeling that she was wasting her time. It did not bode well for their future.

With his arms crossed and his eyes unable to meet hers, Antonio eventually admitted he had sensed for some time that something was not quite right, although even he had not considered it had gone that far. He also admitted his hurt was compounded by the fact infidelity had been one of the few topics they had spoken about at length prior to their marriage, along with their desire to eventually try for a family at some stage when they were both ready. He'd believed that whilst they had niggles in their relationship, as most people experienced, especially in those early years as they learned to live with each other, on those two big ticket items they were on the same page. Clearly that was not the case.

Charlotte had begged Antonio to forgive her, to give her a second chance and an opportunity to explain. He listened patiently as she argued Miles had been a mistake, a silly distraction that had filled her lonely hours, one that had simply got out of hand whilst he was away. She never blamed Antonio directly for abandoning her, although her admission that she had been flattered and charmed by the attention Miles showed her, and how she was made to feel wanted again, appeared to strike a deep chord with him.

She could almost feel the hurt that comment caused, as deep down he recognised he had not always put his wife, or their relationship, first. Especially this last couple of years, as his business developed and it demanded more of his time and attentions, and certainly not these last few weeks, after the death of his father and all the complications managing his estate had brought. He had felt he needed to be there to support his family as they had relied upon him, so he had done what every dutiful son would do. Even at the expense of his own wife's feelings or wellbeing, it would now appear.

Antonio was the first to admit they had grown apart, and somewhere along the way had forgotten the essence of what had drawn them together in the first place. That physical, almost magnetic attraction, that had left him with the same satisfied smile he had seen on her lover's face, had long since gone. He surely had to take some of the blame on that front, so if giving her the benefit of the doubt and trying to put them together again was what he needed to do, then surely it was worth a try. Although the shape and size of what that might look like continued to baffle him.

As Antonio had reflected on that over the last couple of weeks, he'd kept bringing himself back to the same question. What did he want long term, and was his own life drifting along without real purpose too? His businesses were not stimulating him anymore, nor providing the distraction or challenge he needed. Things had carried on without him quite nicely, and getting himself back into the cut and thrust of restaurant life had proved difficult and unrewarding. Certainly some changes would be required on that front too if he was to regain his mojo.

Yet he definitely did not want a relationship where the trust had gone, or where he was no longer enough for the other party. He had too much love to give and too much self-respect to allow that to happen. So, whilst he recognised his mistakes, for him to continue to invest his emotions in a relationship that was not going to last seemed pointless. All relationships have risks, Antonio knew that more than most, and his and Charlotte's had always been an attraction of opposites, rather than one of kindred spirits. But already feeling at rock bottom, after what Theresa had told him, was Charlotte's deception the final straw?

As he stood at the window watching her taxi slowly drive away, he felt surprisingly detached from the whole situation. She was gone from his life, temporarily at least, and there had been no tears shed from either of them. Simply an acceptance that they both needed space.

He looked at his watch, recognising he too would need to leave in the next few minutes, if he was to get to the restaurant in time for the meeting he had arranged with one of his key suppliers. He felt no great desire for that either. The restaurants now no longer excited him and Philippe could more than handle the meeting, so what was the need for him to rush, especially in this weather? The heavy dark clouds and unceasing rain perfectly reflected the melancholy mood he found himself in.

His life was crumbling around him, with so much of that happiness he had once felt seemingly having fallen away over recent months. Nothing was giving him any real pleasure anymore.

As he texted Philippe to let him know of his change in plans, Antonio was reminded of the text he had received from Theresa, over two weeks ago now. The simple text he had chosen not to respond to, but had never forgotten. Asking how he felt, checking he was okay.

Antonio now accepted, even with the passage of time, he was still far from okay. In fact, so much had happened in those intervening weeks that the betrayal of Theresa and Lucía had almost been overshadowed by the betrayal of his wife. He had not spoken to anyone about either set of problems, opting to keep his own counsel, mainly for fear of what others might think, or how they could exploit any weaknesses he might display. He was ordinarily a very private man and certainly someone unprepared to burden others with his problems or worries. Perhaps this time, though, he did need to speak to someone, someone who could help him deal with what was going on in his head, and more specifically in his heart.

For Antonio the idea of professional therapy or counselling was an anathema, believing there was no reason to pay good money to talk to someone, especially when friends or family were around to listen. Whilst some of his friends may have recently fallen away, his family was still there. So why on earth should he not turn to them? He realised he had not properly spoken to either Lucía or Theresa since his return to England, choosing to deal directly with the solicitors, then simply informing them what was being done. He had needed space from them too.

As if experiencing a lightbulb moment, Antonio suddenly understood, with everything else that was going on in his life, it was time to reply to Theresa's text. It was time to reach out to the other women in his life; the women who no matter what they had put him through, he still loved. After all, they knew him better than anyone, and more importantly loved him, unconditionally.

Chapter 21

By the middle of December, a matter of days before Christmas, Antonio was sitting at Heathrow airport, having finally put his plans in place to leave England. He was surrounded by families going on their Christmas break, ready to enjoy a week or two of winter sunshine, away from the bleak British weather. Like him they were eagerly awaiting the flight to be called, although unlike him they presumably had their return travel plans already made.

Antonio had spoken to Philippe one evening a couple of weeks previously, explaining his need to get away.

"I'm thinking of taking a bit of a sabbatical," was the way he attempted to describe it, as they sat and chatted over a beer. The restaurant was quieter than usual and Antonio had called Philippe into his office, in order to give them some privacy. "I need some time away, Philippe, to refocus and consider what I want from my life. If you're willing to take over the restaurants for me, that would be a great relief. I wouldn't feel comfortable keeping them open otherwise. I've considered shutting them for a while, whilst I get my head together, but I don't think that would be fair on the rest of the team, would it? They have their mortgages to pay, and my mid-life crisis isn't going to help them, is it?"

Philippe could see the anguish in his friend's face as he struggled to articulate the pain he had been going through and smiled supportively.

"In reality, you've effectively been covering for me and running things for the last six months anyway, so you'll probably not notice any difference. This time, though, you'll have complete control, and I'll contact my solicitor to draw up an agreement to reflect that, if that would help?" he added ruefully, acknowledging how much he had relied on his friend, and unwittingly taken that support for granted.

As the two men chatted, Antonio eventually confided in Philippe that the loss of his father had hit him much more than he had imagined, and had even gone on to admit that his relationship with Charlotte was not going well either. He had not gone as far as sharing any news about his parentage though, as that, in Antonio's mind, would have been a step too far.

He had added that ordinarily he would have simply thrown himself into work to get through it, but as the restaurants were not challenging him anymore, that would have simply compounded his problems. He was at an all-time low, and he knew that something needed to change in his life, particularly if he was to stave off the feelings of depression that were beginning to creep in. Mental health issues were thankfully something Antonio had limited experience of, personally or with the people around him, so he had never been in a position where he had given it much attention. However, he was sufficiently attuned to his own body to realise some of the early signs. He was listless, had lost his appetite and was struggling to sleep, and nothing seemed to motivate him, not least in the way it had done previously. He realised that unless he did something radical to manage his own wellbeing, self-help may no longer be enough.

Philippe had listened carefully, checking his own body language and being very discreet in the way in which he chose to respond. He had noticed for some time that all was not well with Antonio, and had heard some weeks ago that Charlotte had left home, moving to live in an apartment by herself. Rumours of her affair had begun to spread, especially as Miles Davenport was a well-known and somewhat colourful character around town. Sadly, news travelled faster on the grapevine than most people gave it credit, with social media having a lot to answer for, in his view at least.

Philippe had simply waited for Antonio to confide in him, if that's what he chose. He was uncomfortable to raise the question, or pry into his boss' personal life without being invited. He classed himself as a long-term friend, a fellow proud Spaniard, an unofficial business partner even, but they had never had the type of relationship where either of them had openly discussed their feelings before, unless it was what they felt about the latest menu, or the wine selections for the restaurants. After all, men don't do that, do they? Philippe accepted, rightly or wrongly, bottling up feelings, rather than showing any sign of weakness, was how most men deal with their issues.

Here, though, Antonio was showing a side of himself that was completely unexpected. A rawness Philippe had not witnessed before, an honesty that had obviously come at a cost. He was making himself vulnerable by opening himself up, in a way that showed a great deal of trust in his friend. Philippe had to respect him for that.

"Take what time you need, Chef. I'll keep the ship afloat in your absence, so there's no need to worry on that front. And if you need me to do anything else, or want to talk more, then I'm here for you. I imagine I speak for the rest of the staff when I say that, too. Take a break and don't come back until you're ready."

Antonio's relief on hearing those words was palpable and as he hugged his friend he struggled to keep the tears from his eyes. It had taken a lot for him to reach out and he was overwhelmed by the support he had received.

Charlotte had been less supportive, less sympathetic, fearing that if Antonio was out of the country, back in the bosom of his family, it would not help her chances of rebuilding their marriage. Living in Maddie's apartment was, in her view at least, a temporary solution; a solution that gave them each space whilst they sorted themselves out. She had hoped a little distance would focus her husband's mind and show him what he had been missing out on. Each morning, she had expected a phone call, asking her to come home, even suggesting they meet up to talk about finding a way to get through this somehow.

Throughout their time apart, Charlotte had deliberately not contacted Miles, believing she needed to demonstrate to Antonio that it had been a one-off episode, a moment of madness, not the start of an affair capable of threatening their relationship in any way. Their marriage after all had to count for something, surely?

Although she would be a liar to say she had not been sorely tempted to pick up the phone, knowing even a brief message to check in with him would have been a mistake. Especially as having sex with Miles still played out in her head, almost on repeat, the vividness of it capable of blanking out her other thoughts. He had been such an attentive and passionate lover, instinctively knowing what her body craved and making her feel wanted, at a time when that was all she needed. She was not in love with Miles, but loved being with him and loved how he made her feel, and even though the time Antonio caught them had only been their third sexual encounter, already Charlotte was beginning to feel hooked. That rush of adrenaline it gave her was almost addictive, and something she had missed.

So, when Antonio's call eventually came, inviting her around to the house to talk, her spirits and hopes were raised. She paid attention to the way she dressed, to the way she did her hair and makeup, even to the underwear she chose to wear, just in case. After all, it could be the start of their reconciliation process and she needed to look her best. Be prepared for any eventuality. She needed to look contrite and irresistible all at the same time, a look that she was at pains to perfect as she added the last touch of lipstick in front of the mirror before her taxi arrived.

From the moment he had opened the front door, though, it was obvious all her attentions had been for nought. He looked dishevelled, unshaven and clearly not in any mood to seduce her, or impress her on any level. Inviting her in, and moving directly to the kitchen where the coffee was already prepared, he immediately began to explain how he was feeling. The word *love*, or any residual feelings of that nature that he might have had towards her, was never mentioned.

Charlotte felt his monologue left little room for her to interject about her own expectations or feelings, or how she was doing, let alone how she was managing or coping without him. There was also no mention of Miles, or her affair, or of anything of any significance whatsoever. Not as far as her life was concerned at least.

The more he spoke, the more incredulous Charlotte became. She was seeing a side to her husband she had not witnessed previously, and it was not one she particularly liked. The essence of what he was saying eventually moved from feelings to actions, outlining what he sensed he needed to do with his life. The words 'they' or 'their' rarely featured in what he said. He was informing rather than discussing, describing his plans succinctly, to the point at which it began to feel more like a business meeting, than the attempt at reconciliation she had been hoping for. Moreover, his plans barely gave any thought to how it might affect her, or their marriage, or where she fitted in, if indeed she did. Their relationship was almost incidental, a minor hiccup in Antonio's bigger picture, something that no doubt would be dealt with in due course.

So, when the invite did eventually come for her to move home, it was to live in the house whilst he was away. "After all, there's no point in having an unoccupied property, or in you paying rent, is there?" Antonio had asked, adding that as he had no idea when he would be returning, it made no sense for her not to be there. He was leaving and would be in touch at some point, should his plans change.

Whilst Charlotte tried to hide the disbelief from her face, it was clear his decision was made. It was not up for discussion at any level, or with anyone, let alone his wife.

As the call could be heard to finally board the aircraft, Antonio experienced a sudden lightness to his mood. He smiled at the cabin crew as they checked his boarding card and directed him towards his window seat. It was a feeling he had not felt for some time. He realised he was no longer burdened by the businesses, the house or his marriage. He had dealt with the practicalities and emotional sides of each before he left, some admittingly more successfully than others. Now they would all chart their own course whilst he was away. He was relaxed that the business and house would be cared for, Philippe and Charlotte would respectively attend to those, especially as they both had a vested interest in ensuring no harm came to either. And in terms of his relationship with his wife, well the jury was still out on that.

Antonio had already lost enough sleep without worrying any more on that issue, although the question of whether he still wanted to fight for their marriage, as he had previously thought, or whether that dynamic had changed following her infidelity, still played large in his head. He was not a quitter, at the same time he seriously questioned whether there was anything left worth fighting for.

Spending so much time apart had certainly given them each plenty of space to think, yet after their meeting he suspected Charlotte had perhaps reached a different conclusion to his own. Arriving at the house, he had not been immune to her charms, as it was clear from her appearance she'd had different expectations for their meeting than his. Old feelings had been stirred, he was man enough to admit that, and whilst a weaker man may have succumbed, not Antonio. Not this time.

The look on her face, and her obvious hurt at the words he'd used to explain his feelings, had left him confused. After all, she was the one who had cheated, so what did she expect from him? Simply to forgive and forget, then wait around for the next time, all the time wondering whether he'd return home to find another man in his wife's bed each time he left the house? He was the injured party, although anyone seeing the look she had given him when she had left the house would not have believed it. She was contrite, that much was for sure, but otherwise any trust he'd once felt was being severely tested. No, they were not out of the woods, not by a long stretch.

At least, though, he had started the process of listening to his body and doing what he felt was needed to repair his own spirit. What he did longer term with his life, his marriage, his business, or even when he would eventually return to the UK were questions for another day. All he needed to concentrate on today was the welcome he would receive when he walked back into the finca later that evening. Lucía and Theresa were expecting him, and after the heartfelt discussions that had taken place over recent days, he knew that it was not all going to be plain sailing when he returned. There was still a lot more talking and importantly a lot more listening that needed to take place.

He had a clear sense, though, that he was going home, and whilst he acknowledged he was leaving a small part of himself in England, a part that could not be ignored indefinitely, he was taking the important parts with him. His heart and his spirit, both of which were in need of repair.

Now, settling back as the plane eventually took off and headed south towards the Canarias and the winter sunshine, he realised that was enough for him to concentrate his energies on for the time being. He had the sure knowledge that the rest would fall into place, one way or another. Karma or destiny, or however you chose to term the future unknown, would invariably play its part. Over that he had no influence, whatsoever.

For a moment, as he stared out of the window, he was reminded of a comment Theresa had made to him, many months ago as they sat on the flight going over to his father's funeral. She reminded him he would become what he was destined to become, nothing more, nothing less. So, rather than fear what that might involve, Antonio finally accepted the need to relax and simply let life take him where he needed to go.

A new chapter of his life was about to be written, the thought of which gave him a sudden frisson of excitement.

Chapter 22

It was a beautiful early spring morning; the sun was shining and the birds were tweeting high in the trees behind the house. The windows were wide open to let the gentle breezes waft through, providing some light relief from the intense heat.

Antonio was sitting at the kitchen table at the finca, quietly going over some paperwork with Lucía. He was patiently talking her through what it all involved, surprised that she had hardly any interest in what needed to be done. He had called into the post office the previous day to collect the latest pack of papers the solicitor had couriered over from Lanzarote, with a note saying they needed his attention, before requesting Lucía to sign them. Good progress, in terms of sorting out both Mateo's and José's estates, appeared to be being made, however each week it was surprising how many new sets of papers arrived, or decisions needed to be taken. Probate was taking a lot longer than expected, although given the relative complexities involved, or the fact the two estates were effectively being settled in tandem, perhaps that was to be expected.

In the meantime, a regular amount of money had started to trickle into Lucía's bank account, making everyday life at the finca easier than it had been for many years. Proceeds from the commercial properties and income from the fishery, as well as dividends from shares amounted to a sizeable chunk of money each month. Whilst some of the shares had been sold, or investments traded in, the majority were still held and being managed by an agency on the Spanish mainland. Overall José Pérez' portfolio was doing well and it was clear, from Antonio's perspective at least, that the old man had had a good head for business.

So far, from the sums involved, Antonio was reassured it had been the right decision to retain the commercial properties, maintain the share portfolio and offload the house and *Pesca Pérez* business, as he had originally suggested to Lucía. A buyer for the main house had easily been found and a good price agreed, with the transfer of *Pesca Pérez* also agreed in principle, although neither could complete until probate had been granted. When the final monies from those sales arrived, it would make Lucía a very wealthy woman indeed.

Lucía however appeared indifferent, almost detached from it all. Money was of no real importance to her. Provided she had enough to keep the finca going and put food on the table, the rest was irrelevant. Antonio and Theresa were at pains to get her to think otherwise, or to give any serious thought to how the money could be used to help improve her own life and the lives of her wider family and friends. Having it sitting in the bank, gathering dust, was of no use to anyone.

The Return

"Come here and help me, Anya. Yaya will teach you how to make tortilla, and then we can have some for our lunch. Do you want to help too, Maya? You can wash those other potatoes before we put them onto boil." Theresa had been busying herself making a selection of tapas in the kitchen, leaving Antonio and Lucía free to speak. She was also keeping her eye on Carmen's two daughters, whilst she had driven into the local town to visit her solicitor.

Carmen and her husband, Juan, were going through a difficult period and she was planning on divorcing him, although before she dropped that particular bombshell she needed to know where she stood, particularly with regards custody of their children. Carmen was not the easiest of women to be around on the best of days, with Juan hot-headed too, so the combination of them together invariably left the atmosphere charged. Their relationship had teetered on a knife-edge for a while now, and Juan's latest drunken bout for Carmen had been the final straw.

Over the last few weeks, watching her swan around the house, her moods vacillating on a daily basis, her demands becoming more outrageous, Antonio had some sympathy for Juan. His own wife could be high maintenance, but it looked like Carmen could easily give Charlotte a run for her money any day of the week. And the fact she had returned to the finca shortly after Christmas, with both girls in tow and their bags stacked in the car, announcing she had left him and had come home, had made living in the small house a challenge. There was proverbially no room at the inn, with all four bedrooms already occupied. Lucía in the main bedroom, with Sofía still living at home in her own room and Theresa and Antonio using the two spare rooms. Antonio had offered the girls his old room and with its two twin beds it was ideal, allowing him the luxury of sleeping on the downstairs sofa. Meanwhile Carmen had bunked down with Sofía – an arrangement neither woman was happy with.

After a couple of nights of broken sleep, Antonio, fearing the house could not accommodate three more bodies, let alone six sets of female hormones, decided to move out. He found himself a fully-furnished, two-bedroom penthouse property to rent. It was in a more modern apartment block in one of the adjacent towns, just five minutes' drive further down the mountain from the finca. Having already bought himself a car, he was independent, and it enabled him to visit the finca whenever he chose, or to tour the surrounding towns and villages, refamiliarising himself with the island of his birth. After all, a man in his thirties, living back at home again with his mother was not the coolest move he had ever made. Regardless of everything else that was going on around him, he still had his own life to lead.

Now, watching Anya and Maya working with Theresa, creating the various traditional dishes they would have for their meals for the rest of the week, Antonio was transported back in time. Back to the time when he too had stood alongside his mother as a young boy learning to cook. Learning to create the same traditional dishes the island was as famous for today as it has always been. That was where his passion for food had originally been ignited, and the cuisine that had inspired his own restaurants all those years later. Simple effective techniques, using the freshest of local, affordable and seasonal ingredients. He smiled as he listened to the questions the girls asked and the answers Theresa provided, so patient in her responses as she explained what she was doing, the delight on her face as she passed down her wisdom to the next generation. Antonio was suddenly filled with inspiration, the nugget of an idea beginning to form in his mind.

"Yaya, you look like you're enjoying yourself," Antonio observed, "and the girls look like they are, too." He still called Theresa grandmother, and treated her as such, especially when they were around other people. It was one of the things they had all agreed upon. No one could see any value in doing otherwise, or making their news public. Not for the time being at least as the risks were still there. People had long memories in their small village and with all the legal wranglings that were going on in parallel, any questions would only muddy the waters. So, in the interests of keeping their private lives private, they had reached an accommodation. They would remain silent, with no one, not even Sofía or Carmen, aware of the change in the family dynamic. Lucía, Theresa and Antonio were happy to keep it that way.

"Yes, it's good fun and I'm enjoying passing on my knowledge. It's years since I've had the opportunity to do that, and it's great to have such wonderful students, who are willing to learn," she said, smiling over at her two grand-daughters. Maya had her arms deep in water, washing the potatoes that would eventually become *papas arrugadas*, or wrinkly potatoes as the locals referred to them, and Anya was being trusted to whisk the eggs for the tortilla, the large bowl carefully held in her arms. "Nowadays, with all the convenience food in the supermarkets, youngsters can't be bothered to cook at home. They lead such busy lives and have probably never had the time to learn to cook, or had anyone to teach them for that matter. I feel it's such a shame, especially as we don't want our old traditions to fall by the wayside, do we?" Theresa let out a gentle sigh.

Since her return to Tenerife for Mateo's funeral, over seven months now, she had not experienced any great desire to return to England. It was almost as if she had forgotten the life she had lived in London, with nearly thirty years effectively airbrushed out of her life. She hardly spoke about it and was not missing the hustle and bustle of London one iota. She was simply happy to be back with her family and able to feel useful again. City life, with all its demands had become tiresome, the endless social activities she would engage in to help fill her days had long since given her any real enjoyment. Since Duncan's death she had basically gone through the motions, almost living a half-life, without any real sense of purpose. And then when Mollie died, less than twelve months later, pining her master's death no doubt, even those simple pleasures of walking around the parks, or the company of the dog on an evening, were gone.

With her sudden departure from London, when the phone call had come in about Mateo's death, Theresa had simply packed a bag and left. Her house had been locked up and secured, otherwise abandoned. Then after deciding to stay around to help Lucía, she had employed a local agency to go in and give it a deep clean. There was no saying what state the fridge or freezer would be in by then, or when the bins were last emptied. At some stage she knew she would need to return to London to attend to it, for now, though, she was happy. It was one less thing to worry about and after all, she had all she needed with her, the important things at least.

"I was wondering......." Antonio began, cautious about voicing the idea that was starting to form in his head, "Mama, what do you think about the concept of taking people in, to teach them how to cook, perhaps?"

Lucía raised her head, conscious there was a discussion forming to which she was not party. "Antonio, don't be ridiculous. Whatever makes you think I would want to do that? This house is small enough, without having more people cluttering up the kitchen. Inviting strangers in who we know nothing about. Why should we, and how on earth would we cope, even if anyone would be interested in learning how to make paella anyway? I'm not sure where that idea's come from, but I don't think it's a good one at all!"

"Mama, I'm not talking about taking over your kitchen, or inviting strangers into your home, for that matter." He knew Lucía had no vision for the future and was equally not one of life's risk takers, so pitching any idea to her was always going to be a challenge. However, the more he thought about it, the more he began to feel excited at the concept. In fact, it was similar to something he had considered starting back home but had never quite got around to. Other pressures had always got in the way, and at the time he'd had no headspace to get it off the ground.

He could tell however, by the expression on Theresa's face, that she was not as dismissive as her daughter. Theresa had more experience of what Antonio was capable of in the food and restaurant industry, and he believed she would back him any day. In fact, that was exactly what she and Duncan had done all those years ago to help get his first business off the ground. Duncan had found some premises in an area of London that was on the up; premises that he knew with the right investment over time would make a killing. He bought the property and gifted the use of it to Antonio, with that being the springboard he had needed to start his first restaurant. Over the years those early risks that they had taken had paid back tenfold.

"What I was actually thinking about was that perhaps we could develop a small culinary school, developing some of the land you have around the finca. A place where people could come and take courses, and learn some of the skills Yaya was talking about. We have more than enough land to build on, and we could even create some accommodation, if that was an issue, potentially out of some of those old outhouses. It would be good to regenerate them, don't you think?" Knowing Mateo had fallen to his death from one of those made the mere mention of them something Antonio had to be careful about. However, whilst they remained in the condition they were the memories would never go away, and by converting them into habitable accommodation the overall prospect would be more attractive and potentially more profitable.

Sensing Lucía was now listening to the idea, and even giving it some thought, he continued. "I know the finca is a little remote, so we wouldn't want that to be an issue, would we Mama? I'm sure we could easily attract the business, especially if I trade on the restaurants' reputation. There are plenty of people who would enjoy the idea of a week in the sunshine, learning to cook and enjoying a glass of homemade sangria or two, whilst watching the sunset on an evening. We could start small, then expand if the business is there."

The more Antonio spoke, the more the excitement became evident in his voice. His idea was gathering momentum and he realised he would even be prepared to invest his own money in it, should Lucía be unprepared to back it. It would be just the type of project that he could throw himself into with gusto.

"Think about it, Mama, we could showcase the area, the fantastic products we have here on the island, that in turn will provide a lot of business to the surrounding villages. We could employ local workers and that would help the overall economy too, as well as share some of your good fortune around. Above all, we could all have some real fun into the bargain. What do you think?" He waited for her reply, desperate to read the stoic look on her face that was not giving anything away.

"Well, I'm certainly sold on the idea, Lucía," Theresa announced, hoping her enthusiasm would help convince her daughter. "In fact, I'll even dig out my old recipe books and start thinking about some tutorials, or is that getting a little ahead of myself?" she questioned, laughing.

"I think that might be a bit premature, Yaya," he replied, nevertheless grateful for her support. "Although I could certainly see you'd be a great hit with the students, especially if these two are anything to go by," he said, smiling over at Anya and Maya.

Eventually Lucía looked up. "Alright, why don't you give it some more thought, and talk to a few people to get an idea of costs. I'd be worried if we couldn't afford it, or if it put what we have at the finca at risk. Your papa worked so hard for what we have……"

"Mama, we can more than afford it. In fact, it will be a drop in the ocean in terms of what you've inherited, and in terms of risks please don't worry. I will be here to manage it, I can assure you of that."

The Return

Antonio had just found himself a new project, one into which he could wholeheartedly throw himself, and as he looked around their small kitchen, watching the faces of those around him light up, he could see his excitement had become contagious.

Chapter 23

As Antonio was happily spending his time in Tenerife, developing plans for the finca, Charlotte was rattling around their old house. She had barely spoken to her husband for weeks, and even if she had she would have struggled to know what to say to him. To say she was in a real predicament was perhaps the understatement of the year and time was certainly against her.

Shortly after Antonio had left, around mid-December, Charlotte discovered she was three months pregnant. With everything that had been going on, and all the complexities of the situation between herself, Antonio and Miles, she had completely missed the all-important signs, putting her missed periods down to a mix of anxiety and stress. It was not something she had looked for and even now the concept of being pregnant sat heavily with her.

It was her friend Stephanie who had noticed it, one evening the week before Christmas. They were preparing to share a bottle of wine, before heading out into the city for cocktails then dinner. She had arrived at Charlotte's house for the weekend, with plans of hitting the stores high on her agenda the following day. She needed some last-minute Christmas presents for her two children, as well as that must-have outfit for the New Year's Eve party she and her husband were hosting at their house.

She and Charlotte had booked an expensive restaurant, just off Knightsbridge, for some fine dining, with plans to wash it all down with some vintage champagne. Although looking at how tired her friend was, Stephanie now questioned whether they would be leaving the house at all that weekend.

"Should you be drinking another, Char, in your condition I mean?" she had asked innocently, as Charlotte started to pour them both a second glass. To which Charlotte had looked at her questioningly, unsure at first what she meant. Then as Stephanie's eyes fell to Charlotte's stomach, and the small bump that was barely visible, it became obvious.

"Oh my god, you don't think I'm pregnant, do you?" was all Charlotte could utter, putting the glass down and steadying herself before she fell. "I know I've not been feeling too well recently, but I never imagined that to be the cause. I can't be pregnant, can I?"

"Well, I'm no expert, but it certainly looks like that to me and I should know, having already suffered that condition twice! You'd have thought I'd have learned the first time, wouldn't you?" she laughed. "Anyway, more importantly, congratulations. What will Antonio think? I guess once you tell him, he'll be on the first flight home, won't he?"

Stephanie knew all too well about the difficulties Charlotte was going through with her marriage, and also knew about Miles and the sorry state that particular relationship had got her into, although she had not been at all surprised when Charlotte eventually admitted to what had been going on between them. Stephanie had sensed the chemistry between the two during their weekend away in Bath, and had even felt a little envious about the attention her friend had been receiving. Although now with a baby on the way that would all be behind her, she imagined.

"Yes, I imagine he'll be as surprised as I am," was Charlotte's weak response, not at all convinced of his imminent return, nor of the need for congratulations.

Stephanie, reading the concerned look on Charlotte's face, questioned, "Char, it is Antonio's, I presume? You're not worried, are you?" Miles' name was not mentioned, although it hung unspoken in the air between them.

"No, I'm not worried and I'm sure if I am pregnant, which is a big 'if' at the moment, it will be fine. It's not something we've discussed recently, or something that was even on the horizon, especially with everything else that's been going on, but I'm sure he'll be happy." The conviction in her voice was unconvincing.

The following week, once she had eventually had it confirmed by the doctor, even though the test kit from the chemist had already confirmed it with ninety-nine percent accuracy, it was still a massive shock.

Now, a further two months down the line, the idea of impending motherhood still did not sit comfortably with her. Especially not the prospect of being a single mother, given the likelihood of Antonio wanting anything to do with it was next to zero. No matter how Charlotte worked her dates out, or imagined things otherwise, there was no way she could convince herself, let alone her husband, that she was carrying his child.

At twenty weeks pregnant, with the twenty-three week time limit for a legal abortion looming ever closer, she was fast running out of time, or options for that matter. Should she tell her husband or not, running the risk that he would use that as further ammunition to end their marriage? It already felt perilously clear that the concept of divorce would be entering their discussions before too long, and the existence of an illegitimate child could well be held against her when it came to any divorce settlement. After all, she could not hoodwink even Antonio into accepting it was his, given he could easily work out the dates for himself. There was also no hiding the fact they had not slept together for such a long time either, and certainly not since she had been caught with Miles. It would not take a rocket scientist to reach the obvious conclusion, and knowing that, he would not want to bring up another man's child, of that she was certain.

Alternatively, should she bite the bullet and tell Miles, in the hope he would want to do the honourable thing and take some responsibility for the situation? It takes two to tango, as the old adage goes, and both of them were adults who knew the risks of what they were getting themselves into. It was right that neither had set out to create a baby, although neither of them was naïve enough not to realise that what they were doing often had that result! Why on earth had they not thought to take any precautions?

As Miles had not been in touch for some time, contacting him now, out of the blue, would appear strange. Charlotte had certainly missed him and the banter they had enjoyed. She even conceded the sex had been fantastic too, laughing as she realised the absurdity of that observation, especially in the context of her current predicament.

Perhaps she should message him, but the grapevine suggested he may have gone back to his wife, in an attempt to rebuild their relationship. Charlotte had been surprised at that, especially having been told by Miles himself that they had reached the end of the line and were contemplating a divorce. If she told him about the baby, would that change his attitude, and would she want it to, anyway? He had been good fun and a great distraction, but long term could she see herself wanting to have a relationship with him, only in respect of rearing a child? She imagined his wife might have something to say about that as well, especially if they were making a go of their marriage, second time around.

Or should she just book and appointment at the private clinic and be done with it? She had the brochure and details to hand, and all it would take was a simple phone call to arrange. Abortion was something she had strong feelings about and had never fully supported, not without good reason. Was this good reason, or would she be taking the coward's way out? As by quietly and discreetly getting rid of the pregnancy, Antonio would never need to know about it. They would be free to resume where they had left off, presuming that is, he ever planned on coming back to her.

None of the options appealed and no obvious solution came to mind. She would think on it some more, and make her decision in the morning. After all, another day wouldn't make any difference, would it?

Chapter 24

The following afternoon, Antonio was alone at his apartment, going through some papers and scanning the internet, making notes and scribbles as he went along. He liked to keep abreast of the news, or read some of the foody features he found on other restaurants, even read about other chefs and what they were up to in the kitchen; always keen to see the new trends, or discover who was doing what in the industry.

One of the advantages of the modern apartment he was renting was its Wi-Fi connectivity. It was fast and reliable, meaning he no longer needed to call at the patisserie each day to access his emails or surf the net. The downside, though, was he missed the daily café con leche he'd become partial to, to say nothing of the wide selection of pastries and cakes the place had to offer. He'd enjoyed meeting and chatting with the locals too, considering himself now one of them, no longer an outsider. Especially as his Spanish had continued to improve the more he used it, realising he rarely reverted to speaking English these days. He was certainly blending in, his formal clothes replaced by shorts and casual shirts, his skin benefiting from its exposure to the fresh air and sunshine, and with each passing day Tenerife was starting to feel more like home.

His mood was lighter too, and he was especially excited at the prospect of developing the culinary school. He, Theresa and Lucía had talked at length the previous evening and as the night wore on even Lucía was beginning to believe the idea could be workable. He and Theresa had thrown around some wild and whacky suggestions over dinner, assured each time that Lucía would rein them in. She still needed to be fully convinced on the merits of his proposal, although by the end of the evening she had started to see the fun side to what they were considering embarking on. The idea of converting the outhouses was above all something that really appealed to her. Walking past them each day these last few months, a constant reminder of how and where Mateo had met his death, was anguish for her.

Now all Antonio needed to do was put some flesh onto his idea and see whether it was really as workable as he imagined. Would he get the approvals from the local council he needed to do the development, would he be able to find the architects, the designers, the builders he would need to bring it to life, or the staff who would help run it, both in terms of the upkeep and the trainers? Theresa clearly saw a role for herself there, and others in the surrounding towns may want to be involved too. Although having some more qualified people could be what was required for the kudos they would bring. That would need some thinking about.

Above all, would he be able to sell the concept to the public and bring in the trade it would need to generate in order to make it a viable concern? He was sure he would, he just needed to get it all down on paper and start the process of getting some wider stakeholders bought in. His business head was slowly starting to reawaken, and he quite liked the feeling it was giving him.

So, when the phone rang, he picked it up without really thinking.

"Hola," he answered, automatically assuming his native tongue.

"Oh, is that Mr Pérez, Antonio Pérez?" the caller asked.

"Yes, sorry. How can I help you?" he replied, realising the caller was speaking in English.

"Right, well this is a little delicate," he began hesitantly. "I'm Doctor Hyde, calling from St Thomas' hospital in London. Would I be correct in assuming your wife is Charlotte Pérez?" he checked.

"Yes, Doctor, Charlotte is my wife. Why is there a problem, or do you need to contact her? It's just that I'm not in the country at the moment, so you may want to contact her directly at home. I can give you her number, if that would help."

"No, Mr Pérez, that won't be necessary. We have your wife at St Thomas', so it was you I needed to inform of her whereabouts and her general condition."

"Oh, right, I understand, thank you," Antonio replied, momentarily lost for words. "Is Charlotte alright, has there been an accident or something?"

"Yes, your wife is okay, however she was involved in a traffic accident this morning. The police are still assessing the scene, but I understand she had to swerve quickly to avoid a motorist, and in the process the car veered headlong into a lamppost. She suffered some minor cuts and bruises, and there's a little concussion we're continuing to monitor, so nothing too worrying on that score, although I'm sad to have to inform you that she miscarried in the process. It's too early to say exactly what the cause of that was, but I believe she may have not been wearing her seatbelt at the time. I fear it's the mistake many pregnant women make, especially in their later stages when it can become uncomfortable, or there's a concern about the airbag potentially releasing ...."

Whilst Doctor Hyde began to ramble about the pros and cons of seatbelts and airbags, Antonio could not quite believe what he had just heard.

"Sorry to interrupt you, Doctor, did you say pregnant? I fear we may be talking at cross purposes, about the wrong Charlotte Pérez perhaps. Is there any way you could be mistaken?   My wife, to my knowledge, was not expecting a baby."

Doctor Hyde went quiet for a moment whilst he re-checked his notes. "I don't believe so, Mr Pérez," he began, now feeling more than a little uncomfortable about the way he had handled the call, even the veracity of the notes made by the medical staff who had been the first responders, or the assessment of the junior doctors who had attended Mrs Pérez in A&E, when the ambulance had brought her in. The results of the D&C procedure however were undisputed. The loss of blood and the signs all indicated a pregnancy in the second trimester, four to five months was the estimate. He confirmed the house address with Antonio and described his patient, by way of reassuring himself, although in Doctor Hyde's view there was no confusion. "And your details were clearly listed on her notes as her next of kin, her point of contact in the case of an emergency."

"Right. Thank you for that, Doctor."

Antonio had no idea what else to say, or what he was expected to do or think about the information he had just received. His wife had apparently been pregnant, in fact some months pregnant, a condition he had not known anything about. It wasn't as if she had just found out, or had simply not got around to telling him, unsure of perhaps saying anything until the doctor had confirmed the tests.

If that was the case, what on earth was her motivation for keeping it to herself? It was true, since coming to Tenerife, they were not speaking nearly as often as they had done previously, nor were their conversations as intimate as they had once been, before her affair. He would call maybe once or twice each month, to discuss the practicalities of the house, or enquire about something specific. Occasionally she would call him too, if anything unexpectantly came up. They rarely spoke about how they were spending their time, day to day, with discussions about their feelings well and truly parked.

Although, recently they had started to open up a little more, with the atmosphere between them not as cool as it had once been. Nevertheless, they were still carefully avoiding discussing their feelings, or anything too personal. Neither was ready to open up that particular hornet's nest, not for the time being at least. Charlotte, for once, appeared confident with her independence, rarely moaning to Antonio about having to cope by herself, even joking about some of the scrapes she got herself into without him around. In turn, Antonio occasionally spoke about his apartment, his trips to the shops and drives around the island, although he rarely confided about what he was really doing in Tenerife, or how much he felt at home there. It appeared at some level at least, they were both benefitting from the space that had been created between them.

Even so, there had been plenty of opportunities for her to have raised the subject of her pregnancy, as uncomfortable as that might have been, if she had wanted to. After all, it was not the type of question she would have expected him to ask arbitrarily, was it? "How was your day, are there any problems around the house that I need to address and oh, by the way, are you expecting a baby?"

The more he thought about it, Antonio realised even Christmas and New Year had passed since they had last seen each other, with on both occasions it being customary to share good news. They had spoken on each of these big days, even laughing and joking about some of the traditions they would not need to do this year, given they were apart. Charlotte had said she had no intention of putting the decorations up, or buying a turkey for one, and Antonio had even admitted to being thankful he wasn't being dragged around the shops looking for presents for the in-laws, or having to feign interest when listening to his mother-in-law recount more stories of Charlotte as a small child. In his mind, there had certainly been plenty of opportunities, with the thawing of tensions between them making it easier to raise the subject.

That meant he had deliberately been kept in the dark and the more he pondered that, and specifically the timings the doctor had referred to, he began to realise what her motivation may have been.

"Please remind me again, Doctor, which hospital did you say you were calling from, and what ward has my wife been moved to? I could perhaps phone them directly and ask to speak to her. Importantly, is there anything specific you need me to do, recognising I am not in the country at the moment?"

As the doctor spoke, Antonio reached for a pen and some paper, scribbling down the numbers he was provided. In terms of what he needed to do, or the timings around any discharge, the doctor could not advise him, other than to suggest a call to the ward the following morning might be a good idea. "By then, they may have more of an idea of your wife's overall prognosis, including what their plans are for her discharge. Otherwise, I have nothing more to tell you, so good afternoon and thank you for your time, Mr Pérez."

As Antonio put the phone down, he was now almost certain any child could not have been his, and that left him in an even deeper quandary than before. Where on earth did that leave him and Charlotte now, especially if Miles was still in the picture, as he clearly was? Any chance they may have had of rebuilding the trust that had been lost now appeared to have gone completely out of the window. He could not see any way back from this, and frankly was not sure he wanted to try, even if there was a way.

Chapter 25

The following morning, as Charlotte lay in the hard bed in her private room at St Thomas' hospital, feeling sore as well as sorry for herself, one of the young nurses walked in. She was carrying a tray on which her breakfast had been laid out. A half-filled glass of orange juice, a bowl of bland looking cereal, a slice of anaemic toast, with a lukewarm cup of tea in a pale blue cup and saucer.

"Good morning, Mrs Pérez. How are you feeling today?" She smiled over at her patient, the cuts and bruises still visible after three days, before placing the tray on the small table at the end of Charlotte's bed. "I believe the doctor's planning on discharging you later today, provided everything is still okay after his morning round, Sister said earlier. I'm sure that will brighten up your morning." Charlotte didn't reply.

The nurse pulled back the curtains and announced, "It's a beautiful day. Spring is certainly on its way, isn't it? Although there's not much to look at from this window, I'm afraid. Just traffic. No daffodils or spring lambs on view for you today." She was feeling quite chirpy, and hoped her mood might be contagious, as it was obvious the woman in the bed needed a lot of cheering up. The nurse had read Charlotte's notes so was well aware of her accident, as well as the miscarriage she'd suffered. With a young baby of her own, she could only imagine the anguish she must be going through as a consequence of losing a much-wanted child.

"Thank you," Charlotte eventually replied as she looked at her breakfast tray, clearly uninterested in touching it. She was not feeling at all cheery and although she was grateful for the attentions of the nursing staff, she just hoped the young nurse would leave her alone to wallow in her grief. The pain killers were more than capable of dealing with the bruising and physical injuries she had incurred, yet they did nothing to address the grief she was feeling. That unexpected and unexplainable grief at losing a baby, one that as recent as the day of the accident she had considered aborting. There was no justice in the world. One minute she didn't know whether to keep it, the next she couldn't imagine living without it.

Those few months when she had carried her child, unsure of what she wanted to do about it, or even whether she wanted to keep it, had really messed with her emotions. Putting the question of the paternity of it to one side, she had never realised until that moment how maternal she had been. She and Antonio had initially talked about having children, and how they might at some point fit into their lives. It was not something that had been discounted, yet it was equally not high on their agenda. Charlotte enjoyed the highlife, the socialising and time to indulge her own passions. She had not seen how a child would slot into that, and the thought of losing her figure whilst she ballooned was almost frightening. She had a wardrobe of designer dresses and maternity wear was not for her.

Equally Antonio was immersed in his businesses, concentrating all his energies on building his reputation, making a name for himself in the cut-throat hospitality industry. He couldn't afford to step back and prioritise a child over everything else, regardless of the fact they could afford to employ nannies and others to do the heavy lifting in terms of child care. No, he'd had too much to lose too.

The value of what you lose is seldom appreciated until it has gone, Charlotte now came to realise as she lay in her hospital bed. She was lost in her thoughts and had begun to believe that God was playing tricks with her. Perhaps even punishing her in some way for all the indecision she had gone through, or more likely her behaviour leading up to the accident. Cheating on her husband was one thing, but not telling him she was pregnant by another man was clearly on another level entirely. What had she expected to achieve by keeping that from him? It was her fault she had lost the baby, and along with it any chance of getting her husband back.

Antonio had phoned the hospital the previous evening, the duty nurse in charge bringing the phone handset into her, before quietly shutting the door as she left the room.

"It's your husband, Mrs Pérez," she had said, her face displaying a mildly concerned look as she spoke. "He couldn't get hold of you on your mobile, so he's phoned the ward directly. I'll give you a little privacy so you can speak to him." As a private patient at the hospital Charlotte was receiving excellent attention. Whilst none of the medical staff had any idea about her background or circumstances, it was still obvious to them, from the fact her husband had not rushed to her bedside after the miscarriage, that something was amiss. Their discretion was noticeable.

"Antonio, hi," Charlotte had begun, unsure how to continue. "Nice of you to call."

"Hello, Charlotte," he replied quite formally. "How are you feeling?"

"I'm not doing too well, I'm afraid," Charlotte began, struggling to disguise the tears within her voice. "I've had better days."

"Yes, I imagine you have. I understand from the doctor you've had a car accident, something to do with swerving to avoid a cyclist and hitting a lamppost, I believe he said. Is that correct?" Antonio began in an attempt to keep the conversation factual, at the same time gently prodding. He was anxious to hear what Charlotte said next, unsure whether she was aware of the conversation he'd had with the doctor, or in fact had any idea he knew about her miscarriage. Hence his need to approach with caution, testing the waters before he said too much, especially as the doctor may have inadvertently disclosed personal information that in hindsight he should not have done. He was also careful not to use an accusatory tone, or look to place any blame, as it was already clear from her voice how upset she was. He certainly did not want to say or do anything that would add to her anguish.

"Yes, I've got some cuts and bruises, and the car doesn't look too good either. I can't imagine the damage I've done to that.....or the damage to......" she sobbed, unable to get the words out.

"Take a deep breath, Charlotte, and tell me what you mean. After all, no one else was injured, the car's easily fixed, the cuts and bruises will soon heal, so what else has been damaged? Can't you talk to me, at least tell me what's worrying you, especially if you want me to help you in any way?"

Charlotte went quiet on her end of the phone. "Antonio, I can't. I'm so sorry. I can't even find the words myself, let alone talk to you about it," she spluttered, her sobs getting stronger. How was she expected to put into words how she was feeling, let alone tell him? Especially when he had just said no one else had been injured, unaware her baby had been killed. A baby, whom until that time she had never known or loved, but now felt was more a part of her than life itself. A baby she had in fact been responsible for killing, albeit accidentally, with the memory of the clinic and the number in her telephone, ready to book an appointment for the termination, haunting her every waking moment.

"Talk about what?" He hated the fact he was trying to push her into telling him. At the same time, he feared that unless he prompted the situation, he would never be any the wiser. She had kept the news of her pregnancy from him for so long, and now that it was no longer an issue, she probably could no longer see any reason for coming clean or telling him the truth. A truth that appeared destined to remain an unspoken secret between them. A truth that ultimately was capable of splitting them apart.

After a further prolonged silence, during which Antonio realised Charlotte was not going to say anything more, he continued. "So, what are your plans, for when you're discharged, I mean? I'm assuming they won't keep you in for more than a day or so, will they? Do you need me to come home or collect you, or put some plans in place to come back to London for a while, until you're feeling yourself again?"

Charlotte had given some thought to this one already, and whilst she desperately wanted to see her husband again, even feel his arms around her once more, in fact anyone's arms around her would be nice, she was not in the right frame of mind to see him. Not for the time being. But with Miles out of the picture, what other option did she have?

Also, if he did come home, it would become increasingly difficult to continue to avoid the subject, or explain her frequent mood swings. The doctor had already prescribed her some medication to help her cope and calm her down a little, suggesting that whilst it would take time for her to get over the shock of what had happened, the prescription was not intended as a long-term solution. He'd advised her to take good care of herself, kindly pointing out that the heart didn't heal nearly as quickly as the rest of the body, so she needed to be patient with her recovery. He had smiled benignly as he spoke, gently patting her hand as he left her room.

"Thank you, that's very kind of you, Antonio, but I'm already sorted. I've arranged with my parents to go and stay with them for a short break. It's been a while since I've seen them, so a few days in the countryside will help, don't you think? Mother says she's looking forward to me visiting, and to pampering me, so I wouldn't want to disappoint her, would I? Father will drive over and collect me whenever the hospital decides to let me go. I think being private means they're not as anxious to push me out the door, than if I was simply NHS," she said in an obvious attempt to make light of a sensitive situation.

"Well, if you're sure you're okay," Antonio replied, embarrassed at how relieved he felt with her response. He'd had no immediate plans to go back to the UK in any case, and with everything else that was going on, he was reluctant to be away from Tenerife. Unless it was really urgent, and Charlotte was certainly neither making it sound urgent, nor giving him any reason to come home. It felt like she had already moved on, with other people around her to care for her. Antonio did not feel at all needed, emotionally or otherwise.

"In that case, why don't you let me know when you get there safely, and I'll phone you later in the week, perhaps? Hopefully by then you'll be feeling a little stronger too, and we can have a longer talk. There will be things that need sorting, with insurances and such. I'll also arrange for someone to go around to the house and secure everything, as I imagine no one will have been there for a few days?" Antonio tried to keep the question out of his voice. He couldn't remember what days the cleaning lady went in, or if in fact she still did. More importantly he didn't care to imagine if Miles had moved himself in already, however implausible that idea might be. The question of what role Miles was currently playing in his wife's life remained a complete mystery to him.

"Thank you. I hadn't thought about that. Yes, there will be plenty of things to sort out, I'm sure. I'm tired now, though, so can I say good night and speak to you in a few days, when I get to my parents' house, like you suggested? Good night, Antonio, and thanks for calling." And thanks for caring, she added quietly to herself once she had hung up and just before the next wave of tears arrived.

Now, with the morning's arrival and the news of her imminent discharge having just been announced, the reality of actually spending time in her parents' countryside manor suddenly loomed large. Their house was certainly grand, the furnishings somewhat dated, yet with every amenity and labour-saving device on offer. Mainly, though, it was dark and over-stuffed, piles of endless objects her parents had amassed crowding every spare inch of floor or wall space. Even her childhood bedroom now housed antiques that were being stored, given there was no longer any room to display them downstairs. They competed for space with the plethora of dolls and stuffed animals her mother had encouraged her never to part with, filling the shelves above her bed and the tops of the wardrobe. She and Antonio had slept in that bedroom on occasion, with Charlotte recalling how creepy it had felt having the dolls stare down on them, especially if she and Antonio were being intimate.

Well, this time, at least sex wouldn't be an issue, although their sad eyes would undoubtedly be a further reminder of what she had lost. No baby to play with the toys that had so lovingly been kept.

And the idea of being cossetted away, being fussed over by her mother and cajoled by her father, was one with which she was not particularly enamoured. He would be forever trying to involve her in some activity or other, arguing idleness was not good for the soul, and her mother would be forever feeding her, attempting to rebuild her strength with a bowl of soup or something else she had cobbled together in the air fryer. After her husband's cooking, her mother's meals could never compete, and no end of kitchen devices would ever succeed in adding taste to the bland offerings she concocted.

On the plus side, an hour's drive outside London meant she would not be bumping into friends or nosy neighbours, which mercifully was a blessing. She was not in a mood to speak to anyone. Quiet country walks with her parents' dogs to distract her sounded charming. Although after a few days, with just her parents and the dogs for company, that position might easily change.

Chapter 26

By the end of May, Charlotte had been back in London for some weeks, deciding ten days with her parents was more than enough for her to cope with. Her mother had constantly asked questions and pried into her marriage, asking where Antonio was and why he was not with her. Without answers herself, Charlotte found this line of discussion both distressing and upsetting. She had no idea where her relationship was going, or if in fact she still had one. Antonio was still in Tenerife and had made no attempt to come home.

For him life had presumably largely gone back to normal. Nothing at all had been said on the subject of the miscarriage. Charlotte had decided that what he didn't know wouldn't harm him so continued to speak as if nothing had happened. Conversations between them remained straightforward and to the point. In response, Antonio respected her privacy and did not press for any more information than she was prepared to offer. They discussed the practicalities of normal life, with the easy banter that had begun to emerge before the accident no longer evident in their conversations. It was clear they were drifting further apart, with neither making any real effort to reverse the slide.

Miles did not know about the child either, and as sorely tempted as Charlotte was to contact him, she had managed to resist it. He was still married and according to sources he and his wife were working on repairing their relationship.

"So, what are you doing next weekend, Char?" Valarie asked. They had all met for lunch in a wine bar in Soho before hitting the shops. Valarie and Stephanie had come up to London the previous evening and stayed with Charlotte. They were spending the day together before catching the train home. "I presume you've got something good planned for your birthday? Have you asked Antonio if he's thinking of coming home for the occasion?" she added with a questioning look.

"No, I've nothing arranged and I don't believe Antonio has any plans whatsoever for coming home, full stop, let alone for my birthday. I can't imagine it's even on his radar. I think the ship's well and truly sailed on any chances of us rebuilding our relationship, I'm sad to say."

"Are you sad, though, or are you just lonely?" Valarie asked, provocatively. "It's not good for you to not have a man around, you know – and it is months since, well, you know…."

Charlotte smiled, unsure whether her friend was referring to the miscarriage or when she had last had sex, although given the two were so clearly related it was almost a moot point. Valarie and Stephanie were the only two friends with whom Charlotte had felt confident enough to share the news of her miscarriage. After all, they had both known about her affair and had needed an explanation when she suddenly went off radar after the accident. Stephanie had already suspected the pregnancy, so lying to them any further would only have exacerbated the problem.

"That's a good question, Val, and one for which I don't have a ready answer," Charlotte replied with a mournful look in her eyes. "I guess I'm sad my marriage isn't working out as I'd hoped, but I'd be a liar to say it had been perfect, especially these last twelve months. If it had been, I suppose I wouldn't have looked twice at Miles, let alone got into bed with him, would I? Moreover, if Antonio had been happy, he wouldn't have chosen his family and life overseas, over me, would he?" She then looked across at her friends, with a wicked smile on her face. "I'll also admit I am missing sex, especially sex with Miles, although not so much with Antonio, I hasten to add. I think if I'm being really honest, ladies, that fizzled out a long time ago," she giggled in an attempt to hide her embarrassed admission.

"Well, what's stopping you contacting him again? I'm sure Antonio isn't living life as a monk over there, is he? He's bound to have a few women on the go. Men, in my experience, don't seem to know how to avoid it, so why should you?" Valarie was in a mischievous mood, buoyed up by single-handedly drinking virtually the full bottle of wine.

"Val, you can't say that!" Stephanie chirped in, almost spluttering on her wine in the process.

Valarie had an interesting take on fidelity, and having been cheated on by at least her last two partners she was now at the stage where it was less important in a relationship. Whereas Stephanie was still very much the monogamous type of woman, blissfully married to a man she believed to be faithful, with her happy homelife and adorable children. It made for an interesting mix of ideas and advice whenever the friends got together.

"Steph, stop being such a prude and top your glass up! It's time you loosened up a little and got real," Valarie chided, unprepared to give up on the subject, and particularly not after the gossip she had heard the previous day. "Char, so what's stopping you contacting him again, especially now he and his wife are finally splitting up? I'd say now was as good a time as any to get your juices flowing again, wouldn't you? And preferably before someone else beats you to him. Miles is a very attractive proposition, and would be a good catch. I certainly can't see him staying available for long."

"Where have you heard that?" Charlotte questioned.

"Oh, someone mentioned it the other day, at the gym, I think. I can't remember who, but apparently his wife was seen out with another man, and by all accounts they looked to be quite close."

As Charlotte sat pondering what Valarie had just said, it gave her plenty of food for thought. Perhaps it was time to draw a line under whatever she and Antonio had been dancing around for the last few months, because although she had absolutely no idea if Valarie was right in terms of whether her husband had found someone else, their current arrangement was certainly not working for her.

And importantly, if she acted quickly and messaged Miles, perhaps her birthday night might not be as much as a washout, or as lonely or as boring, as she had previously suspected it might be.

As Charlotte was drawing a line under their relationship, so too was Antonio. He had waited months for the old feelings for his wife to return, listening for nuances in her voice or the odd word of encouragement whenever they spoke. No apology or any feelings of remorse, or any outpouring of feelings in any way, had been expressed by either of them in terms of what had happened, or where they now found themselves.

Those old adages that time is a great healer, or even absence makes the heart grow fonder were not working for him, or Charlotte it would appear. So, no matter how many times he tried to think otherwise he could no longer see any reason for fighting for their marriage. His wife had given him no signs of encouragement, or if she had they had not been noted. They were friendly when they spoke, courteous even in their dealings, but that was as far as it went, and in all their time apart neither one of them had ever suggested they meet up, not once. That alone spoke volumes.

Around the finca Charlotte's name was rarely mentioned, with the wider family no longer enquiring after her either. It was almost as if Theresa and Lucía had read the writing on the wall far earlier than Antonio, and as neither Carmen nor Sofía had ever had much time for their sister-in-law, to them it was no great loss. They had all noticed how relaxed and happy Antonio was, with him never showing any signs of discontentment or anxiety about being apart from his wife. And if Antonio was happy that made them happy too.

By the end of May, Antonio was deep into the planning stage for their new venture. He had drawn up a business plan and had received tentative backing from the local authorities to his ideas. It was quite an adventurous development and most people appeared supportive of what he was proposing and commended the amount of investment the family was planning to inject into the area. It all boded well, and when the final plans were drawn up and costed, they would have something more formal to seek approvals against.

He had also spoken to Philippe and some of his restaurant friends, all of whom were equally supportive of the plans and willing to work with him to find suitable chefs and clients to make it a success. There was also talk of inviting guest chefs to Tenerife to do specific dishes, even hosting celebrity events to get its profile known, particularly in the early days when it was building up its reputation.

"I think between ten to twelve clients at a time should be more than enough to break even, with one, possibly two courses running every month. Then if we add in the extra income from offering accommodation, or other experiences, we should easily be in profit, perhaps even within the first year, provided we ignore the initial investment and set up costs, that is. Those will need to be amortised over a few more years, but that shouldn't be an issue," Antonio was mumbling away to himself, whilst looking at the spreadsheet on his laptop. He was preparing for a meeting with some of the members of the local business council later that day, who were also interested in learning more about the plans.

Lucía wiped her hands on her apron and looked over at the screen. It was full of numbers and figures and she could not make head nor tail of it. Nevertheless, she was now fully bought into the concept and was getting quite excited by it. News was starting to filter around the area about what the Pérez family was contemplating and whenever she was out and about people would stop her and ask, anxious to pick up any information, or more likely learn where all the money had come from. The family was just a normal family, so for them to suddenly be investing hundreds of thousands of euros into their finca was almost incredulous, although they quite liked the sound of what was being proposed. They especially liked the sound of the extra work and hence money it would bring to their area. Lucía had explained how they intended to employ local workers and tradespeople to do the necessary building and conversion work, as well as the jobs that would be created running the place once it opened.

She was also happy that the issue of probate had finally been settled, in respect of both Mateo's and José's estates, the process of which had finally allowed *Pesca Pérez* to be sold along with the house where Mateo's grandparents had lived. When the money hit her bank account, Lucía could hardly believe her eyes. Until that point it had been something she could not quite get her mind around. After all, she had no knowledge of José, or any of the Lanzarote family interests, so for her to suddenly inherit it, lock, stock and barrel was beyond anything she had ever imagined. She was a simple woman who would never have need for the great riches that had inadvertently landed in her lap, so provided she had what she needed, and her family was provided for, she'd want for nothing else. A new kitchen and an upgrade to the finca's plumbing were all she really wanted. The concept of Antonio investing the money, for the purposes of growing it further, washed completely over her head.

Carmen and Sofía however had other ideas and were keen to help Lucía with suggestions of how they could spend the money, with for Carmen her divorce from Juan being her top priority, along with finding a new home for her and the girls to live. Having spent the last few months crammed in with her mother, sister and grandmother it was time to move out and move on. Juan's drinking had got worse, along with his behaviour when he was drunk, with Carmen seeing no reason whatsoever for putting up with it for a moment longer than was necessary, or having her children witness it. But they needed their own space, and as much as she loved her family, living at home with them was not her idea of living.

After the solicitor had advised she would have no problem with custody of her daughters, adding that in her view it was a straightforward case of unreasonable behaviour, she had received Carmen's instruction to file the papers. Now all she needed to do was wait for the divorce to be finalised, and hunt for a property. "Something with a small swimming pool would be nice," she suggested hopefully, looking at Lucía for support, as Sofía simply rolled her eyes at her sister's audacity.

Sofía equally believed it was time for herself to move out. She had just turned forty, so well past the age when living at home with your mother was considered acceptable. Having the money to live independently, though, had never been an option previously, as although she held a good administrative job, working at one of the local estate agents, the pay was low. By the time she'd funded the garage for the regular repair costs to her battered-up old Fiat, and had contributed towards her own living expenses, her salary was gone. At least Lucía no longer needed money from her to meet the bills at the finca, so that was a bonus, and with the money her mother had given her to buy a new car, it meant she was already feeling a lot better off. Thankfully she did not have expensive tastes, unlike her sister.

Importantly, Sofía had her eyes set on getting a job at the cookery school, and had already dropped a few hints to Antonio that she could manage the office for him. After all, she was experienced in dealing with clients and running an office. The handling of the paperwork, along with the financial and legalities of running a business would be second nature to her, to say nothing of her excellent IT skills, all of which were transferable. Above all she would love the chance to become directly involved in the family's new venture. The job at the estate agents was fine, but it was not challenging, and it was boring. Sofía needed more fun in her life, and from what she had already gleaned about the cookery school, it certainly sounded fun.

Theresa had watched quietly from the side-lines over recent weeks, as her family came together over the planned new development. The general mood and atmosphere around the finca had lifted, and although there were still moments when grief sneaked in unexpectantly, by and large her family was moving forward with their lives. There was a shared purpose, with everyone finding something to be grateful for, or to get involved in. She had even dug out her old cookery books, as she had suggested, and was looking at ideas that she could present to Antonio. Deciding what foods to cook was still a long way off, but for Theresa it was something that was giving her a great deal of pleasure, especially when she found some of the older or perhaps long-forgotten recipes, which she'd decided to adapt for today's living, today's methods. After all, the things they taught needed to be suitable for modern ways of living, she argued. Not many families, she imagined, would have the outside stew pots, wood stoves or open fires her ancestors had used to prepare and cook their peasant foods. And who in their right mind these days would consider butchering a rabbit, or de-heading a tuna fish, when the supermarkets or local markets would sell it pre-prepared and ready packaged?

Reading into the history of Canarian food and understanding how it had developed over the years, including where some of the influences had come from, was also interesting. Theresa still had an active brain and by carrying out some basic research she was able to point Sofía towards some relevant articles. Sofía had suggested she could compile a leaflet, or a small brochure, to help explain what they were offering at the school as well as support the marketing that would eventually be required.

To Sofía, reading about the evolution of food within the Canary Islands proved fascinating, most of it information she had never learned about in school. Its early connections to Africa and the trade in goats; to Spain, with their ample supplies of wine and olive oils; and even to Portugal, for their tangy mojo sauces, which was a particular favourite of hers, eaten with freshly baked bread. Then there was the introduction of potatoes, peppers and corn to the islands, as trade routes from the new worlds of America opened up in the fifteenth and sixteenth centuries, along with some of the more exotic spices arriving from Asia around the same time. To say nothing of the banana plants from Southeast Asia, or the tomatoes, believed to have come from Europe when the Spanish arrived there from Mexico.

Those early banana plants eventually resulted in swathes of banana plantations becoming a key feature of the islands, as were the acres of tomato cultivations. Both of which were responsible for generating a thriving industry for the island, one that continued to account for a large proportion of its economy; staple foods that continued to form the basis of the majority of the wholesome dishes the locals still cooked, and foods the tourists had come to love too. The more Sofía delved into it, the more her excitement grew.

"Right, Mama," Antonio announced around an hour or so later, unable to hide the tiredness in his own voice. It was three o'clock in the afternoon and Lucía was still working away in the kitchen, Theresa was having a siesta before dinner and Carmen was collecting the children from school. The house was surprising peaceful. "I think I've done all I need to for now, so I'm going to head back to my apartment for a quick shower and to get changed, and perhaps something to eat before I head out. I'll call you tomorrow to let you know how the session goes, otherwise I'm heading into Santa Cruz for the day. It's time my wardrobe had an update, so I'm going to see what I can find in the shops. Do you want anything picking up while I'm there?"

"No, thank you, Antonio." Lucía smiled, happy to see her smile reflected in his face. He had such a handsome face, and although she could see he was happy, she could also sense a certain sadness behind his beautiful blue eyes. All of their lives had changed in such a short period of time, and as truly grateful as she was that they had weathered the storm that had threatened their family, as far as Antonio was concerned, she feared that storm was not quite over. There was something going on that she did not understand, with the maternal instincts in her suggesting it was something she should not ignore.

Feeling bold, she asked "It's Charlotte's birthday next weekend, isn't it? When you're in Santa Cruz, why don't you look to buy a gift for her, perhaps even have it mailed over? If you hurry it shouldn't be too late in arriving."

"No, Mama, I don't think that's a good idea," he sighed, the smile instantly being wiped off his face. "I suspect the only thing Charlotte is looking for from me at the moment is a divorce." He had attempted to keep his feelings bottled up all day, carefully avoiding speaking to anyone about it until he had his own mind worked out first.

Lucía looked on confused.

"I got a message from her, yesterday evening, saying we need to talk. From the way it was worded, the inference I took from it was she's looking to formally separate. I think she's had enough of the way we're currently living – still together, yet having completely separate lives."

"Oh, Antonio, I'm so sorry," Lucía replied, wrapping him in her arms. "I knew things weren't going too well between you, and that you needed space to work things through, I just hadn't realised it had got to that stage. How do you feel about it?"

"Frankly, I agree with her. I don't want to live a half-life either. I know I'm partly to blame as I've probably not tried as hard as I should to meet her half way. I also know I can be single-minded, even stubborn when it comes to my work. I just don't feel like the effort is worth the reward anymore. My heart is not in fighting it. She's moved on, and if I'm honest I think it's time for me to do the same." It was the first time Antonio had actually voiced those words, and he could feel the relief course through his body as he did so.

"In fact, whilst I'm in Santa Cruz I'm going to make an appointment with a solicitor to understand my options." Seeing Lucía's questioning look, he explained. "You see, there's a pre-nuptial agreement in place, that protects Charlotte and her family's assets. It effectively means I can't access her trust fund. I seem to recall it was worded reciprocally, but at the time we were looking to get married I was a relatively unknown chef, so I'd have had nothing to lose and potentially everything to gain if we did split. Her parents wanted to protect her, especially as they never thought we were a good fit. I was not their ideal son-in-law.

"Now the tables are turned. Because, as you know, when Duncan died he left me the freehold to the three properties in London, where the restaurants are, plus the house we live in, as well as a substantial sum of money for me to spend or invest. So, on paper,

I am very comfortable. Charlotte's family was more interested in looking backwards and not forwards, so only protected what she had, not what she would have. And as she hasn't worked since we married, everything she now spends is down to me. Hence, I don't know where that leaves me. I guess I need to have some idea before I reply to her, because I don't want to walk into something unwittingly, or put the businesses, or my properties, at risk."

As Antonio picked up his laptop and kissed Lucía goodbye, she could sense the storm she had feared was closer than even she had imagined. How he was going to navigate it was anyone's guess.

Chapter 27

The summer months passed in a flurry of activity as the building works finally got underway and by the end of October there were clear signs that real progress was being made. There was still a long way to go, particularly in terms of the construction of the new building that would house the cookery school itself, but the renovations on the old outhouses were taking shape.

Over the summer they had been cleared of all the redundant machinery Mateo had accumulated over the years, equipment he couldn't bear to part with or face throwing away. They had then undergone a total renovation. The stone work had been repaired and new roofing had been laid, along with a series of new windows and doors installed for added security. The external look was still one of refurbished outbuildings, as keeping the rustic feel was important for the image they were creating with the cookery school, although the interiors had been completely remodelled. They now provided a series of individual bedrooms, already wired and plumbed to accommodate the en suites each room would have fitted in due course. When decorated, they would be modern airy rooms, with all the home comforts their clients would expect, including high speed Wi-Fi. Antonio was insistent that the finca needed to be brought into the 21st Century, as far as that particular technology was concerned at least.

The main house was also being remodelled, with a double extension being constructed to the rear of the property, which would provide an additional bedroom and en suite bathroom on the first floor, and a larger space below to house the modern kitchen that would be installed. A separate room, that would work as office space, was also being created. Overall, it would provide a much more comfortable environment, as well as a more private bedroom for Lucía that had the added benefit of beautiful sea views over the valley below. The renovations also included scope for putting an en suite in for Theresa, by knocking two of the existing bedrooms into one. The old layout, with the single bathroom upstairs and only one internal toilet, had been difficult for some time, especially with so many people living in the house, and the small bedrooms had felt cramped, with everyone having to make do and share.

Now there would be much more space, although Lucía often wondered whether it was worth it, especially given Sofía had eventually moved out into a nearby apartment, and Carmen and the girls were due to move into their new home in the coming weeks. She and Theresa would rattle around in the house she argued, although secretly she was looking forward to the peace and quiet it would provide. Her own bedroom would be a haven for her to escape to whenever the business got too noisy or life too difficult. The first anniversary of Mateo's death had come and gone and whilst Lucía still missed him every day, she was keeping herself occupied with all that was going on around her. A small piece of her believed Mateo would have been proud of the way she was coping, and the positive way she and the family were responding to life without him. That thought gave her comfort in her darkest days.

As Antonio drove through the gates of the finca and approached the house, he was pleased with the amount of progress that looked to have been made in the short time he'd been away. There was still a lot of activity on site, but the chaos appeared to be orderly. The foreman was outside the outhouses and waved in greeting as he saw Antonio get out of his car.

"Buenas tardes, Señor Pérez, welcome home," the jovial man shouted over, showing his toothy grin as he smiled. He was munching away at a large bread roll, that looked to be stuffed with cheese and ham.

"Gracias, Manuel. Good day to you, too. Is everything going well, or is there anything you need me to attend to?"

"No, Señor. Work is going to plan. Do you want me to update you now, or later?" His foreman was obviously on top form and wanted to share that with Antonio.

"Give me a few minutes, Manuel. Enjoy your lunch and then we can talk. I just need to speak to Señora Lucía first."

Antonio smiled as he walked towards the house. Manuel was a real character, with a healthy appetite and a figure to reflect it. He had come highly recommended and was proving to be both trustworthy and a hard worker. The team he had working with him clearly respected him too, and knuckled down, which augured well for everything being completed on schedule. After the week Antonio had just had, he certainly needed that boost.

He had flown back to the UK to meet with the lawyers and finalise his divorce settlement from Charlotte. It had felt quite emotional to see her again after so long. She was looking well and happy, and greeted him politely, if a little professionally with the lawyers around. Had her behaviour or manner towards him wavered in any way he was unsure what he would have done. The divorce was still not sitting comfortably with him, but it was clear she had moved on, and was even content with the settlement that had eventually been reached. There was no coming back from her perspective, and if he was truly honest with himself, he wasn't sure he wanted that either. It just felt like they had failed, and that was what really didn't sit well. He hated to fail at anything.

Over the last months the lawyers had worked hard to interpret the pre-nuptial agreement in light of the obvious change in Antonio's circumstances, balanced against its original intent, which had always been heavily slanted towards protecting Charlotte's interests. Charlotte's solicitor had initially argued in favour of the agreement being made void, believing with Antonio's current wealth it would be more beneficial for her to seek half of his assets, even at the expense of her own wealth having to be assessed.

Antonio's solicitors had maintained the agreement needed to be upheld. After all, he argued he did not want, or expect, anything from Charlotte, or her family's estate per se. He secretly knew that unravelling their complicated affairs would prove difficult, conscious her parents had put a large proportion of their assets in their daughter's name over recent years, for purposes of tax management and estate planning. They were adamant this was not to be investigated and hence were not cooperating on any front. Antonio did not want to play dirty, although when he raised this privately with Charlotte, her solicitors were forced to back down.   Fearful of precisely what her parents' estate planning might have involved, she had no desire to see them done for tax evasion, or worse.

A great deal of toing and froing between them eventually arrived at a settlement they could live with; one that above all protected Antonio's businesses and properties, whilst providing Charlotte with a one-off financial payoff. It was sufficient to allow her to buy herself somewhere else to live and would not see her destitute, not as her trust fund remained untouched. And with no children to consider, and Charlotte being deemed to be financially independent, there was no ongoing maintenance payments awarded.

Whilst she had argued for some ongoing allowance, given she was not in employment, at least until the point at which she remarried, she had backed down after the disclosure process revealed her previous pregnancy and subsequent miscarriage, a fact Antonio's solicitor was swift to point out had been withheld from his client. It was clear from Antonio's reaction it was not new news, and equally clear he knew he had not fathered the child.

Charlotte was mortified, her embarrassment difficult to hide as she sat opposite him and read his expression, the knowing look in his eyes. She'd always believed her secret to be safe, so to discover he had known all along made it even more difficult to digest. Coupled with the fact he suspected Miles was back on the scene, if not someone else, immediately put her on her guard. A casual comment, dropped into their conversation during a coffee break earlier that day, was all it took. Her body language had said all he needed to know.

Antonio was unsurprised to realise his soon to be ex-wife had already begun another relationship. After all, she was a very attractive woman who enjoyed the high life. Staying at home, alone, was not in her DNA. Nor was he surprised she had hoped to keep her affair under the radar, correctly fearing it would worsen the outcome of their own settlement.

What he hadn't realised at the time, though, was that it was a resumption of her old affair, or the fact Miles was going through parallel divorce proceedings with his own wife, where similar discussions around sharing the spoils of their marriage were taking place. So to continue to argue would only muddy the waters and make the overall picture worse for all concerned. Hence once she'd realised the cat was proverbially out of the bag, Charlotte lost any remaining fight and simply capitulated, swiftly instructing her solicitors to move on. After all, life was difficult enough.

So, whilst the settlement was all agreed and the paperwork signed, and as far as the lawyers were concerned a job well done, that did not make Antonio feel any better. Walking out of their offices, knowing all that remained outstanding was a rubber stamp to put the final nail into the coffin of his marriage, he realised his life was never going to be the same again. Approaching forty, it was time to start over.

Flying back to Tenerife a few days later, though, had felt right, and as Antonio had boarded the plane for the first time it truly felt like he was going home. He had largely put his affairs in order at the restaurants, meeting with Philippe and some of his other advisors to ensure everything was being managed efficiently. The businesses were doing well and although Antonio was pleased, it did not fill him with anywhere near the same level of excitement or pride as it had once done. His name was still technically over the door, but it was Philippe's direction and decisions that were driving its success these days. Antonio had effectively become no more than a sleeping partner, content to see his investments grow without getting his hands dirty, or more importantly without standing in the way whilst someone else ran things.

He'd also met with a property management and lettings agency that specialised in high end rentals and arranged for his house to be put on a long term let. Without Charlotte in the property, he was concerned about its upkeep and overall maintenance and needed the assurance that someone would deal with that. The property was in an excellent location, and he was assured it would be snapped up within hours of being advertised. The market was buoyant, with currently a high level of interest in rentals, although the agent was quick to assure Antonio of their rigorous vetting process for potential clients, especially when he saw the look on Antonio's face. The last thing he needed was a family of hillbillies moving in, or squatters trashing the place.

He and Charlotte had met up at the house one final time to discuss what they needed to do with the contents, removing whatever personal possessions they each wanted to keep, which amounted to surprisingly little. There was no debate, no arguing about who took what, or fighting over the best china. Their clothes, the odd painting, photographs, some books and a few miscellaneous items were all they each needed. Antonio, having already recovered his chef's knives from the restaurant, had little use for anything else. It was all very amicable and the more they discussed specific items they realised there was nothing about which they felt particularly sentimental. It was all just 'things', replaceable pieces of wood or metal. Things that would not fit into their new lives anyway, and things that neither of them wanted around as a constant reminder of what had gone wrong in their marriage; they were better left in the house for the new tenants to enjoy. It was time for each of them to move on and look forward. A clean slate was all they needed.

"Hi, I'm back," Antonio announced quite loudly, as he walked back into the finca. The noise of heavy drilling could be heard in the background and for once the old kitchen was empty. "Is anyone home?" Walking through the house he located Lucía almost screaming at the workmen, desperate to get her voice heard over the commotion. The noise had upset her quiet morning before continuing into the afternoon, and frankly it was all starting to get too much for her. Her simple orderly life had been overrun by a house load of workmen and she was beginning to feel quite stressed by it all.

"Mama, is everything okay?" he asked, trying to weigh up the situation, personally unable to see anything untoward.

"Oh Antonio, thank God you're home," she replied, visibly relaxing at the sight of him. "It will be, now that you're back and you can sort this whole mess out. I'm going for a lie down!"

The builder and Antonio exchanged a glance, and smiled, both watching as she put her hands in the air and sighed, clearly at her wit's end with all the disturbance.

Chapter 28

Christmas came and went without much ado in the Pérez household. The workers had a few days rest and Antonio spent his time largely going over the updated plans for the development. Over recent weeks further progress had been made, and he even felt they could be ahead of schedule, which was almost too good to believe.

The accommodation block, or more correctly the converted outhouses, were now fully equipped in terms of the electrical, plumbing and communications wiring. They had also been tiled and painted, with new lighting fitted. Overall, they were looking very impressive. The furniture for each of the bedrooms was on order; nothing too lavish, simply comfortable items that were in keeping with the theme of the overall development. Rustic, homely and traditional. There were twelve small self-contained rooms, a mix of singles and doubles that at maximum capacity could sleep twenty people. As courses were being limited to twelve clients initially, some provision had been made for visiting chefs, should they want to stay over. Antonio knew the nearest decent hotel was a good drive away, so imagined most would welcome the opportunity of staying local, and as he was hoping to attract some of his own friends to be guest chefs, he would welcome it too.

The cookery school was a short stroll across the working farmyard to the main house, which itself was nearing completion, meaning Lucía's blood pressure had almost returned to normal. She was even beginning to show some excitement at the prospect of the finished project. Kitchen appliances and other deliveries were arriving by the day, with the new furniture she had picked out for her bedroom due any day.

She'd recently taken a trip into Santa Cruz with Theresa, to mooch around the shops, and had been talked into spending some of the money she'd inherited on herself. "A new wardrobe deserves some new clothes," Theresa had argued as she'd encouraged her daughter to splash out, with Lucía later admitting spending the money had felt a lot better than she had imagined. For someone who had never been used to having money, the fear of spending it, and being left with none again, remained a constant worry.

Antonio, however, was most excited about the progress on the new build that would form the cookery school itself. It was situated to the rear of the finca and accessed by a separate road, with its own private parking facilities. Its location benefited from being in the shade of the fruit trees, with windows that would provide plenty of natural light and enable the warm breezes to blow through, thereby ensuring temperatures were managed, especially during the hottest parts of the year. Being in the mountains could become extremely hot, especially in the summer months when temperatures soared.

It was a single storey building with a demonstration-style kitchen, where some of the more technical aspects could be taught, with a separate work area where the clients would recreate their own food. There was also a communal dining area and a comfortable break-out area, with a small bar, where clients would be encouraged to congregate for dining – even sharing some of the food they had created, over a glass or two of local wines or Sangria. There was still a lot of work to be done to fit the school out to the professional level it needed to be, but the basic structure was almost complete.

Antonio, imagining that by early summer they could be ready to start taking their first clients, had begun working with Sofía on the marketing campaign. She had really thrown herself into the administrative side of setting up the business, with some of her ideas proving to be quite inspired. Antonio was impressed with her work ethic and her overall commitment, and had to admit her IT skills were better than his own. Working together so closely had enabled him to see a side of Sofía he had never fully appreciated. She had for too long been under her parents' shadow, living at home as the dutiful spinster daughter, old before her time in both mind and body. So now, at forty, to be finally emerging and finding a passion for life brought a genuine smile to his face.

It had also brought a smile to her own, he had noticed, realising she was making much more of an effort with her appearance. Her new haircut and smarter clothes showed what an attractive woman she was under all the dowdy layers, and living independently in her own apartment was giving her a lot of interesting topics to talk about. It was exposing her to a life she had never really experienced; friends and socialising, neither of which she had appreciated the value of before. She felt alive and excited, a feeling that was almost alien to her.

By 5th January the whole of the household was excited. It was the eve of *Día de Los Reyes*, or King's Day, which was the day Spanish children typically received presents from the three Wise Men. The tradition, dating back centuries, is for the children to clean their shoes the previous evening and leave them outside the door before going to bed. The Kings or Wise Men would then drop presents into them whilst they slept. When they awoke, they would open their presents and celebrate the day with parties, festivities and parades. It was one of the biggest festivals of the Spanish calendar.

Theresa had been busy the previous day baking the *Roscon de Reyes*, the traditional cake eaten for breakfast on the morning of King's Day. She had carefully placed the tiny figurine of the king into the batter, before putting it into the stove, with tradition stating that whoever has the slice with the figurine in is treated like a king, or a queen, for the remainder of the day. To avoid arguments, this year she had added an additional figurine and marked on the cake where they were hidden, so that both Anya and Maya could each find one. It was not the correct thing to do, but preferable to an argument for the rest of the day, and with all the work ongoing around the place she felt it was advisable to keep stress levels down.

On the morning of 6th January, the brightly decorated cake took pride of place in the centre of the kitchen table awaiting the family's arrival. It was still early and Theresa was sitting in the kitchen alone, enjoying a quiet moment ahead of what would be a manic day. The winter sun was slowly rising over the horizon and the cloudless blue sky promised a beautiful day ahead. It never ceased to amaze her how much better she felt with the weather here, recalling the number of dark and dank winters she had endured in London over the years, wrapped up against the bitter wind, or fearful of going outside in case she slipped on the icy pavements.

Lucía would be waking shortly, and within a couple of hours any peace she was currently enjoying would be shattered. Carmen was due to arrive with Anya and Maya around ten o'clock, with Sofía and Antonio arriving together around the same time. Antonio had offered to collect Rosa too, who was no longer good on her feet. Theresa had noticed her friend had aged more since her son's death, with her every movement appearing to be an effort these days. Walking the short distance to the finca was proving harder by the day, but she was family and it would not have been right for her not to have been included.

After a late breakfast, and the enjoyment of the cake, they were all driving down the mountain to one of the neighbouring towns, to join in with the church parade. Anya and Maya were dressing up with the rest of their school, and had been badgering their mother all week to finish their costumes. They were excited, and over recent days their excitement had become contagious as the whole family prepared for the celebrations.

For Lucía, along with the celebrations there would be a tinge of sadness. She'd recently commented how Mateo would ordinarily have been carrying one of the religious statues or flags around the square, proudly holding it aloft as the parade processed around the town. It was another of those annual traditions the church had in which he had always got himself involved.

"Antonio, would you be prepared to stand in and do that, in place of Papa?" Carmen had asked, noting the sadness in her mother's voice whenever the parade was mentioned. "I know they were looking for male volunteers to make up the numbers. Anya and Maya's teacher sent a note home only last week, asking if any of the dads would volunteer. I've no intention of asking Juan, because I want to keep him as far away from the school as possible, but there's no reason why you couldn't do it, is there? Even start a new family tradition," she'd added, smiling over at her mother, noticing the faint smile along with the tears in her eyes at the suggestion.

Antonio, realising he had been railroaded by Carmen once again, and unable to say otherwise, had simply nodded. So, it had been decided, Carmen would contact the school as soon as she got home with the name of another willing volunteer.

"No doubt someone will be in touch with you, if there's any instructions or information you need before the day," Carmen had added, smiling mischievously, having got her way. "Brothers are so easy to manipulate," she thought, laughing to herself, "unlike husbands!"

Chapter 29

Two weeks after King's Day parade, Antonio was outside in the farmyard. He was talking to Manuel, the foreman, going over some details that needed to be clarified before the workmen continued. They were taking a short break under the shade of the trees, with Antonio conscious that had Manuel not been on-site a few might have even drifted off into an afternoon siesta. It was around two o'clock in the afternoon, and for once there were dark clouds in the sky, with the potential for a thunderstorm or downpour later that evening. They had spent the morning securing the site in case the winds got high, for fear of any damage being done. After the heat of the winter sun, the cloud was providing a degree of welcome relief for the workers.

Carmen drove in and parked alongside the main farmhouse, her actions, as she got out of the car and almost ran to the front door, making it obvious she was panicking over something.

"Carmen, is everything alright?" Antonio shouted over. He was unused to seeing Carmen so rushed or so flustered. With Juan no longer on the scene, continually winding her up or antagonising her, her life appeared to be a lot calmer and much more organised, so for her to be in an apparent dither now was a little concerning.

"Oh Antonio, I didn't see you there. Yes, well no, not really. There's been a problem at the house. The toilet won't flush and there's water everywhere. I think a pipe, or the boiler has burst, or something, so I need to call a plumber out, quickly before the whole house floods. But I've got to get the girls collected from school. They finish in less than fifteen minutes and I can't abandon them. They will be worried if I'm not there waiting, so I need Mama to go get them for me. I rang the house, but she didn't answer, so I've had to call round. I'm running out of time," she said looking at her watch.

"Calm down a minute, and stop panicking will you. Mama's not in. She and Yaya have gone to visit Rosa in hospital. I don't imagine they'll be back for another hour or so."

Rosa had taken a bad fall the previous day. Thankfully there was nothing broken, just a bad sprain to her leg, and some inflammation and bruising. Walking had become increasingly difficult anyway, but this new injury had made it impossible, so the hospital had been unprepared to discharge her and were keeping her in for a few days.

As he said this, Antonio could see the colour drain from Carmen's face, so offered a solution. "Why don't I go and collect the girls for you and bring them back here? And perhaps one of Manuel's men can drive back with you and sort your plumbing out. That shouldn't be a problem, should it Manuel? Could Raul perhaps go to Carmen's as there's not too much left for him to do here today, is there?"

"No problem, Señor," Manuel smiled. "I will go and wake him," he laughed, noticing Raul under a tree with his eyes closed.

"Thank you, Manuel. And Carmen, I'll drive down to the school now and then ring you when I've collected them. I might even call in at the pasteleria and get them both an ice-cream or a cake, so don't worry if we're not back for a while. Mama can feed them here, if they're not too full after their treats. They could even sleep over, if you wanted, if Raul can't fix it tonight."

"Oh Antonio, you're a saint," she said, kissing him, her relief evident. "Thank you so much."

Thirty minutes later Antonio was running into the school playground, dodging the other parents who had already collected their children and were making their way home. He was about ten minutes late and out of breath, having struggled to find anywhere to park close to the school gates. He could see his two nieces, standing awkwardly with a lady, looking around and waiting for their mother to collect them. At their ages, they should have been able to walk home by themselves, but their new house was around five kilometres away from their primary school, and not on an easy bus route. And given they would be going to secondary school within a short space of time, Carmen had decided it was easier to keep them in their routine, rather than face the unnecessary upheaval.

The Return

Anya and Maya were an extremely close unit and with only eleven months between them, and in the same academic year, they were often mistaken for twins. It was a fact they played on frequently. Their features and build were very similar and with their long thick dark hair and brown eyes making them almost identical, coupled with their tendency to dress in matching outfits, it made the process of distinguishing them even more difficult. Antonio had taken a while to realise their game, and now, aware of how often they played tricks on their friends and teachers alike, was always on his guard.

For all their confidence, though, they were still of an age where they were easily embarrassed, with the slightest of things capable of setting them off, or making them feel uncomfortable. And if one of them felt it, almost by telepathy the second one did too. The recent split of their parents had on occasion been difficult for them to handle, and being at the centre of many of their arguments had left its mark.

Carmen had become sensitive to this and was conscious of some of the damage hers and Juan's behaviour had wrought, their constant bickering and fighting had clearly not gone unnoticed. So she was now overly protective of her daughters and had consequently asked the school to keep their eyes open for any behavioural changes, or anything that could indicate a problem. Above all, she had been adamant that unless she instructed otherwise the girls could not be allowed home with anyone other than herself. Juan, although not a danger in himself, had to be kept away. More of his badmouthing of their mother was not what Carmen wanted for her daughters.

As Antonio ran up to the girls, their teacher was therefore immediately on her guard. Señorita Rodriguez, whilst she recalled seeing the man at the King's Day parade, and vaguely remembered he had something to do with the family, had never been formally introduced to him. She had no idea of either his name or his relationship to the girls, if in fact there was one. It was most probable he was their mother's new partner. She was well aware of the recent and quite acrimonious split the children's parents were experiencing, and their mother's specific instructions to keep the father away from the girls, under any circumstances. She had to respect that, and knew it was not her position to offer either comment or judgement.

So, all things considered, she had absolutely no intention of letting the children go with a perfect stranger, even if the girls recognised him. Anya and Maya remained quietly standing by her side. They were more than a little embarrassed by the fact their mother had still not collected them, but smiled when they saw Antonio approaching. They liked him and thought he was funny, with his balding head, his bright blue eyes and his little round tummy.

Isabella Rodriguez was relatively new to the island. She had moved there just under twelve months previously, from Valéncia on the Spanish mainland. She had seen the vacancy come up and felt like a change of scenery would suit her nicely. It was shortly after the break-up of her own relationship, so getting far away from Valéncia had suddenly become a priority for her. She needed to be away from the familiar reminders that would pop up whenever she turned a corner, or crossed a road in the old city. Things that would remind her of the happier times, or even bring back some of the memories she fought hard to forget.

Isabella had so far made few friends on the island and for the time being was preferring to keep herself to herself. She was normally quite sociable, but with her recent experiences she was reluctant to get too close to anyone, especially men. Above all she was unwilling to engage in gossip, or join in with the other teachers as they speculated about parents or other staff members during their breaktimes. It was so destructive, something she had discovered at her own cost, when her own life had been the subject of the gossips' tongues.

She still recalled the moment when she had walked into the staffroom and had sat quietly in a corner, hoping for an undisturbed few minutes break, to catch up on some marking between lessons. It was a stressful time for Isabella, as her wedding was less than ten days away, and there were still a few things remaining that needed to be sorted. Her fiancé, Tomás, was not being too co-operative either, meaning she was finding herself having to pick up most of the last-minute organisational issues and it was all becoming quite tiresome.

As she had sat down, she could overhear two of the other female teachers talking. They were almost whispering behind the cabinets, occasionally giggling and completely unaware of anyone else's presence in the room. Although she tried to blank out their conversation, and did not want to be accused of eavesdropping, when she inadvertently picked up that it had something to do with her best friend and her fiancé, she found herself automatically tuning into what was being said. Her best friend was also on the teaching staff, so was a familiar character to them all.

When she realised what they were actually saying, her mind struggled to register the words. She could hardly believe it. They had apparently been seen in a very intimate embrace outside a bar, kissing in a way that went well beyond the bounds of friendship. The words "his hands were all over her," and "she was drunk, but clearly encouraging him," had reportedly been overheard by a male teacher as he had left the bar the previous Friday night, around midnight. He had also reportedly seen them walking off together, both tipsy.

Isabella was shocked, initially unprepared to believe what she was overhearing. At the same time, she felt paralysed, unable to move or allow herself to be seen.

The bar they were speaking of was one with which she was familiar, one that was close to where Tomás' apartment was located, and one she had occasionally visited. It was a lively, modern bar with loud music and flashing lights, and a dance floor that got crammed the later the evening became. It was not her scene, yet very popular with the younger crowd.

The night in question was one she knew Tomás had been out drinking, supposedly alone. He'd mentioned going for a quick drink after work. She recalled ringing him later that evening, her message going direct to voicemail. The following day she had also struggled to get hold of him, realising it was much later in the afternoon when he'd eventually contacted her. The memory was clearly etched on her mind. She recalled pacing her bedroom at home waiting for him, knowing they needed to go to the tailors to get the final fittings done for his suit and realising they would be late.

The more she was forced to listen to the gossips and the speculation that was clearly doing the rounds in the school, the more the thought he had possibly slept with her best friend that night started to form in her head. Someone she trusted, and even earlier that day had spoken to in the corridor, chatting away as if nothing was untoward. She was her bridesmaid, the friend who would stand beside her at the altar steps when she made her vows. Vows to love and honour her husband and remain faithful to him, until death do us part. Then he would do likewise.

What a joke that would have been, if the gossips were right, which invariably they did turn out to be.

Isabella had questioned Tomás later that day, and although he denied everything, it was clear from his behaviour and body language that he was lying;

with his nonchalance suggesting it was not the first time something like that had happened, or potentially the last.

The following day, her friend also reluctantly confirmed it, admitting it was a silly one-night stand, nothing serious, just something that had got out of hand after one too many tequilas shots. She begged Isabella to forgive her and not to cancel the wedding, or lose their friendship, based on her one stupid mistake.

Isabella, heartbroken, embarrassed and feeling completely duped was not in the mood for forgiveness, so regardless of her friend's or her parents' protestations cancelled the wedding. Her mother had simply shrugged, suggesting she should turn a blind eye, almost implying it was acceptable behaviour, and her father had told her at her age she should just get married and be done with it, before it was too late! The suggestion was left hanging in the air that at nearly thirty years old she was an old maid, someone at whom no one else would look twice. Better to take what was on offer than be swallowed by pride.

Isabella knew she had not been graced with beauty nor had the best of figures, nevertheless her parents' open acknowledgment of that fact was hard to bear. She had always accepted she was far from the prettiest girl around, with striking as opposed to soft features. However, she'd believed she was loved for who she was, not how she looked. Apart from which, the trust had gone, something that did not bode well for any future relationship. If he could cheat on her before their wedding, then he would have no qualms in doing so afterwards. It was better to know the type of man he was now, rather than later, was her sense of the situation.

Given her parents disagreed with her and given their attitude, which Isabella knew to be morally wrong, she felt she needed to be somewhere far away from them, and far away from the wider crowds. Somewhere in private, where she could lick her wounds and attempt to rebuild her life. If marriage and children were not to be, then so be it.

So, when the job vacancy on the holiday island of Tenerife came up it fitted her brief perfectly. Neither her parents nor her fiancé would come looking for her there, and even if they did, she would not be interested. She was moving on. She was a good teacher and a good human being and none of that was going to change, regardless of whether she married or not. She did not need a ring on her finger to define her.

She was also very diligent, so bringing her thoughts back to today, she knew there had been no contact with the school to say the girls were to be collected by anyone other than their mother, hence when Antonio approached and tried to take them away from her, she naturally objected.

"I'm sorry, I cannot let you take the girls. They are to be collected by their mother only, unless we're advised otherwise. Today that has not been the case."

She stood there resolutely taking their hands, even though the girls appeared anxious to go with him.

"Their mother has been delayed and has asked me to collect them," Antonio had argued, believing that would be sufficient enough reason. Why else did she think he would be there, he wondered to himself.

"I'm sorry Señor....."

"Pérez, Antonio Pérez," he replied, offering out his hand politely. "I'm their uncle, so there's no problem with me taking them," he repeated, calling the girls over. "Anya, Maya, shall we go for an ice-cream?" he asked, clearly in an attempt to prise them away from their teacher, who continued to stare quite sternly at him.

Isabella remained completely oblivious to his charms. She'd already had to deal with enough of the politics of school life today, and Señora López's continued delay, to say nothing of having to deal with this stranger, was only adding to her woes. She just wanted to get home, feed her dog and eat. She had missed lunch and was desperate for some food. She had a healthy appetite and even the mention of the ice-cream had set her stomach rumbling.

"That may very well be the case, Señor Pérez," she continued, unmoved by his assurances. "However, until I get notification from Señora López herself, the children will remain under my care." She glanced down at her phone to see if there were any messages she had missed, unsurprised to see the screen remained blank.

Until then, safeguarding was a principle Antonio had barely given a second thought, although once the realisation that he had put their teacher into a difficult position took hold, Antonio suggested, "I'll ring my sister now, if that would help? Then you can speak to her yourself. It's just she's had problems with the plumbing and was struggling with time..." he began to babble as he rang Carmen's number.

After a few rings the answerphone took over, forcing Antonio to leave a brief message. "Carmen, phone me immediately. There's a problem at school." Whilst he did not want to sound overly dramatic, at the same time he needed her to ring back soon, so had to inject some degree of urgency into his voice. Otherwise, by the look on the teacher's face, they could be in a stalemate for some time.

As they were standing in the playground, the caretaker came out and nodded over at Isabella, a questioning look in his eyes. He was anxiously waiting to secure the main entrance gates, and given all the other children and parents had left he was wondering how long they would be.

"Is everything alright?" he enquired, also noting the unfamiliar face and wondering whether he needed to wait around to offer Señorita Rodriguez any support. He quite liked the new teacher and had a lot of time for her, and wouldn't want any harm to come to her.

"Yes, thank you, Dominic. I'm just waiting for a parent to be in touch," she replied, looking around, hopeful to see the girls' mother running towards her.

"If you need to secure the gates, though, please do. I don't want to hold you up, and I have my keys with me so don't worry. I can easily go through the other gate when I'm ready." Once the children had gone home, staff traditionally used the rear entrance anyway, so it was no inconvenience to her, although that didn't help today's situation, as all the children had clearly not left.

After another ten minutes Antonio could see she was starting to get anxious and had noticed she kept looking at her watch, as if she needed to be somewhere else.

"Look, if you want, why don't we go and wait in the café across the road, with the girls? Then as soon as Carmen rings, I can let you know, and we can sort this out. At least that will enable the caretaker to lock up," he said, looking over in his direction, where he continued to prowl, obviously unprepared to leave the teacher alone. "I'm sure my sister will be horrified with all the fuss she's created." Isabella looked at him, clearly weighing the situation up.

"I'll even treat you to an ice-cream, or a coffee if you'd prefer?" he suggested, with a reassuring smile, once again trying to win her over.

At a loss for any better suggestion, she reluctantly agreed. A small smile formed on her lips as she replied. Her feet were getting tired and above all else she was desperate for a drink. "Okay, thank you, Señor. That's very kind of you."

"Antonio, please," he replied, still unaware of her name. He had not thought to ask, and felt a little awkward mentioning it now, given she had not introduced herself. He quite liked her smile, though. It had lit up her face, resulting in her no longer looking as stern as she had, which was a positive. "Now come on girls, shall we show your teacher the best way to eat ice-cream, whilst we wait for Mama to be in touch?"

They both giggled as they let go of their teacher's hands and took hold of Antonio's, leaving Señorita Rodriguez to follow in their wake, wondering what on earth she had just agreed to.

Chapter 30

It was after seven o'clock in the evening when Antonio arrived back at the finca with the girls. He had sat in the café opposite the school for nearly four hours, patiently waiting for Carmen's call to come through. When eventually it had, he was able to hand the phone over to Isabella, who simply smiled when she ended the call. She said goodbye to the girls and thanked Antonio for the drink and the snack he had bought, before going on her way, feeling more than a little embarrassed by the events of the afternoon.

"Oh Antonio, I am so, so, sorry," began Carmen, as soon as they walked into the house, immediately running to hug her daughters, who looked no worse for their adventure. "My phone was dead and Raul had switched the electricity off in order to deal with the water leak, so I couldn't recharge it. It was only after I arrived here and plugged it in that I got your message. I started panicking when I heard the message. I'm so sorry to have wasted your time, Antonio, and what must Señorita Rodriguez think of me!"

Carmen was absolutely distraught at the thought of the teachers gossiping about her behind her back, or worse still laughing at her, which no doubt they would once the story came out. She imagined their opinion of her would be even lower than it currently was, believing they already saw her as a neurotic woman, obsessed with the thought of someone trying to kidnap her children.

"Don't worry about it. I think she saw the funny side, eventually," he replied. "I have to say she was quite intimidating initially, and I feared at one stage she was going to call the police, or security at least. A guy questioned her in the playground and I thought she was going to report me to him for child abduction. She had no intention whatsoever of agreeing to me bringing them home, not without your approval. She was very professional, if quite scary I might add."

"Well, at least they're safe, and by the looks on their faces they've already eaten," Lucía observed, her voice a little jaded. She and Theresa had got home earlier from their visit to Rosa at the hospital and were feeling tired. They had not eaten and with all the fuss had not even planned their meal. Suddenly having to feed everyone seemed a chore she could well do without.

"Yes, they've both eaten, Mama. A mix of ice-creams, donuts and then pizza and chips – in that order, I'm afraid," Antonio admitted, looking over at Carmen. He was conscious she was trying to get the girls to eat more healthily and this afternoon's adventures had not helped her cause. In his defence he added, "We were just going for ice-creams, and then when it took so long for you to call, we had some drinks and cakes, and then later still the girls were getting fidgety so I ordered them some food. I hope you're not too annoyed?"

Before Carmen had time to reply, Anya chirped in. "It wasn't just us who were hungry, you had some chips too, Uncle Antonio. You and Señorita Rodriguez shared a plate, don't you remember?"

"Yes, and you both had a burger, too," added Maya, not wanting to be outdone by her sister.

"Yes, alright. We've all eaten," he laughed a little embarrassed to have been outed by his nieces. "I felt sorry for Isabella, given she was obviously hungry. It was getting late and I couldn't let the girls eat in front of her, not without ordering for her too, could I?"

"No, of course not," Carmen replied, her eyes raised at the way Antonio had mentioned the teacher's first name. There had been a definite gleam in his eyes that had not gone unnoticed. "So, it's Isabella, is it? I always wondered what her first name was. I've never been on first name terms myself," she teased.

"Well, if you ever find yourself alone in a café with her for four hours, then you'll know what to call her, won't you!" he replied quite pointedly. "Touché," he thought, cutting off any further discussion on that topic. "Anyway, Mama, how was Yaya Rosa? Has she caused enough commotion at the hospital yet for them to discharge her?"

"No, Antonio, and it's looking like she will be there for a while longer. Her body's not responding as well, or as quickly, as they'd hoped to the treatment, so they want to keep her in for observation. I said you might go tomorrow to visit her and take her some food, if you had time. The hospital food is not good, she says, so I'm worried she's not eating."

"Yes, Mama. I will call in tomorrow and take her something tasty," Antonio offered. He knew Rosa had a good appetite, like his own, so the thought of her being off her food was worrying.

"Provided he's got time. In between all his work and having afternoon tea with Isabella again," Carmen teased, winking at Antonio.

"Leave him alone," Theresa chided her granddaughter. "Isn't it time you took the girls home and got them showered and ready for bed, Carmen? After all they've had a busy day and will be tired."

Antonio smiled over at Theresa, grateful for her intervention.

Driving back to his apartment an hour or so later, he mulled over the afternoon. It had not panned out at all as he had expected, sitting around in a café chatting, when he really should have been on site with Manuel, overseeing the building works. He had phoned Manuel to explain his dilemma and arranged to catch up with him early the following morning. There was still a lot to be done. At the same time, he could honestly say it had not been an entirely wasted afternoon.

When they had first entered the café, he could not read the teacher at all. She had maintained her stern manner throughout their exchanges. She was protective, vigilant and obviously determined not to let the girls out of her charge; unprepared to release them into the hands of some unscrupulous character, a complete stranger.

At the same time, she had been willing to come along with that same stranger for a drink. Antonio had not applied any pressure, simply made a request to wait somewhere more comfortable, until the call from his sister came in. He imagined she had weighed up the danger of going with him, against the risk of not, and decided in his favour. That in itself had been a small win. He liked to think his charm had not been entirely lost on her.

As she had drunk her first cup of coffee, her demeanour had remained quite guarded, with her constantly looking around and watching for the café door to open, or waiting for Antonio's phone to ring. Over time, though, as the girls relaxed with their ice-creams, joking and laughing with Antonio, so she began to, too.

After about half an hour her jacket came off and she released her hair from the clip she had been wearing. The café had got warm and she was making herself more comfortable. He was surprised to see how long her hair was when it was released, as it cascaded down her back almost to her waist, ramrod straight and luminous in the sunlight. In his experience few girls grew their hair so long these days. Charlotte had medium length blonde hair, just below shoulder length. Hers was nowhere near as long as Isabella's, or anywhere near as natural or shiny. Years of colouring and expensive treatments had obviously taken their toll.

And when she took off her jacket, Antonio could see the pretty blouse she was wearing, the pastel shades suiting her olive skin, and the merest outline of her body. As he caught her eyes, he looked away, embarrassed to realise he had been caught staring. Isabella had what his grandmother would call a comely figure, not at all like the toned and slender frame of his wife – ex-wife, he corrected himself quickly. She looked like she enjoyed her food too, unlike Charlotte who had been known to pick at a lettuce leaf, which as a chef Antonio found rather unnerving. He enjoyed his food, and enjoyed other people enjoying his food, so cooking for Charlotte had always been a challenge.

At the point at which Antonio decided to order pizzas for the girls, Isabella had been unable to disguise the noise of her stomach, churning with hunger, for a moment longer. The coffee had been nice, but she needed food. So his suggestion for them to eat had been welcomed, provided she could buy her own meal, she had insisted. Antonio had smiled at this and agreed. It had not been worth the hassle of fighting with her again, not over something as trivial as the cost of a burger. She had begun to relax and to open up, so why ruin it now?

Over the food they had begun to chat. Nothing too taxing or too personal. He had learned she was new to the area, as was he. She talked a little of Valéncia as he did London, although neither mentioned the reasons that had brought them to Tenerife, nor professed to be missing their previous lives. She talked a little about her teaching and her love of children, with a passion that was impossible to ignore. He spoke about his love of food with the same level of passion, and found that it was a subject on which they appeared to have a lot of common ground.

Feeling no need to impress her, Antonio had made no mention of his own expensive restaurants, or his ambitious plans around the cookery school and certainly no mention of his great personal wealth. He just played it down, simply admitting to being a chef who was currently enjoying a sabbatical whilst recharging his batteries.

By the end of the afternoon, he had felt extremely relaxed in her company. They had enjoyed a pleasant few hours, chatting away with no agenda, no hidden motives. It had felt good to talk, even perhaps to have made a friend. It was a long time since he had made a new friend of his own. Most of his friends back in London had been couples, or friends of Charlotte's that she had introduced into their circle, none of whom he had chosen to keep in touch with after his divorce. They were people who were not cut from the same cloth as himself. People who were more comfortable in Charlotte's world than his. Isabella would not have fitted into Charlotte's world and, as he now realised, neither had he.

So, the idea of meeting up with Isabella again, for a drink or maybe a meal, as friends, suddenly sounded quite appealing. It would do him good to get out a bit more. Although as he let himself into his apartment, he realised there was a small fly in the ointment as far as that idea went. As they had parted company, it had never occurred to him to ask for her mobile number, or offer his own. After all, there had been no need for them to be in touch again, had there? Therefore, unless he was brave enough to approach Carmen, with the suggestion that he pick the girls up again, he had no immediate way of contacting her. He would need to think about that.

Chapter 31

January and February passed in a haze, with Antonio barely having time to think, let alone make arrangements or consider socialising. Work had significantly ramped up on the overall project and by the end of March there was a clear end in sight. The whole family was starting to take a collective sigh of relief at the idea that it would not be long before the workmen were off site, with life able to get back to normal. Although what normal would look like once the clients began to arrive was anyone's guess.

All building work on the outhouses had been finished and the furnishings had finally been installed, with new beds, bedroom furniture and soft furnishings all neatly arranged. They looked almost as if they had been set up and staged, as agents did with showhouses, with the overall effect very professional, at the same time appearing comfortable and relaxed.

Carmen had offered to choose the fabrics and linens, and no one could deny the look she had created was absolutely stunning. The project had certainly demonstrated her flair for interior design, and her creative skills had been piqued, leaving her imagining if that was something she could take up as a career for herself. If ever she had time, that was, with two small girls to look after – although with Juan now completely off the scene and her daughters shortly off to secondary school, she did feel she would need something to occupy her time.

Sofía was also in her element managing the marketing side of the operation, along with running the administrative side of the business for Antonio. She had taken a series of photos of the bedrooms and uploaded them onto the brochures she was creating, along with the photos of the cookery school she had taken earlier, and ones of the communal areas where clients would be encouraged to relax between courses, or in an evening if they chose to stay at the finca. The internal areas had been fitted out with comfy chairs and a small bar, again in a relaxed colour scheme, and the outside terrace had tables and chairs arranged around an open fire pit that would keep people warm in the evening. A few fleece blankets had been placed in the photo to enhance the effect. The mountains could get extremely hot during the daytime, but equally very chilly in the evenings, especially during the winter months. She had thrown in a few scenic shots of the area too, views and vistas from the finca, the odd sunset shot, along with contact details and directions to the airport. As it was assumed most clients would come from overseas, accessibility was a concern and something they may need to consider. A taxi service, perhaps from the airport, even a mini bus – but was that over thinking it?

The overall effect, however, looked very professional and was ready for Antonio to review and share with his friends in London. They were looking to get their comments, and hopefully their endorsement, before final printing or uploading onto the website she had created. So whilst it had been a busy few months for Sofía, she was revelling in the challenges it was providing her and was constantly surprising herself at the positivity she was feeling as a result. In fact, both she and Carmen had changed so much in the last twelve months. Sofía recognised how much more confident she now felt, how more alive. Having always lived in her younger brother and sister's shadows, she was now enjoying her own limelight and it felt good. Carmen in comparison had calmed down considerably, and was the happiest anyone had seen her in a long time. Without the stresses of money worries, or the constant antagonism she had felt living with Juan, always on her guard against him and his behaviour, she felt much freer. Freer to enjoy herself and her children, and freer to express herself in a way that she was comfortable and confident with.

"Sofía, these look really good. You've done a great job, in fact you both have," Antonio added, recognising it was a team effort. Carmen and Sofía were anxiously standing by and watching over him as he read the final version. He had to admit that they had done a fantastic job, and the harmonious way in which they had worked together was a credit to them both.

"I think it's about ready to email over to Philippe and the others, to get their views. Philippe has been putting the word around and he's already got quite a lot of interest, I understand. Hopefully it all sounds promising," he added. Sofía and Carmen smiled at his reaction and the praise they were receiving.

"I've also now settled on the lecture programme too, and I've secured a few good names to come and be our guest chefs. So, once we've got the final dates agreed, we can lock all those names in. I'm hoping those first speciality weeks will sell out quickly, although the basic package ones should be fun too. A little more relaxed perhaps, and more rustic – but the same basic content."

Antonio, working with Theresa and Lucía, had selected a range of dishes that would be recreated by the students. Mainly traditional dishes, but with some more contemporary Spanish fare, including dishes of his own creation that currently featured on the menu at his top London restaurants. He was planning on demonstrating those himself, and was encouraging Lucía and Theresa to volunteer to cook some of the others. He believed it would add to the authenticity of the school, especially in the early days when it needed to establish its name, if there were real Spanish home cooks involved. People who cooked these rustic dishes on a daily basis and could also talk with passion about the freshness of the ingredients and the manner in which they had been harvested.

He was yet to convince either Theresa or Lucía to stand up and give the demonstrations themselves, though. Either way, he had a series of names of other people who would happily step in and work at the school if they were not prepared to do it; chefs he had worked with over the years, as well as a handful of local women who had stepped forward to offer their services. The whole idea of the school had certainly captured the locals' imagination.

"I think, before we send it we should agree some dates. It's no use offering a course if people don't know when it will be held, is it? And without fixed dates we won't be able to take bookings either. Let's get the diary out, shall we, Sofía?" he suggested, suddenly feeling nervous that once dates were fixed it would all become real.

It was Friday afternoon, the end of a long week, and Sofía's preference was to head home, although seeing Antonio so focussed she agreed.

"Let's try to organise our launch event around the end of June as a speciality one, with dates for two basic ones in July and two more in August, one speciality and one basic, perhaps. That gives us three months from today and should be sufficient for now, don't you think? We can then tweak the programme based on feedback, in time for the autumn and winter schedule, once we know what works well and where the interest lies."

The basic courses were five days long, with the specialty ones only four days, with a VIP dinner included on the first night. Overall, taking account of all the recurring activities of setting everything up, and the cleaning processes on completion of each course, including supporting any travel arrangements clients would have, it would likely be a ten day end-to-end activity. Two a month was therefore more than sufficient to cope with. There was scope to develop a more intensive programme, expand the course content, with even scope to introduce different cuisines over time. For now, though, they wanted to feel their way and not run before they could walk. If the financial investment failed it would not be the end of the world, however, given the amount of emotional investment the family had made, no one wanted to even consider that as a possible outcome.

Having eventually settled on the dates, and sent them over to Philippe with the brochure, Sofía and Antonio looked at each other, nervously laughing at the enormity of what they had done. It was after eight o'clock in the evening and the others had long since left them to work alone in the office. Carmen had taken the girls home around six o'clock and Theresa and Lucía could be heard talking outside on the terrace, relaxing with a drink and watching the sun set over the horizon.

"Wow, this is real now, isn't it, Antonio? What have we done?"

"I think we both deserve a drink, don't you?" Antonio replied, looking over at Sofía. There was a satisfied smile on both their faces. "Why don't we drive home and meet up in the bar, in an hour's time, say? My treat."

"I'll pass, if that's okay," she replied tentatively. "It's just I've already arranged to meet someone tonight, for a drink."

Antonio simply nodded, unwilling to pry or push the issue. Sofía had never been one for dating and until that point had never had a serious boyfriend, with her occasional relationships usually petering out after the first or second date. Living at home, she had little to offer a prospective suitor, by way of conversation or anything else. She had never had an intimate relationship either, and now at forty had long since given up on the chance of ever meeting anyone, let alone finding someone to settle down with.

Life was not all bad, though, and over recent months she had found much more to amuse herself and occupy her time. She had joined a gym and had started taking the occasional classes; Yoga, Pilates. It was introducing her to more people and allowing her to make new friends. She was finding new experiences to challenge her thinking and by itself that was providing more interesting things for her to talk about. Looking back, moving into her own apartment had been the catalyst for her rebirth, followed by her new role and the challenge that gave her. Dealing with so many different people also gave her a depth of confidence she had never felt before.

So, when a chance meeting with a man in the lobby of her apartment block, as they were waiting for their lift to arrive, led to them striking up a conversation, she was quite pleased with her reaction. Ordinarily she would have kept her head down and said nothing, whereas she had looked up, smiled and said hello. She had been met by a set of kind eyes, belonging to a man with quite distinguished grey hair, who was perhaps a few years older than herself – around his mid-forties she would guess. And from his accent and the way he dressed she imagined him to be Italian.

Over subsequent days they bumped into each other a few more times. He was new to the area and regularly asked her questions; where to buy certain things, what day did this or that happen, and did she know how to contact the caretaker for the building? There was a leak in his bathroom that needed fixing, he had advised. All quite mundane topics, but things that got them talking. After a couple of weeks, he suggested going out for a drink, to the bar across the road from their apartment block.

"It's nothing fancy, just better than talking in the corridor," he had said in his almost perfect Spanish. By this time he had established she lived alone, and having not noticed any men callers, felt emboldened. "I could meet you around nine o'clock Friday night, if you'd like? And if you're hungry, we could always go for something to eat afterwards. I normally eat quite late."

Tonight was the night. So, as it was a very long time since a man had asked her out, let alone a good-looking Italian, as much as she would have enjoyed a celebratory drink with Antonio, the idea of meeting her new friend held much more appeal. And realising how late it had already become, she knew she would need to hurry home, if she was to have time to shower and change into something more appropriate. The old Sofía would never have considered dressing up for the occasion, happy to go out in whatever she had been wearing all day, whereas the new Sofía was a different person and was already considering what to wear. After all, Italians always dressed well, so she did not want to disappoint him.

And whilst it might not be a date, per se, it was the closest she had come to one for a long time; she remained ever the optimist. Being Friday night too meant no work in the morning, or nothing to rush home for, so she could stay out as late as she wanted.

Chapter 32

Once Sofía had left, Antonio had not wanted to go directly home, to his empty apartment and dinner for one. He knew that as soon as he did, he would simply open up his laptop and continue to work, unable to switch off or relax. He would pour himself a beer, pick away at his takeaway and continue where he had left off, with his spreadsheets laid out in front of him. That would be him for the evening. The door would be locked to the outside world and eventually he would head for bed, with the prospect of a weekend ahead of him. Two whole days without any plans, other than the promise of visiting a sick relative in hospital. He had needed a distraction tonight, a chance to break out of the rut he had fallen into, although when Sofía had said she had other plans he could see little alternative. There was no one else for him to call on.

Whilst his apartment was furnished with everything he needed and was perfectly comfortable, it had a very impersonal feel about it. Clean lines and minimalist furnishings. The walls and surfaces were bare of anything that would give a clue to the type of person who lived there. There were no pictures or photos around, no mementos or books, or anything else that would allow a visitor to read anything into the mind of the occupant. It simply had the feel of a high-end bachelor pad, somewhere transient without fear of any roots being laid.

It mainly suited Antonio. After all, he had chosen the apartment. It was somewhere local to live, somewhere that served a purpose, especially in those early days when his life was in turmoil; somewhere for him to continue to live when being under the cramped roof with his family was no longer feasible. Since then, and his subsequent divorce, he had done little to change anything, happy enough to plod along. He had not chosen to take anything from his London home to make the apartment more attractive, and had quickly declined Carmen's offer to add some softer feminine touches, using her recently acquired interior design skills. Knickknacks or scatter cushions did not appeal to him, moreover he did not need any reminders of his earlier life.

But now, if living in Tenerife was where he saw his future, a more long-term arrangement might be needed. Living out of boxes in a two-bedroom, albeit a penthouse apartment, and feasting on takeaways was not his usual style. He was a wealthy man, a successful chef, yet someone who you'd argue had gone almost into hiding in a remote hilltop town. It was just a lifestyle he had drifted into, without any thought or consideration of the consequences. He had become a loner, leaving the finca each evening to return to his solitary and bachelor type existence in his sterile apartment.

Other than Sofía, no one had visited him, and even then, she had only called around when passing by to drop some papers off. He had never actually invited anyone for a meal or a drink, never cooked for anyone, and in terms of female company, well that had simply been non-existent. He had been so busy over recent months that socialising and making friends had not been top of his agenda. There was always too much to do to justify taking time out for himself. Although was that simply an excuse, a mechanism he had employed to protect himself from further hurt or rejection? Charlotte had hurt him more than he had realised, leaving him painfully aware that was a place to which he did not want to ever return. His confidence had taken a real beating.

By the time he pulled up outside the Indian takeaway to collect his usual Friday night order, he was feeling more than a little despondent. To think, he had been on a high less than an hour ago, and now after the short drive home was feeling completely jaded. A sudden storm had arrived, and the rain was coming down quite heavily, conspiring to make him feel even more miserable.

As he made his way to the Indian restaurant, careful to side-step the puddles, his head covered as he ducked to avoid the rain against his face, he quite literally bumped into a woman, dithering in the doorway of the takeaway, knocking her sideways and forcing her to drop the carrier bag she was carrying. The contents spilled out, all over the pavement. She had been fiddling with her change, counting the loose coins back into her purse, and partly in Antonio's defence, had not been looking where she was going either.

"I'm so sorry," he said, bending down to help the woman, who was obviously struggling to preserve whatever she could of her meal. The poppadom looked beyond recovery, although the content of the rest of the boxes was probably okay, Antonio's crude assessment of the situation suggested. "Here, let me help you."

"Thanks. It was probably my fault, anyway. I should have been looking where I was going. It's just that I thought he'd undercharged me, and I wanted to check before I left. It's not my usual takeaway, so I'm not used to the prices, but it seemed low. I thought I'd give it a try, but now with all this rain, I'm beginning to wonder why." She looked down the road to see the rain cascading. It had become torrential all of a sudden, and given she had walked to the restaurant was not looking forward to her return journey.

As she looked up and met his eyes, she could see a glimmer of recognition. "Hang on, I know you, don't I? Haven't we met somewhere before?" She was desperately trying to place his face or where they had met, and then it suddenly clicked and she smiled. "Yes, it's Antonio, Maya and Anya's uncle, if I recall correctly. We had a long coffee break together, a few months ago. Isabella Rodriguez, their teacher, in case you've forgotten." She laughed at the memory. "That day I was convinced you were trying to kidnap them. I'm so sorry about that. Apart from which, it was so embarrassing the following day, trying to explain my behaviour to the headmistress."

"I hope you didn't get into any trouble – you were only doing your job, after all," Antonio replied, recalling the afternoon.

"No, it was just that I'd locked myself out of the school, so I had to call the caretaker to get access when we left the café. It was late and the rest of the staff had long since gone. The problem was, I was convinced I'd picked up the right keys and I hadn't. They were the keys to the gym cupboard! And my handbag, with my car keys and apartment keys in, was still in the classroom. Without them I couldn't get home. And all I could think of was my poor dog who would need feeding and walking. My elderly neighbour looks out for her at lunchtime and takes her out for a short walk, but I'm usually home by four o'clock, at the latest, so I take her out then and give her some dinner."

Antonio struggled to stifle a laugh as she spoke. She was clearly feeling none of the reserve she had on their initial meeting.

"And here I am again, embarrassing myself in front of you, again," she smiled at her admission. Antonio was reminded of her lovely smile.

"Hey, no problem. In fact, let me buy you a fresh takeaway. It's the least I can do, and then I'll drive you home, if you'd like?" He'd noticed the look on her face at the heavy rain, and surmised she had walked, realising that if she had it would neither be too far, nor out of his way to take her home.

"Thanks, there's really no need, I'm only a couple of blocks away. And in terms of food, I'm sure there's enough left that I can rescue. I'd ordered enough for two anyway, and there's only me to feed," she admitted. "The dog's not allowed Indian food, too spicy," she added making light of the situation. "In fact, you've probably saved me from eating too much, as I really do need to start cutting back on what I eat. I do like my food, as you can probably tell." As she said this she breathed in, as if to disguise her small tummy.

Antonio chose not to comment on her weight. Having been married to Charlotte and knowing how sensitive women could be on that subject, he knew to stay well clear. From where he stood, though, Isabella looked to have a rather shapely figure, one he personally couldn't see anything wrong with. He also quite liked a woman with a healthy appetite.

"Well, just let me collect mine and then I'll drive you home anyway. The storm looks like it could get thunderous, and I wouldn't want to be responsible for you getting hit by lightning as well, would I?" Isabella tried to say no, however Antonio insisted.

As he had been standing there, listening to her talk, and watching the way her lips moved and her eyes light up as she spoke, he began experiencing the weirdest sensation in his gut; one that was clearly telling him he could not afford to let this woman slip through his fingers again. It was a completely bizarre feeling, and if asked he would be unable to explain where it had suddenly sprung from, or what it meant.

He had never thought to ask for her mobile number that time they had met, having never seriously thought they would be in contact again. She was simply the girls' teacher. He knew nothing about her, or she him, for that matter. And whilst he had to admit she had on occasion popped into his thoughts over recent weeks, he had never followed it up. Other things had always distracted him.

Now, though, it was almost as if his gut was telling him there was an ulterior motive for asking to drive her home, as when he dropped her off, which he fully intended on doing, he would know where she lived. And even if he had still not managed to get her mobile number by the end of their journey, which was something he needed to work on, at least knowing her address would be a step forward. In turn, that would make it easier for when he collected her the next time, because one thing was for sure, he fully intended spending more time with this woman.

There was something about her that made him laugh. She was good company and he realised he enjoyed their banter. There was also a quirkiness about her, an innocence that he liked, with a look that was quite unique. Nothing pampered or false about her appearance. A completely natural beauty. She was not his normal sort – if he'd ever had one – and she would certainly not have fitted into his smart London set, or his previous life. Her dress sense alone would have marked her out in the crowd. None of that mattered, though, as right here and right now the woman appeared to be exactly what he needed. A friend, someone with whom he believed he would enjoy spending his time, and someone whom he felt wouldn't judge or restrict him in terms of what he needed to do with his life. Someone who would allow him to be himself.

It was almost as if the stars were telling him he sorely needed Isabella in his life. So all he now needed to work on was getting her mobile number and convincing her of that fact too, without frightening her off for good.

Chapter 33

Two weeks later and it was Maundy Thursday, the beginning of the Easter holidays. The children were breaking up from school and fiestas and parades would be held around the island, in the towns and villages, as people celebrated the Christian festival. In their area it would culminate in the Easter Parade after the Easter Sunday service. There was a general feeling of merriment in the air.

Work had now been completed on the finca, with Lucía and Theresa delighted with their new bedrooms and en suites, to say nothing of the spacious new kitchen that had soon become the heart of the home, as was fitting. Work had also been completed on the accommodation block, with Carmen the first to point out that the furnishings looked amazing. The cookery school was also progressing well, with the workmen at the final fixes stage, ironing out those inevitable little niggles that appeared from nowhere. Just another week or two before all workmen would be off site, finally allowing Antonio, Lucía and Theresa to be able to start experimenting with their new appliances. They were desperate to familiarise themselves with all the workings of the facilities before the school went live, and with the arrival of their first students at the end of June time was running out.

Lucía was starting to demonstrate a degree of excitement at the prospect of presenting her skills to the students, all her previous inhibitions apparently now addressed. Neither Antonio nor Theresa was quite sure what had changed her mind, or if the feeling would last, but were happy to see her smiling again. It was obvious she was feeling much brighter about life in general, with a renewed spring in her step, along with an acceptance that her life had not ended, as she had previously believed following Mateo's death. It had simply meandered in a different direction. So, whilst it may have taken her nearly two years to get to that point, for now she was prepared to go with it. Lucía knew that having her mother and Antonio back in her life would never replace her husband, although it had certainly helped to distract her from her grief. And as Theresa kept saying, she had to live her life – whatever there was left of it, or how it turned out to be. Mateo would not have wanted her to do anything else.

There had also been an extremely positive response to the brochure and marketing material that had been issued the previous week, following Philippe's comments on their draft. As a result, a stream of enquiries and some early bookings had been received. Sofía was starting to feel the pressure of fielding the enquiries, whilst still getting herself familiar with the IT system in place, at the same time as arranging interviews for local staff. They were looking to employ a team of cleaners, drivers, kitchen staff and other general trades to help with the running of the school, and keep the gardens and exteriors clean and tidy. Some of the landscaping still needed to be completed, but by and large the finca was looking very tidy, and a massive improvement from the sight that had welcomed Antonio nearly two years previously. He recalled the rusty gates hanging off their hinges, broken equipment littering the farmyard and the outhouses, with their caved in roofs and rotted window frames. Now the ramshackle buildings had been reborn and local trees and indigenous planting would line the entrance, with cactuses and even the odd banana tree being brought in to improve the overall look of the place. First impressions counted and Antonio believed planting some of the local flora was another great way to showcase the island.

Importantly, the sign had now been positioned at the gates. "*Maestro Pérez – Escuela de Cocina,*" it declared. A school of cookery, with the great teacher, Chef Antonio Pérez as its figurehead.

So, with the initial course diarised to run at the end of June, and less than ten weeks to go before their first guests arrived, the levels of excitement and trepidation were building in equal measures. There was still a lot of work to be done.

Antonio was feeling pleased with progress, at the same time he recognised he was starting to feel exhausted. He was not sleeping as well as he should, his mind never capable of fully switching off. He was forever running over lists in his head, mentally ticking off what had been done, then lying awake worrying about those things that were still outstanding.   He knew the rest of the family were feeling that way too.

Carmen came waltzing into the kitchen, wafting her arms in the air and clearly at her wits end with Anya and Maya, from the snippets of conversation Antonio could hear. He and Sofía were both sitting in the office and exchanged a look that said "best to keep out of this one!" She had just driven them both to school and they were driving her mad. School was breaking up later that day, and the prospect of nearly two weeks of having them under her feet was not filling her with excitement.

As he sat at his desk, he realised Carmen wasn't the only one who needed a break. They all did. A chance to recharge their batteries before the final push.   He got up and walked into the kitchen, indicating that Sofía should follow him.

"I've been thinking, why don't we all have a couple of days off? We're tired and I think it will do us good to have some time away from here. What do you think to a day at the beach tomorrow, or we could even take the children to a water park on Sunday?" he asked, looking around the room. "The workmen won't be here tomorrow anyway, so we could easily put the phones to answerphone for a day or two over Easter. As far as I know we're not expecting any deliveries, are we? What do you think?"

"I'm not sure, Antonio. I was planning on visiting Rosa tomorrow, to check in with her. Then I was hoping for a quiet day on Sunday. A chance to put my feet up," Theresa began, not warming to the idea of a day out.

"Yes, I agree with Mama," Lucía added. "I don't want to go to the beach or the water park. It will be too hot. I'll probably just rest and put my feet up. There's a series I might watch too." Since Wi-Fi had been installed, Lucía had discovered Netflix and was known to occasionally lock herself in her bedroom and indulge in her newly found passion of binge watching.

It was not quite the response Antonio had expected, yet perhaps understandable from Lucía's and Theresa's perspectives. "What about you, Sofía?"

"I've already made plans, Antonio," she replied, quite sheepishly. "I'm spending the weekend with my friend, Lorenzo. We're going to drive over to Puerto de la Cruz for the day," forgetting to mention they had booked a hotel and were planning on spending one, maybe two nights together. They had been dating now for several weeks, the occasional dinner out or drinks in the bar after work, kissing quite passionately as they walked back to their respective apartments. So far, that was as far as it had gone. She had never invited him into her apartment, nor accepted an invitation into his. As the proverbial forty-year-old virgin, she felt scared he would think of her as frigid or inexperienced, both of which to a degree was true – so whenever the kissing got too intense she would back away, leaving him confused and frustrated. Sofía liked Lorenzo very much, and found him extremely attractive, but something was preventing her from the actual act of sex. She had read about it, and had watched enough television to know what it involved. Sadly, though, that was as far as her experiences went.

Lorenzo was increasingly feeling rejected, a feeling he was unused to. He was a healthy man, in the prime of his life, with a healthy sexual appetite and with no strings attached saw no problem with two consenting adults getting it together. It was only sex, not a promise of happy ever after. He had bedded enough women in his time to know the score, so could not see what her problem was. She was an attractive woman, with an amazing figure; one he was not embarrassed to admit he was anxious to experience for himself.

Then one evening after a few drinks, when he pushed the point, issuing a direct invitation to go back to his place, making his intentions very clear, he was shocked at her admission. The panicked look in her eyes as she backed away almost scared him. Sofía liked him a lot, he was not blind to the signs, yet this was a whole new experience for him. Lorenzo did not know what to do or say, so simply left her at the door without pushing his point any further. That was not his style.

This weekend however was his attempt to right a situation, one he'd never found himself in before. A seduction that he hoped even Sofía could not resist. Until then he'd been happy to take it at her pace, however his anticipation was now running high. He did not want to put it off any longer.

Whereas Sofía was still nervous. Even now, for her the outcome was far from a foregone conclusion. That final act of sex, and how it might play out without the Hollywood glamour or soft lighting, remained a worry. She bit her lip as she thought of what the weekend might entail, unsure whether she would stay the course of two nights with Lorenzo and a double bed, or would she find herself hot tailing it back home, on the bus, before breakfast.

"I've got a great idea, Antonio," Carmen piped up, fearing she was the only one without any plans, yet feeling she above everyone was the one who needed some space. She'd had a thought, and to her it was simply ingenious. A thought that would involve two whole days without the girls, an idea that really appealed to her. "Why don't you take the girls to the beach, or the water park, or wherever you fancy? You can even have them to sleep over, as an extra treat. In fact, why don't I go home now and pack them some things? That way you can pick them up from school and return them to me - sometime Saturday, late evening perhaps, even Sunday morning at Mass. How does that sound?"

Realising that once again Carmen had managed to bamboozle him, he simply gave in. After all, what else did he have planned for the next couple of days? Nothing. "Okay, but for heaven's sake, Carmen, please phone the school and let them know this time. I wouldn't want to have to go through all that trouble again," he replied, resigned to the idea of entertaining his nieces for the weekend.

Although, it would give him a chance to see Isabella again, he thought to himself, suddenly warming to Carmen's idea of collecting the girls from school. Keeping them overnight on Thursday and Friday, even Saturday was a bit of a push, as what on earth could he do to entertain them for nearly three days and nights, especially given childcare was not his forte? So much for his idea of a few days off work to rest and relax!

It was perhaps worth it, though, if he could see Isabella for a few minutes in the playground and maybe have a chat. With all his previous good intentions gone by the wayside, he had still not contacted her, so perhaps this might finally present him with the opportunity he needed. It might even lead to him building up the courage to invite her out for a drink, making him question once again what it was that he was so scared about.

Chapter 34

As term ended on Thursday lunchtime, Antonio arrived early at the school gates, along with the other mothers and grandparents equally anxious to pick up their charges. Whilst Anya and Maya were unlikely to be expecting him, at least today the school was. He had stood over Carmen, patiently waiting until she had made the phone call, unprepared to even consider driving to the school until she had done so.

"Uncle Antonio, what are you doing here?" squealed Anya as she ran towards him.

"Is Mama not with you, is there something wrong with her?" Maya asked, more suspicious of his motives for turning up, and worried Carmen may have had some kind of accident.

"No, everything is fine. Your mama suggested I collected you. She also thought you might want to come home with me tonight. We could spend some time together, even have a sleepover, if you wanted?" he asked, unsure what the girls' reactions would be to that idea, having never slept over before.

Maya looked over at Señorita Rodriguez, who was standing a few metres away, her eyes questioning whether it was alright to go with him, because the last thing she wanted was a repeat of the previous occasion. That had been very embarrassing in class the following morning, when a couple of the boys started talking about her and Anya, questioning what they had been doing the previous afternoon, joking that she and her sister were teacher's pets. They had been seen sitting in the café, with their uncle and their teacher, having a meal, and everyone wanted to know why. So now everyone in the school knew about it and Maya felt they were being laughed at behind their backs.

Isabella walked over to them, smiling. Before the end-of-school bell had gone, she had made an effort to quickly straighten her hair and check her teeth for the remains of any of her lunch, before leading her class out to the playground. For some reason, when the head mistress had told her Señor Pérez was collecting Anya and Maya, authorising her to let the girls go with him, she had felt an unexpected flutter in her stomach. She didn't quite know why, nevertheless she wanted to look her best. The first time she had seen him she had embarrassed herself with her stern and controlling manner, and the last time she had dropped her takeaway at his feet, marginally avoiding ruining his smart shoes. She was hoping third time lucky, at least in terms of avoiding any embarrassment.

"Ah, buenas tardes, Señorita," Antonio said, instinctively returning her smile. "There's no need to worry today, I am authorised to take them."

"Yes, I believe so, Señor," maintaining the formality when in earshot of the other parents. She had already noticed a few glancing over in her direction. "Maya, Anya your mother phoned earlier to advise the school that your uncle would be collecting you today, so there's nothing for you to worry about," she said reassuringly to the girls.

"Yes, I was thinking we could head to the beach later and then have some food out, maybe a pizza?" Antonio added to the girls, equally reassuringly.

Maya was still suspicious. Her mother had been acting weirdly that morning, arguing with both her and Anya over nothing. She was not at all sure what was going on and as the concept of sleeping over was one that had never been discussed before, why was it being suggested today? Why were they being packed out of their house, without being given a proper explanation?

"If we are going to the beach, I'll need to go home first, to change and get my swimsuit," she said, looking down at her uniform, as if it was obvious she was not dressed for the occasion. Moreover, she was aware a trip home would at least assuage some of her concerns about her mother's welfare. One of her friends' mothers had left home without telling anyone last term, just upped and gone with another man, simply abandoning her and her brother without any explanation. With a boy in the year below them, his mother had died suddenly. She'd had an accident on the motorway, when a truck crashed into her, and the doctors had been unable to save her. He had to go and live with his grandparents miles away. She remembered they had said prayers for her in assembly and everyone had cried.

Anya, sensing her sister's concerns, suddenly became worried something had happened to their mother too. Small tears started to form in her eyes.

Isabella, noticing Anya was unhappy, wrapped her arms around her. "What's the matter, Anya? It sounds like your uncle has a fun weekend planned for you and your sister. There's nothing to cry about. In fact, I wish I had a trip to the beach planned, and pizza. It sounds very exciting." She spoke in a gentle tone, in an attempt to encourage the girls, realising Antonio was at a loss what to say or do to appease them. It was clear he had little experience of dealing with children, or handling their concerns. He smiled over at her, grateful for her support.

"I want to go and see Mama." Maya's look again questioning Antonio. "Are you sure everything is alright?"

Anya then joined in with the chorus, echoing her sister's cries. "I want to go and see Mama, too."

"Hey, don't cry," he said, bending down to hug them. "I know, why don't we phone your mama now and you can both talk to her? Then if you still want to go home, I'll take you. How about that?" They both nodded and Isabella smiled on, suddenly a lot more impressed by his negotiation skills.

Antonio dialled Carmen's number and after a brief discussion with her, he handed the phone to Maya. Maya spoke to her mother for a couple of minutes before handing it to Anya. Mainly the girls listened and nodded as the conversation progressed. All the time Antonio and Isabella watched on, exchanging the odd glance, both intrigued by what was being said.

Anya then handed the phone back to Antonio with a smile on her face. "Mama says if we are staying over, we don't have to go to bed early, as there's no school tomorrow. So I think we should stay, Maya, and we can watch Netflix in bed, and eat chocolates."

Maya eventually conceded. Carmen had reassured her she was alive and well and that nothing was untoward. She had even gone on to say that she thought it would be good for them to spend more time with their uncle, mischievously suggesting it might cheer him up, as he was feeling a little down. "Okay, but I'll need some more things if we're staying overnight, so can we drive home anyway?"

Antonio let out a sigh, relieved, if a little surprised it had taken so long to convince them to go with him. "There's no need, it really is all sorted. Your mama's put your things together and your bags are already in the car. Have a good look, and if there's anything she's missed, there's always the shops." He hated having to resort to bribery.

"Well, have fun on the beach and enjoy the rest of your weekend, girls. You'll have to tell me all about it in a couple of weeks," Isabella said, briefly waving as she watched them chatting away, before turning to go back into the classroom. She had smiled as she noticed their three heads close together, clearly giggling over something.

The playground was now empty and the caretaker would be out soon to lock the gates. It was the end of term and nobody had wanted to hang around or chat longer than was necessary. Everyone it appeared had places to go, people to see – apart from Isabella who was facing a quiet weekend alone, to say nothing of the rest of the holidays that stretched out ahead of her. Nearly two whole weeks of moping around by herself, with no one or nothing, other than her dog, Peca, to amuse her.

She had just reached the entrance door to the school, when she could hear steps running up behind her. She turned to see Antonio, almost out of breath as he stopped in front of her, small beads of sweat starting to appear on his bald forehead. "We were just wondering, the girls and I that is, if you wanted to join us at the beach. If you're busy, or you would rather not, then I'll understand. It's just I'm not big on building sandcastles, and I could do with all the help I could get," he said, anxiously leaving the question hanging.

"Well……" she replied, desperately trying to find the right words to say yes, but at the same time struggling to play it cool. After all, she did not want to come across as desperate or needy. "If you put it that way, and you really need my help, then I suppose that would be fine. I'll need to go home first, though, and feed my dog," she said smiling. "Apart from which, I'll need to go home to change into my swimsuit, because I don't imagine you've got that packed in your car too, have you?" she laughed.

Antonio laughed at her response. "No problem, shall I pick you up at your apartment, in around an hour's time, then?" he questioned. "I can remember the road, I just don't have the building number. In fact, why don't you give me your mobile number and then I can ring you when we're outside?"

"Thank you, that sounds good," she replied, giving him the information he'd requested. "I'll see you shortly then." She smiled as he walked off again and waved at the girls, who by now were giggling even more by the gates.

If she was honest, she had warmed to Antonio the first time she had met him, although the circumstances that day had been extremely difficult. She'd had to maintain a professional air, unable to fully relax in his company or let her guard down. She had enjoyed chatting to him, though, and they had talked quite openly about a lot of subjects, appearing to have quite a few things in common and some shared interests. She had then found him even funnier the night of the takeaway, obviously not bothered by the way she had embarrassed herself, or the fact she had looked bedraggled in her scruffy clothes, her hair wet from the storm.

She had even imagined from his body language he liked her too, so had been disappointed when he had simply dropped her off and waved goodbye, without saying a word, simply leaving her to enjoy what was left of her takeaway for one. And the fact he had not been in touch with her since, or asked for her mobile number at the time, she'd taken as a sign he was not interested. Perhaps she had been wrong, or perhaps she was reading too much into it, looking for something that clearly was not there.

Was she so desperate, or was it more the case that given it had been quite some time since she'd last had a boyfriend, she was just out of touch? She had clearly misread kindness for interest. He'd probably had no interest in her whatsoever, or not at least in the way she would have liked.

Although today, she had to admit her stomach had done a bit of a summersault at the news he was coming into school, and then another when she had seen him waiting in the playground, playing it cool with the other parents. She had also not missed the way he had looked at her, almost entreating her support with the girls. So maybe he was interested. Only time will tell. Either way, as Isabella floated back into her classroom to collect her bag and jacket, she suddenly felt a lot more excited about life in general.

Any excitement, though, was short lived, as a sense of panic soon set in. What on earth would she look like in her swimsuit? Over recent weeks, whilst she had tried to lose some weight, there was no evidence of it having gone anywhere, and she was very conscious of those extra kilos she carried. She really didn't want her body to turn him off, just as it had her ex-fiancé, Tomás, who'd had no difficulty whatsoever finding someone much more attractive to fall into bed with.

No, perhaps it would be easier all round if she called him and cancelled, before it was too late.

Chapter 35

Easter Sunday morning arrived and the sun shone brightly through the apartment windows. The curtains were closed, however the light still managed to seep through the small tears in the cheap fabric, casting shadows on the dated bedroom furniture. Isabella knew she really needed to repair or replace them, and if she intended staying around she should start to make the apartment look more homely, put up some nice pictures or get some soft cushions, even some new bed linen – anything to make the place feel loved, more personal.

Since she had arrived, the small one-bedroom apartment had never truly felt like home. It was furnished with other people's things, items she would not have chosen for herself. Things she would gladly have thrown away if she had the money to replace them, which clearly on a teacher's salary she did not. It had simply been a place to return to at the end of the day and somewhere safe to leave the dog while she was at work.

Having broken up on Thursday afternoon, school had barely been shut for more than a day, with over another week's holiday left to go. Ten more days, for which Isabella had yet to make any firm plans. Other than the Easter Sunday church service at eleven o'clock later that day, her diary was completely empty.

Her class would all be there, well at least those who attended Sunday Mass regularly, which was not as high a percentage as she would have liked, or those who were not away on holiday, which given the time of year would reduce the number further. Nevertheless, a good proportion should be there, and fingers crossed they would remember their lines as they led the prayers.

The last term had flown by so fast Isabella feared she did not want to wish this new one away as quickly, with another year gone without much being achieved. She was approaching thirty and what did she have to feel good about? She almost hoped she could stop the clock, or at least rewind it a little.

Now, rewinding it to the previous Thursday evening would be a good place to start, she thought, smiling to herself as the memories of her afternoon on the beach started to flood her consciousness.

Antonio had picked her up outside the apartment as planned, his car already packed to the rafters, with a picnic, towels and everything imaginable the girls would need for their time on the beach. Carmen had obviously gone to town, sending bats, balls, inflatables, flippers, goggles, even fishing rods – unsure what adventures her brother had planned for her daughters. More likely not wanting any excuse for them to come home, citing they had forgotten something. Antonio had confided in Isabella he believed his sister may have a new man on the scene, hence her desire for the girls to be out of the house for the night. As yet he had no proof of that, although he also suspected his other sister, Sofía, had a man on the go too. She was, he suspected, going away with him that weekend.

Isabella had laughed. "So you think both of your sisters are skulking around on the hunt for sex, do you? Well, good luck to them is what I'd say," she had added without thinking, leaving her feeling mortified and causing Antonio to blush as he looked away. She had been too forward, making herself sound as if she was playing the same game. It had obviously embarrassed him, and herself into the bargain.

They had then driven to the beach at El Médano, a quiet seaside town in the south of the island. It was an area famed for attracting kite surfers and wind surfers from around the world, known for its strong winds and bohemian lifestyle. The conditions were perfect for the surfers, with the sights they created as they soared high into the skies, or navigated a particular wave, quite spectacular. The beach, with its black sand and gentle tides, was also very popular with the locals, who would come down from the mountains with their families and relax in the sunshine. Antonio had recalled visiting El Médano many years before, as a young boy with his parents and sisters, spending their days playing on the beach or swimming in the sea. So this memory was what had drawn him back to the area with Maya and Anya, he had told Isabella. "It's the perfect place to pitch our towels, and enjoy our picnic," he had said.

As soon as they had dropped their bags, the girls immediately stripped off and ran into the sea, leaving Isabella and Antonio to unpack.

"Well, they look like they're having a great time," Antonio said, looking over at the girls as they splashed around in the water. He had stripped off too, his bright red swimming shorts ready for action. "Shall we go and join them, and have a splash around before we eat?" he asked, acting almost like a big kid, rather than a grown man approaching his forties.

Then looking over at Isabella, Antonio had noticed she was struggling with her swim suit, and more particularly trying to put her sun cream on, her arms doing contortions as she attempted to reach the middle of her back. "Here, let me help you with that?" he laughed, automatically reaching for the bottle and not waiting for a response. "You look like you're struggling, here turn around."

Not wanting to burn, yet feeling like a helpless female, Isabella reluctantly agreed. "Thanks," she replied rather shyly, lifting her hair off her back and turning it towards Antonio.

Isabella had eventually chosen to wear a one-piece costume rather than her bikini, believing it would not expose those extra kilos anywhere near as much. In any event, her bikini, even if it still fitted her, would not have been appropriate. There were children around, children she taught, and the sight of their teacher in a stringy excuse for a garment would not have gone down well.

Antonio gently started to rub the lotion in, starting at her shoulders and gradually working his way down her back. The feel of his hands was so tender, and as he massaged the cream in, careful to ensure he covered all the areas that would be exposed to the sun, Isabella was grateful her face was turned away from him. It had been a long time since a man had done that for her, and she had forgotten how good it felt as her body relaxed with the sensation. Her involuntary "Ahhh....." was difficult to conceal.

When he had finished, he simply turned to Isabella, and offered her the bottle. "Would you mind rubbing some in for me too, please? I made sure the girls were covered before we left home, but I didn't think to put some on myself. You don't mind, do you?"

Isabella certainly didn't mind. It would be her pleasure.

The rest of the afternoon was pure fun. They laughed, they played, they chatted, they relaxed and they ate. The picnic was surprisingly good, with Isabella amazed to see the effort Antonio had gone to. He had mentioned that he liked food and was a bit of a chef, but she had never imagined he was particularly serious about it.

"That was amazing," she had declared when they had finished eating. "You should seriously consider going into that line of work professionally," she had suggested, surprised when he replied, "I thought I'd already told you, I'm a chef. Did you not believe me?"

Later they left the beach and went for ice-creams to one of the heladerias close by. The girls each chose a huge stacked waffle cone with multiple flavours, some of which Isabella had never heard of before, let alone tasted. They laughed as the ice-creams melted, dripping down their hands in the heat of the afternoon sun. It had been a perfect day, a surprising day, and one she had not wanted to end, although, as they headed home, it was obvious that perfect day was nearly over. The sun was starting to set and the girls were dozing in the back of the car, leaving Isabella and Antonio to chat.

"I've had a lovely day. Thank you, Antonio, for inviting me. I haven't been to that part of the island before, so it was lovely to see it. And to spend time with you all, too."

"Thank you for coming with us, it's been our pleasure. I'm not sure I would have managed them alone," he replied looking into the rear-view mirror and checking the girls were asleep before he continued. "Next time, we could go somewhere different, perhaps? I can show you more of the island, if that's something you'd like?"

Antonio, noticing Isabella did not reply, ventured further. "We could go, just the two of us, I mean. Not with the girls. Perhaps even on a date, if that's something that doesn't sound too twee at our age."

"I quite like twee," she replied, with a smile turning to face him. "And I like the idea of a date with you very much. So, yes please, I'd love to see more of the island, and spend more time with you, of course."

So whilst Thursday's afternoon at the beach had panned out a lot better than she had expected, today was another day. It was Easter Sunday morning and she would be seeing him again soon, albeit as part of the crowds at the Easter Parade.

He had not contacted her on Friday or Saturday, no doubt busy entertaining his nieces. And Isabella, fearful of it all being a dream, had not wanted to get in touch either.

Having got back into her apartment and having fed Peca, she had sat on her lumpy sofa and gone over the events of the day in her mind. The more she replayed them, the more she realised she had probably read too much into it. He was simply a friendly man, someone who probably meant 'date' as a drink, or a chat. Nothing more than that.

And why on earth would he be interested in her anyway? She was not particularly attractive, she was still overweight and all things considered had very little going for her. Living alone in a barely habitable apartment, without friends, other than a dog for company. Her parents and ex-fiancé between them had certainly done an excellent job at undermining any confidence Isabella had once had. Now was certainly not the time for daydreaming. Now was the time to be realistic, so she had better manage her expectations accordingly.

Whilst Isabella was bemoaning her lot and questioning her actions, Antonio was whistling away in his apartment, anxiously pacing and waiting for the girls to get out of his bathroom, so that he could take his shower. Having them to stay over for the weekend had been eye-opening, to say the least, and after the parade today he would happily hand them back to their mother, whether she was ready to take them back or not. He was physically and mentally exhausted.

On Friday, he had taken them shopping and treated them each to a new dress and a pair of trainers. Then on Saturday he had taken them to the water park, before going out for burgers at one of the local restaurants for dinner. He had suggested he cook at home, as he was tired after a day on the slides, but they had laughed at that idea, pointing out it was supposed to be a treat, and staying at home was not a treat.

Throughout their stay, the girls seemed to do nothing other than giggle and eat all day, before giggling and eating some more all evening. On all but one of the three nights, they had ended up crashed-out on the sofa in front of the television, exhausted. He had carried them carefully into his spare bedroom, and laid them next to each other on the king-sized bed, fully clothed, before collapsing onto his own bed and falling into a deep sleep. Neither girl had washed, showered or even cleaned her teeth before bed, and if Carmen ever heard about that, he knew he would be in trouble.

"Come on you two, I need to get ready too." He attempted to cajole them. The church service started in less than an hour and he needed to get them there in good time, with their bags packed and everything loaded into the car, as well as make himself presentable. The house looked like a disaster zone, dirty plates and biscuit wrappers all over the place, as well as at least the packaging of two Easter eggs they had already guzzled. He would have to sort the mess out when he got home, as he neither had the time nor the energy for it now. The rest of the family would meet him at the church, and after the parade the plan was for them all to head back to the finca for a family feast. Yaya Rosa would be there too, along with a few close friends.

Antonio would have preferred to side-step it, however Lucía and Theresa had been busy organising food the previous day in preparation, so he didn't have the heart not to attend, or to let them down. He just hoped Sofía and Carmen, both of whom had been otherwise engaged all weekend, remembered to turn up. Otherwise, it would be a long afternoon.

Talking of Sofía and Carmen, Antonio didn't want to allow his mind to wander to what either of them may have been involved in all weekend, although the more he tried to distance himself from thoughts of either of them having sex, the more his own mind wandered to the possibility of himself doing the same, with Isabella.

Seeing her in her one-piece costume on the beach had been a real treat, and at times he had struggled to avoid being caught staring, or worse. He had guessed there was a curvaceous figure under her layers, but he had never imagined it to be as good as it was. She clearly did not see it herself, as she appeared embarrassed once she'd stripped out of her dress. She was forever adjusting her costume, fearful of showing off her ample cleavage or her shapely buttocks, whenever it got wet in the sea, or rode up in the waves. As well as unconsciously patting her stomach whenever he mentioned she should have something else to eat. Why did women believe they were overweight, when really they were perfectly proportioned and simply enjoyed their food? He hated women who were waif-like, scared to eat anything for fear of those extra calories. Charlotte had been like that and it had driven him mad, he now realised.

And her flawless olive skin – so soft to the touch. How he had enjoyed massaging her sun lotion in, letting his fingers linger longer than was strictly necessary. It was just a shame it was only her back that had needed doing, as he would have enjoyed rubbing her legs too, and her arms, with all those fine wispy hairs. They looked equally soft and smooth, yet strong at the same time. Then her neck, when she'd lifted her hair - he still couldn't believe how he had controlled his desire to nuzzle it, let alone control himself when she rubbed the cream into his own back. If ever there was a definition of agony and ecstasy at the same time, he imagined that afternoon on the beach for him would come pretty close.

Antonio had never been good at reading people's body language, or being particularly sensitive to emotions, another of the points Charlotte had regularly criticised him on.   So whilst he was clearly captivated by Isabella, he had never given any thought to the fact that his feelings may have been reciprocated. She was out of his league, surely? He was probably around ten years older than her, slightly overweight and almost bald, as well as having the baggage of an ex-wife to contend with. What could she possibly see in him? Antonio was often guilty of using a self-deprecating manner as a self-protection mechanism, especially where women were concerned, and today was no exception. In all other walks of life, he was confident and charming, but not so when it came to the fairer sex.

He recalled how Charlotte had been one of the first women he had actually felt comfortable around. How in those early days she had been physically attracted to him, and vice versa. He had been much younger and fitter, and with a lot more hair in those days. He had also been ambitious, with a glittering career ahead of him – all of which was an aphrodisiac for women, or so he had been told.

Keeping Charlotte interested, though, once the initial throes of passion had worn off, the ring was on her finger and the time he could devote to her became limited, due to the demands of that same glittering career, proved impossible. He could see that now, and could also see how easily she had been tempted away by the next shiny model to shower her with attention.

He had taken his eye well and truly off the ball, and for that had paid a hefty price. It was something he would not want to be found guilty of again.

His whole life and his priorities had taken a real hit in recent months, and it was not an exaggeration to say that as a result he was not the same person. Emotionally he'd had to deal with the death of his father, the end of his marriage, as well as being faced with the realities of his parentage. To say nothing of the practicalities of dealing with the estates of his father and a long-lost great-grandfather that no one had given any consideration to for over forty years. None of those events had he seen coming, and taken alone each would have had the power to destabilise a person. However, when combined, and coupled with a complete change in lifestyle, a move to a new country, stepping away from the business he had built from scratch, and the development of an entirely new one, well it was more than most people would be capable of dealing with. So perhaps, he shouldn't be being so tough on himself after all.

And if Isabella was willing to go out on another date with him, then it was time to grasp the nettle and go for it. Time to have the confidence to get back into the saddle, the swing of living, whatever risks that might entail for the future. He deserved to move on with his life, as much as the next person, surely?

"Why should Sofía and Carmen be having all the fun?" he thought to himself, as he eventually got in front of the mirror to begin his shave, again desperate to dispel that image that thought was creating in his head.

Chapter 36

The rest of the school holidays went in the blink of an eye, and before too long it was Tuesday morning and classes were resuming. The start of the final term. The end of the school year was finally in sight, with the promise of the long summer holidays ahead of them. The prospect of which meant different things to different people, with teachers desperate for the six-week break and parents worried about how they would amuse their offspring for so long. However, with Easter behind them, it was now a time for everyone to refocus, come what may.

For Antonio, he had to concentrate all his energies back into the final push with the development, especially if they were to stand any chance of the cookery school being a success. His few days' break over the Easter weekend, during which he had allowed himself to temporarily switch off, was now almost a distant memory, albeit a very pleasant one. This last week in the office had been one of the busiest yet, allowing him little if any time to think about anything, other than work.

As he settled back behind his desk, ready to deal with all the emails he'd received during the preceding days, he questioned if anyone ever truly switched off. Several new bookings had come in over the weekend, a raft of bills was waiting to be paid and a range of items that had to be ordered 'today', to avoid deadlines being missed, were all screaming out for his attention.

Sofía stepped in, a bright smile on her face. "Why don't you leave those with me, Antonio, while you go and talk to Manuel? I can easily run through them and prioritise, and deal with what I can before you get back. If there's anything really urgent, don't worry, I'll shout."

Since her time away with Lorenzo the previous weekend, Antonio had noticed Sofía had a real spring in her step, with a glow about her and an attitude that made light of every situation. She had wholeheartedly thrown herself into the new venture and whatever was going on between them, which Antonio still did not want to contemplate, was obviously working wonders for her.

"Thanks – if you're sure?" he asked, rhetorically, as he moved away from his desk before she had the opportunity to change her mind.

In addition to meeting with Manuel for the final snagging of the development itself, Antonio had a meeting in town with a local wine merchant. He was someone he was keen to bring on board, as one of the activities planned for the speciality courses was a master class in pairing wines with certain foods. It was something he was passionate about and something he encouraged at his own restaurants in London. There he employed a sommelier to advise on the best wines to accompany customers' choices of food, whereas here he was hoping the merchant may be able to recommend someone, even offer to do it himself.

He had arranged to meet the merchant at eleven o'clock, in a café close to the town square, so all being well by lunchtime he would have another job ticked off his list. If he didn't dawdle he would have ample time. As he walked over to the school to meet Manuel there was a real spring in his step. Thankfully there was no longer anything major left to do, so Antonio was feeling positive – even on a bit of a high. He imagined it was some sort of residual effect from his Easter break, although that was eight days ago so perhaps not.

Anyway, the break had done him good, some downtime and a chance to refocus, although what that meant in reality, particularly in relation to Isabella, he remained at a loss to explain.

After the Easter parade, he had taken the opportunity of drawing Isabella to one side and inviting her to spend the following day with him. He felt like he needed to seize the moment, rather than allow more time to pass him by. Apart from which, what reason did he have to prevaricate, what did he have to lose? Surely, if she was not interested, she would say so. He had a sense of now or never, and could see no reason to waste the small window of opportunity they had, before the demands of work or school reabsorbed them.

Isabella had jumped at the chance to spend the day together, not expecting their 'first date' to come so soon after the beach trip, if that was what this was.

She had nervously spent the remainder of Sunday deciding what to wear, what would most flatter her figure – something fashionable yet comfortable, especially if they were planning on driving any distance in the car. Nothing too tight around her waist, nothing that would look creased or show sweat marks, and above all nothing that would scream desperate. She wanted to impress, but did not want to come over as easy. Her ex-best friend's one night stand with her ex-fiancé had told her enough about how dangerous a meaningless fling could be, and she certainly did not intend making that mistake. She had to find the right balance, without scaring him off.

Isabella had sighed as she'd scoured her wardrobe, finding it distinctly lacking in anything appropriate, let alone fashionable or flattering. Eventually settling on a pale blue and yellow summer dress that buttoned from top to bottom, and a pair of comfortable flat walking shoes in preference to her usual heels. Looking at herself in the mirror, she felt it was the best she could do under the circumstances.

She really liked Antonio and could even see a potential future with him, if that wasn't too presumptuous after such a short time of getting to know him. Yet what little time they had spent together had felt good, and even though they had not shared too much about their past lives, from what she had gleaned about him nothing had negatively bothered her. His values and ethics were sound, he was a generous and kind family man, with a handsome face and an infectious smile, and a body that was more than acceptable. Okay, he was perhaps more chunky than hunky, but she quite liked that in a man.

So all things considered, any bodily needs she might be harbouring would need to be controlled, at least until she worked out what his motivations were for inviting her out. Was it purely friendship, something more intimate and meaningful, or pure sex he was looking for? And whilst the latter was admittedly very appealing, she had her reputation to consider.

They had spent the day touring the island, before having dinner at an intimate coastal restaurant, where they had shared a huge pan of seafood paella. Isabella declared to the waiter that it was delicious, commenting that coming from Valéncia, the renowned home of paella, she considered herself an expert. Antonio's thoughts had been less complimentary, thinking how much better his own tasted. However, he had simply agreed, not wanting to spoil the moment or get into a debate with a local chef on the merits of cooking rice.

Isabella had no idea of the type of chef he was, nor the type of restaurants he owned, and for now he was happy to keep it that way. That part of his life was safely locked away. Here on the island, he was a different man, a much more relaxed man, and that was the person he wanted her to get to know. He felt no need to try to impress her with his money, his properties or his reputation, as he possibly had with Charlotte. Charlotte had come from a completely different background, was naturally more materialistic, eventually revelling in the attention his wealth and status brought. Isabella, he imagined, would need a completely different approach, if he was to successfully woo her.

They had laughed and joked throughout their day together, easily holding hands as they walked around the various sights and small villages they visited. Isabella was in awe of the island, and Antonio was enjoying showing her the place of his birth. Many of the places they visited brought back childhood memories, times he had spent as a young boy with his sisters, helping their father as they visited suppliers, or made deliveries for the farm – a mix of produce or livestock, depending on the season. Some memories he chose to share, most he kept to himself. It was funny, no matter what truths Theresa had told him, he would always think of Mateo as his father, and Sofía and Carmen as his sisters. Above all else, Lucía would always be his mother. So whilst he accepted the truth, the rest was the version he felt most comfortable living with.

As the evening drew to a close, a slight tension crept in between them. A sense of anticipation perhaps, even expectation of what might happen next. As they had left the restaurant they had kissed, and whilst it felt good, something in her response had not felt right. Antonio, sorely tempted to invite Isabella back to his apartment for the night, at the last minute lost his nerve and instead pulled the car up outside her apartment block. He had mulled it over as they had driven back, unable to decide what her response had meant. There was almost a reserve about her, a tentativeness that left him to wonder if he was expecting too much, or too soon. It wasn't that they weren't both consenting adults. After all, to most people in today's society, sex was just sex. Antonio was still old school, though. She needed to want it as much as he did, and standing in the car park, to him it hadn't felt that way.

By dropping her back at her apartment, he had chosen to leave the ball in her court. If he was invited up, he would go. If not, he would simply drive home. So the fact he was not invited in for a drink, let alone anything else, to him spoke volumes. She was either not interested, or not ready, and regardless of her reasoning he was not pushing it. He would just back off for a while and give her some space. Let her get her head together and then call her again in a few days. He would invite her out for another drink, somewhere informal, and see how the land lay. And if it looked promising, he might even summon up the energy to try again, because his gut kept telling him she was meant to be in his life.

Conversely, as Isabella had got out of his car that evening, she had been unsure what she had done wrong. She believed she had given off enough signs to make her intentions perfectly clear. So, perhaps friendship was the nature of the relationship he was after, after all. Perhaps she had been way off the mark thinking he was interested in anything more.

His kiss hadn't said that, though. His kiss had been warm and passionate; in truth it had taken her a little by surprise, almost knocking her sideways. It was much more than she would have expected from their first proper kiss. It was a kiss that promised something more, yet ultimately failed to deliver. A kiss that had left her nervously anticipating their night together, with the idea of waking up in his bed the following morning, his warm arms wrapped around her something that really appealed. It had been a long time since she had slept with anyone, other than her dog, Peca, and as nice as that was it didn't compare.

Yet the more she relived their day, looking for signs of where it could have all gone wrong, the more she struggled to make sense of any of it. He had been so attentive, so kind and at no stage had their conversation dried up or become awkward. He had made her laugh with his funny mannerisms and his self-deprecating jokes, and in turn he had laughed when she joked or told little anecdotes about her own life. They had appeared to be on the same wavelength entirely, which made it even more incomprehensible why he had driven her home and summarily dumped her at her door, without even a suggestion or hint at the prospect of going back to his apartment for the proverbial nightcap.

There had been no way she could have invited him up to her apartment, though, was there? Her list of excuses was endless. Firstly, it was disgusting and not set up for entertaining anyone, let alone a prospective lover. Also, it hadn't been cleaned for a while, with cleaning one of the jobs she had lined up for later that week, along with dealing with the piles of recycling all over the kitchen. With plenty of time on her hands and an empty diary, what else had she to look forward to, anyway?

The bed linen was also long overdue a change, and the bed had been left with the remnants of her paltry wardrobe still strewn all over it, from her earlier indecision about what to wear. She laughed to herself now, recalling the effort she had gone to making herself irresistible. Ha-ha, so much for her choices!   In term of the rest of the apartment, the old tattered furniture, the chipped crockery, the stained worktops, well, there wasn't much she could do about that, leaving her sure the sight of that alone would have sent him running for the hills, had she taken the risk of inviting him up. It was certainly not a penthouse apartment, or nowhere near the palatial surroundings of the one Antonio claimed to live in.

There had also been Peca to think about. The dog had been left for long enough as it was, and had she brought someone new into the apartment, someone she had never met before, she would have gone mad. She was a nervous dog at the best of times and not good with strangers, especially not strangers who would have forced her to sleep in her basket, rather than the lumpy bed she was used to. It was all an unmitigated disaster and yet another man lost in her life.

The morning had started with so much promise, and now as she cleaned her teeth, before getting into bed, Isabella was beginning to despair. At the ripe old age of twenty-nine, what had she achieved with her life, or more importantly what promise did the future hold? Where had those heady aspirations gone since she had first arrived on the island? She was supposed to be starting a new and exciting life, moving on from a failed relationship, towards building a better future for herself. Accepted, it was never going to be plain sailing, and teaching would never make her rich, yet she had never expected barely making enough money to keep a roof over her head, let alone afford any improvements. She was still low on the salary scale, so hopefully when her pay was next reviewed things would get easier, but paying her bills had been a real wake-up call, with those sizable deductions becoming harder each month.

Above all, living in the hovel she called her apartment was depressing, especially compared to the relative comfort of the home she had left in Valéncia. What was more, living an all but friendless existence was beginning to take its toll. She had hoped, at least on that front, that in meeting Antonio she had turned a corner. All the signs sadly indicated otherwise.

Well, at least she had a few days on her own to think about the conundrum that had become her life. After all, what else did she have to do with her holidays?

Having finished his meeting with Manuel ahead of time, Antonio drove down to the town for his eleven o'clock meeting with the wine merchant. His earlier meeting had gone well, so he was feeling relaxed and in a surprisingly good mood. Everything appeared to be going well in his life at the moment.

As he parked his car outside the café, he was surprised to see Isabella getting into a taxi, outside her apartment block across the street. He watched as she handed a carry-on bag to the driver, as well as a large suitcase, before getting into the back seat and closing the door. She was not close enough to see him, and would not have heard him had he chosen to shout over to her, but Antonio sensed there was something strange in the way she looked, almost agitated and certainly distracted.

He had not spoken to her all week, not since their day around the island the previous Monday, so eight days ago. He had tried to give her the space he believed she needed, and had been more than a little disappointed she had not messaged him or invited him out for a drink, or even simply for a chat. Perhaps he should contact her and check everything was alright, as there was definitely something strange about her behaviour.

He couldn't imagine why she was in a taxi, with luggage, let alone where she might be going. Last week had been the school holidays, so if she had planned on going away, surely she would have gone then? He certainly didn't recall her mentioning anything about taking a trip or a holiday. Then again, why should she? Today, though, was a school day, and by rights she should be in the classroom, not in a taxi, heading in what appeared to be the opposite direction to the school.

As the taxi drove passed him, he could see her head was bent down. She had not noticed him at all and appeared to be on her phone, completely distracted. Antonio was confused, unable to put an explanation to what might be happening. As he was pondering whether to call her and check everything was okay, the wine merchant turned up. He parked his car directly behind Antonio's.

"Ah, Señor Pérez, good day," he said, shaking Antonio's hand. Looking towards the café, he added, "Shall we go in? I believe the coffee here is excellent. If you get a table, I will go and order, and then we can talk through your plans. I believe I have some ideas that you might find interesting."

With that Antonio put his phone back into his pocket and followed him into the café, deciding he would phone Isabella after his meeting, perhaps invite her out for a drink, provided she had no other plans. He really hadn't liked the way it had been left between them and felt eight days was more than enough time for her to cool off, assuming that was what she was doing. If he had come on too strong, he would apologise, because if nothing else he would still value her friendship, if that's all she was prepared to offer.

And in terms of the taxi and the luggage, it was probably nothing and certainly nothing to do with him. He didn't want her thinking he was checking up on her, so better not to draw attention to it, or mention he had seen her, unless she offered the information.

Something, though, had not felt right, yet he was at a complete loss to imagine what that might be.

Chapter 37

After touching down at Valéncia Airport, mid-afternoon later that day, Isabella took the metro towards the city. Her parents' house was situated in one of the less wealthy suburbs, around thirty minutes' walk from the Cathedral, but the metro stop was mercifully only a five to ten minutes' walk from their house. Given the heat of the day, and the fact she was having to drag her luggage, that distance was just about doable. Any longer and she might have resorted to getting a taxi.

She was not feeling particularly good about returning home and the circumstances were certainly not of her choosing, although when she had weighed up her alternatives, what option did she really have? Her father had phoned the previous week, simply advising her it was time to come home. There was little debate, almost an instruction that she was needed and was to return home as soon as possible. Her mother had been taken ill after a bad fall and hence needed to be cared for. It was a daughter's role to do that, he had pointed out, saying he should not be expected to take time off work to nurse his wife.

His phone call had come the morning after the night before, specifically the morning after the night Antonio had abandoned her on the doorstep, leaving her questioning her whole existence. Her resistance was low and as she was already feeling pretty despondent, all her father's call did was add to her woes.

Whilst she had initially maintained a relationship with her parents after leaving home, it was fair to say it had been strained for some time. The occasional phone call, once or twice a week in those early days, letting them know she was still alive, had now become once or twice a month. That was about as much as it amounted to, and even then, their calls lasted little more than a couple of minutes. They had never supported her decision, or her reasons for leaving, making their feelings of disappointment perfectly clear in the process. As such they had little interest in understanding anything about her new life, her career or what living on the island meant to her. Their views remained steadfast and very traditional - a daughter's role was to marry, produce grandchildren and look after her husband. Equally important, in their view at least, the role extended to looking after her parents in their old age or illness. And as their only daughter, and someone who had clearly failed to do anything with regards the first three, it was surely not too much for them to expect for her to deliver on the last.

Had Isabella been in a better place, she would probably have argued against her father's demands a little more vociferously. She would have cited her career at least and the fact she could not leave her job at such short notice. Leaving her students in the lurch, a matter of weeks before they were due to go to high school, was not at all the type of professional behaviour she prided herself on. She might also have said she couldn't simply leave her apartment, packing up all her worldly possessions and just upping-sticks, especially without giving her landlord due notice. There would be implications for doing that, potentially when she began looking for references for future apartments. There was also her dog, Peca, to consider. What would happen to her? She had a responsibility towards her and couldn't just leave her on the streets. Having rescued her and brought her into her home, to now return her to the dogs' shelter, basically abandoning her once again, through no fault of her own, how would that make either of them feel?

Most importantly, if she had been in a relationship, or had friends to talk to or to advise her, then she would certainly not have jumped so quickly when he'd phoned. She would have weighed up her options in a more considered manner, and discussed with the people around her what she could do; maybe take a sabbatical from work, maybe sub-lease her apartment, maybe fly over for a short visit first, then assess the situation before making a final decision. After all, her mother's condition could be more temporary than her father was making out.

However, without the counsel of the wise, her behaviour had simply been to revert to that of a small child, dutifully doing what a parent requests. She agreed to sort a few things out, look at flights and then return home.

The headmistress, a pious and sensitive woman in her late fifties, had been rung and told that regretfully family circumstances meant she had to hand in her notice, with immediate effect. She apologised for any inconvenience, but hoped she would understand. Her parents needed her and she had no alternative other than to go to them.

Her landlord was then contacted and given notice on the apartment. She had paid until the end of the month anyway, so other than losing a couple of weeks rent it was not the end of the world. And her clothes, most of which were still on the floor from the previous day's dressing-up activity, were simply piled into her suitcase. There were little, if any, other personal effects to worry about.

The only upside was that her neighbour, the kind gentleman who lived across the hall, and who looked after Peca during the daytime when Isabella was at school, agreed to take care of her. He said he was used to their daily walks around the park, so would miss the dog and the company she gave him. Seeing the look on his face, Isabella didn't have the heart to disappoint him, so agreed to him looking after her.

She had then sat and waited a whole week, moping around in the apartment, in the vain hope that something – anything – might change before her flight was scheduled. Had Antonio called, or contacted her in any way, and provided her with the slightest of reasons to stay she would have done so without hesitation. But he hadn't. She had not heard a single word from him, a single text. So as she shut the door on the apartment building she felt like she was shutting the door on her life. Returning home like a dejected and failed warrior, having gone into battle for her independence, and lost miserably. In fact, she had absolutely nothing to show for her time away, or equally nothing on the horizon that remotely looked to offer her any form of hope for her future.

Entering the house, Isabella could hear raised voices coming from the room at the back. Despite the bright sunshine outside, the interior was dark, dingy and cool. There was also an unpleasant smell of food in the air, aromas that made her stomach turn. Her parents appeared to be arguing about something, although their words were not clear, and feeling like she did not want to walk into an argument, she made her presence known.

"Mama, Papa, it's Isabella. I'm home." Their voices quietened instantly.

Her father came out to greet her. "About time, we were expecting you a few days ago. What has kept you? Did you not realise your mama needed you urgently?"

"Well, I am here now, Papa," was the extent of her reply. She had expected at least some warmth in their welcome, some gratitude that she had packed in everything to fly over to be with them. Perhaps she had expected too much. That was starting to be the story of her life.

"Good, well you can sort the remains of the meal out. I have started, under instruction from your mama, but as I'm clearly not doing it right," he replied, looking back sternly towards the kitchen, "I will leave it to you to finish. I will be back later." That probably explained what their argument had been about, thought Isabella to herself, as she saw her mother's reaction, although it did not explain the urgency with which he left the house, without a kiss or any other form of greeting towards his wife or daughter.

Turning towards her mother, Isabella smiled at the older woman. She was seated in a high back chair with her leg in plaster, propped up on an old wooden stool. She looked neither comfortable nor well-cared for, with her hair matted and her clothes unkempt, and she looked to have aged in the months Isabella had been away. Whilst she was still only in her fifties, anyone would have been forgiven for assuming she was approaching her seventies.

"Mama, can I get you anything, or at least make you more comfortable?" she asked, taking her jacket off and moving towards the stove to discover what was producing that awful aroma. "What is that?" she asked, removing the lid to the pan. She was unsure what her father had been trying to make and was at a complete loss to how she was going to recover the situation.

"It's rabbit stew. I think the smell is due to the wrong spice being added, nothing more. Your father is not a patient man and does not take instruction well. Hopefully you will cope better." Isabella was surprised to hear there was a distinct lack of warmth in her mother's voice either. She had expected a warm welcome home from at least one of her parents.

"Perhaps, now you're here you could shower me and wash my hair?" she asked a few moments later, expressing a degree more warmth this time. "I have not been able to do that properly since my accident and your papa has been washing me with a sponge and a bucket of lukewarm water. Also, can you fetch me some clean clothes from the closet upstairs when you take your bags up. Nothing fancy, just a dress and a shawl to put over my shoulders should be sufficient."

"Yes, Mama. And then I will make you a drink and you can tell me what's been happening. Papa simply said you were unwell, without any explanation as to what the problem was, or how it had happened. So I had no idea what to expect, or how bad your illness was. I presume you've broken your leg?" Trying not to feel too disgruntled, Isabella looked down at the plaster cast and wondered if this was the extent of her mother's injuries. For if it was nothing more than a broken bone, with a few weeks rest she should soon be back on her feet, although without knowing anything more she had no idea what the prognosis might be. She was no doctor, yet it didn't appear to be anything terminal, nor look like anything that had required her to be summoned home with such haste, or without explanation.

"Why don't you put the kettle on and get yourself sorted first. We have plenty of time to talk, now that you're home. There are clean sheets in the cupboard, if you want to make your bed up, and perhaps you could do mine at the same time. That way the sheets can all go into the washing machine together. The rest of the laundry is in the bathroom. I'm not sure when it was last done, as I don't think your papa has worked out how to use the washing machine yet," she laughed trying to lighten the atmosphere a little. She was pleased her daughter was home, even if she was reluctant to show it.

As Isabella took her bags upstairs to her childhood bedroom and closed the door softly behind her, she had the distinct impression life was about to get a lot more difficult than she had expected. Coming home was not the homecoming she had imagined, nor was it the peaceful haven she had hoped for, somewhere where she could quietly lick her wounds, again, whilst nursing her mother back to health.

As she stood with her back towards the door, she sensed she was in for a rough ride, and as she regarded the cramped bedroom, devoid of any warmth, with the old single bed tucked up against the window, she suddenly longed for her apartment. It may well have been a hovel, but it had been her hovel and somewhere no one had told her what to do. No one at all.

A couple of hours later and Isabella's mother was washed and dressed, wearing a clean set of clothes, as well as some fresh underwear Isabella had managed to find in her mother's bedroom drawers. The first of several loads of laundry was in the washing machine, with a change of bedding now on her parents' bed, as well as her own single bed. The dinner was cooked, the rabbit stew just about recoverable from the mess her father had left, and a dessert had been baked, nicely chilling in the fridge for later. It was fair to say Isabella had not sat down since she'd arrived and she was starting to feel exhausted. It had been a long day already, and with the flight and the travelling, to say nothing of the general lack of cheer in the house, she was finding it all very draining.

Cooking dinner, though, had been enjoyable, and in truth it was one of the experiences she had missed. Her mother was a good home cook, who had schooled her well. Over the years she had encouraged her to experiment with different foods and ingredients, especially sweets and desserts, which soon turned out to be Isabella's passion. As a consequence, from an early age she became confident around the kitchen and enjoyed the products of her endeavours, perhaps too much.

Whilst on the island, though, her apartment had not been well equipped, with only a basic stove and little by way of utensils or baking aids on offer. That severely limited what dishes she could produce, apart from which, there was no reason to make anything special as no one ever visited. Coupled with the fact there was little fun in eating alone, or the high cost of fresh ingredients, she had cut back considerably on what she ate. The plus side was that some of those extra kilos had finally gone, so not all was lost. Being back home, and back in the kitchen again, though, could prove a real challenge, especially if the way she was feeling at the moment was anything to go by. As she eyed the chocolate dessert again, her desire to comfort-eat the whole plateful didn't seem to want to go away.

The table had been set for dinner for the last thirty minutes or so, her stomach was rumbling and they were still waiting for her father to return. He had left the house shortly after she had arrived home and Isabella had no idea where he had gone, or when he would resurface. When asked, her mother had just said he had errands to do, which now that she was home he could get on with. Her explanation was basic to say the least. In fact, she had barely spoken to Isabella since she had arrived, other than to reel off an endless list of chores, and she had certainly not provided any further details around her accident, or illness, or whatever it was that had caused her leg to be set in plaster. Isabella had probed but remained none the wiser.

"Papa is home," her mother said when she eventually heard the door opening, and seeing a second shadow behind him simply added, without any element of surprise, "you had better set another place for dinner, Isabella. It looks like we have a guest."

Isabella looked around to see Tomás standing behind her father. He was smartly dressed, clean shaven and had recently had a haircut. He was also carrying a bunch of fresh flowers in his hand, with a look of pure remorse on his face.

"Hello, Isabella. It is so lovely to see you again. To see you home at last, where you belong. I have missed you so much, my love," he said, with the broadest of grins on his face as he offered her the flowers. "Here, I have bought these for you."

Isabella was surprised to notice it was almost a replica of the bouquet she had ordered for her wedding, the exact same choice of flowers and mix of colours. All her favourites.

Isabella looked from parent to parent as she accepted the flowers, unsure what else she could do given the circumstances. However, seeing matching smiles on each of their faces, satisfied smiles, the penny finally dropped. Tomás' arrival had obviously been prearranged, her father's errand to round him up and make him presentable, now she had finally returned. She recalled her father's words, questioning why it had taken her so long to come, their plan obviously held in abeyance until her actual return. Two hours to get his hair cut, change his clothes and visit the florist, who was clearly in on the prank too, sounded about right.

Isabella felt duped and more trapped than she had ever felt in her entire life, with the more she thought about it, the more she was left wondering whether her mother's injury was all an act too. Had her accident simply been serendipitous, opening up the possibility of Isabella returning, leaving them all to jump on the bandwagon and devise whatever hairbrained scheme they had concocted?

As she continued to look between them, the penny finally dropped. She could sense the clear expectation that this time she was not getting away so easily. This time the marriage would go ahead, come what may. Her parents had got their daughter home, Tomás had got his fiancée back, and she would soon be married off, this time without incident. Before long she would be producing the grandchildren her parents felt were their right, married to a man, who was the best she could expect under the circumstances.

Leaving everyone to live happily ever after.

Chapter 38

By the end of her first week of being home, Isabella was beginning to tear her hair out. She felt frustrated, being treated almost like a captive in her parents' house. Constantly at the beck and call of her mother, who continued to sit with her leg propped up on the kitchen stool, watching over her as she worked away preparing meals for the family. She had even taken to hobbling around after her on her crutches, following Isabella from room to room, as she attempted to bring some semblance of order back into the house. It had been six weeks since her mother's fall, Isabella had eventually deduced, and in that time the rooms had not seen a duster or a vacuum, and the dust was mounting.

Her rare outings to the markets or to the stores to do the family's shopping, or run whatever errands her mother demanded, were among the few treats Isabella had. She wandered around the city by herself, taking a quiet moment to think about her life and what it had been reduced to. Today was market day, and as she sat in an internet café, enjoying a coffee and a pastry, waiting for her phone to recharge, she pondered what had become of her life.

She was missing school, not just the occupation it gave her, but the pure joy of seeing her pupils' smiles each morning, or the delight on their faces when they achieved something new for the first time. Her mother's scowl could never compete. She was mainly missing her independence, though. That ability to make her own choices and decisions and she worried how easily she had fallen back into the role of dutiful daughter. She was finding her parents' wishes hard to discount, especially as she was living rent-free under their roof. In fact, the more she thought about it, the more she realised she was missing nearly every aspect of her old life, yet was powerless to do anything about it. Her previous attempts to step-out by herself had failed and she had neither the heart nor the wherewithal to attempt that again. That desire felt like it had been beaten out of her for good.

It had become clear, from the discussions that had taken place that first night, what was now in store for her, with her initial suspicions being confirmed almost as soon as they had sat down at the dining table. Her parents were once again pushing for her marriage to Tomás, and Tomás in turn was presenting himself as the contrite man. He was begging for her forgiveness and for him to be given a second chance, promising never to be unfaithful again, his eyes imploring her to believe him.

"We loved each other once, enough to consider getting married," he had stated. "What's stopping us from doing the same again? Isabella, will you agree to marry me, please?" As he asked her parents had simply looked on encouragingly, their plates of rabbit stew going cold before them, barely touched.

Whilst it had not been the most romantic of proposals, or settings, over recent days Isabella had been weighing it up in her mind. Her heart continued to fight against it, whereas her head accepted there was a lot of sense in what he had said. They had been happy once, and Tomás was making a real effort with her this time, courting her as he had in those early days. They had gone out to dinner, just the two of them, and chatted about what had happened. He had openly said how it had made him feel, especially when she had simply left, without waiting for an explanation, or even giving him a chance to apologise. He was desperately trying to rebuild her trust and those feelings she had once had for him, that much was obvious to Isabella.

Tomás was not a bad looking man, in fact he was quite handsome and would be a catch for anyone. So, with the amount of effort he was making, Isabella was struggling not to feel something for him again. It was not love, and certainly not trust – not yet at least, and she was certainly resisting his attempts to lure her back into his bed. But was what she was feeling enough, and with little or no alternative could she afford to discourage him, or be choosy, without at least giving him a chance?

He also had a job and his own apartment, so that if nothing else would give her an opportunity to finally move out of her parents' house and no longer be so dependent on them. Maybe she would even have the chance to find another teaching job, although not at the same school she had left. That would be too much, knowing the gossips would have a field day with her return.

But if his feelings or his remorse were as strong as he suggested, why had he never come looking for her? Why had he never tried to make contact, to apologise or ask her to come back? In all that time she had neither changed her mobile number, nor her email address, and had not fallen off the face of the earth, so if he had wanted to contact her, why had it taken him so long? She was baffled. Valéncia was a beautiful city, and one she had previously thought would be her forever home, so all things considered, would it be so bad to settle for what was being offered?

It was all getting a bit too much for her, Isabella realised, as her thoughts continued to vacillate one way and another. Returning home had clearly been a mistake, something she was becoming increasingly aware of each day.

As she took a final mouthful of coffee, ready to leave and catch her lift home, her mobile rang. She had finally managed to recharge it, after buying a new charging device for it earlier that morning from the market. Her old one had either been lost, or more likely left behind in the old apartment, and as her phone had died the day after she had got back home, with everything else that had been going on, recharging it had been the least of her worries. Who would need to contact her anyway?

"Isabella, finally! I've been trying to get hold of you for days. Your calls have just been ringing out, or going straight to messages. Where are you, or more importantly is everything okay? I've been worried about you."

"Oh, Antonio," she replied, pleasantly surprised to hear his voice. Her stomach did that little somersault that was becoming the norm every time she thought about him. "Yes, everything is fine, thank you. There's no need to worry. I'm at home, in Valéncia. My mother is unwell and I'm looking after her."

"Right, well that explains the suddenness, I suppose. I did wonder what had happened when I couldn't reach you, especially when neither Anya nor Maya knew what had happened," he replied, with a sense of relief. "So, when will your mother be well enough for you to return home? I hope it's nothing too serious."

Taking a deep breath, she thought carefully for a moment, toying with what she should say, or how much she should tell him. What would it matter to him anyway? "I'm not planning on coming back to the island, Antonio. I've handed in my notice at school and given up my apartment. After all, there's nothing for me there. Apart from which, my parents need me here."

The other end of the line went quiet, as Antonio struggled to think what to say next. Her response had hit him sideways, but not as much as when she added, "I'm sorry, I'm going to have to go now. Tomás has just arrived, and he's offered to take me home."

They may not have spoken much about their previous lives or loves, but Antonio had a good idea who Tomás was. What he didn't have any idea about, though, was what he was doing back in Isabella's life, barely a week after she had left Tenerife.

Chapter 39

"Antonio, what on earth's the matter with you?" Sofía enquired, looking over at her brother. "You look like you've just seen a ghost. Has something happened at the suppliers? Is there a problem?"

She had just returned from the kitchen, carrying a tray with a hot drink for each of them and a small sandwich with a bowl of homemade soup. Occasionally they went to the village, or the local town, for a break at lunchtime and a change of scenery. Today, however, they were busy, so had decided to camp out in the office and work through, Lucía offering to make lunch for them. When Sofía had left the office to go to collect the food ten minutes earlier, Antonio had been on the phone to one of their suppliers, checking final arrangements for the last of their deliveries. She really hoped there was not a problem.

"Oh, no, Sofía. Everything's fine at the suppliers. They're still on schedule to deliver everything next Monday as planned. No, it's something else."

His mind wandered as he tried to get his thoughts together, his phone still in his hands as he contemplated phoning Isabella straight back to ask what was going on. What she really doing in Valéncia, and what was Tomás doing with her? He recalled her mentioning his name once, and also mentioning she had once been engaged, but it hadn't worked out – without going into the specifics. Had Tomás been her fiancé or just an ex-boyfriend, he couldn't quite recall – and even so, was it the same guy? Tomás was not an uncommon name.

Then again, what right did he have to question her? It was none of his business what she did, or with whom. Hadn't she made that perfectly clear that night? She was not interested in him, so what was his problem?

Yet, the more he pondered it, the more questions he seemed to have. When she first answered his call, she had sounded happy to hear from him, surprised even. He could tell that from the timbre of her voice, that warm tone that he had come to recognise. By the end of the call, though, her tone had changed and she had sounded distracted, almost eager to end their conversation. They normally had no problem chatting or finding things to talk about, but today it had felt strained, almost like she could find nothing to say to him. There was not even a promise to 'speak later', or 'I'll phone you back' if she really was too busy, or Tomás was waiting impatiently for her. To Antonio something had sounded distinctly odd and as he sat, staring out of the window, fiddling with his phone, completely oblivious to anything else around him, his gut was once again talking to him.

"Well, are you going to tell me what's bothering you, or should I just sit here and keep wondering?" Sofía asked after a few minutes, her interest piqued at what was worrying him. It was clear from his behaviour, and the lines on his forehead, that something was seriously wrong. It was so out of character for him to worry.

"Sorry, what did you say?" Sofía's voice drew him out of his thoughts.

"I said, what's wrong? Something is clearly worrying you and I'd like to know what it is, or if I can help."

Antonio thought for a moment how much he wanted to say. Whilst he and Sofía were close, chatting about their love lives was not top of their list of discussion topics. She had confided in him about Lorenzo, though, so perhaps he did owe her the same level of openness. But what could he say?

"I was just talking to Isabella Rodriguez, you know Maya and Anya's teacher," he began.

"Oh right, I hadn't realised you two were close," Sofía replied, a little surprised. "What were you talking about, because didn't Carmen say she had left the school, quite suddenly I understand?"

"Well, that was the point," he continued. "She and I had been going out occasionally, for the odd meal or drink. I had thought there might be something developing between us. I really liked her and then suddenly she just left, without a word. I was surprised and have been trying to contact her all week, to reassure myself that everything was okay. Her phone has been off, though, and today was the first time I've managed to get through to her."

Sofía had suspected Antonio had been dating somebody, but he had never mentioned anyone's name, and she had certainly never suspected it was her nieces' teacher, assuming it to be a local girl, or someone he had met at one of the suppliers, or even online.

"And, is everything okay? Because from the look on your face, it certainly doesn't appear to be." Sofía was beginning to sense there was more going on here than he was prepared to admit. "Have you had an argument, or something? Are you the reason she left?"

"No!" he replied quickly, surprised by Sofía's line of questioning. "In fact, it was quite the opposite. I kissed her, and that was the last time I saw or heard of her, until today."

"And did she kiss you back?"

"Yes, and no. I sensed there was some reserve, so I left it at that. I wasn't sure what was going on. I really thought we had something between us. Then today there appeared to be an ex-boyfriend on the scene, and it's left me confused, especially as she said she doesn't have any plans on returning."

"Who doesn't have any plans on returning?" Carmen asked, walking into the office mid-conversation and plonking herself down on the only remaining chair, clearly exhausted from her morning's activities.

"Señorita Rodriguez," Antonio said. "I spoke to her earlier this morning and she said she had handed in her notice and wasn't planning on returning to the island at all."

"Hold on, wind back. Why on earth were you talking to Señorita Rodriguez? What am I missing here?" Carmen's eyes moved between them, trying to read the room.

Sofía quickly updated her sister on what Antonio had said, putting her spin on some of the details he had chosen to omit. Acceptedly, she was not as worldly wise as most women on the subject of men, having only very recently come to the conclusion they were worth the effort, well Lorenzo was at least, but she sensed there was more of a game being played here than she first believed.

"I think, Carmen, our brother here is in love, whether he knows it or not. And I think he's at a loss to work out what to do about it, or how to go about contacting Isabella, even if he wanted to. Am I about right, Antonio?"

Antonio remained speechless. Love, was that really what he felt? Was that what his feelings amounted to, or what his gut was telling him? Surely not.

"I think you may have well hit the nail on the head, Sofía," Carmen replied, smiling over at her brother and seeing the bemused look on his face. "Well, I never saw that coming, nor by the looks on your face, did you, Antonio!"

"So that just begs the question, what are you planning on doing about it? Because if you are right, and the ex-boyfriend is back on the scene, your options may be limited. You might have to accept she doesn't feel the same way about you, as you clearly do about her." The more Sofía watched his body language, and the way he was responding to their banter, the more she was convinced her assessment of the situation was correct.

"Oh, he's not going to give up that easily, are you Antonio?" Carmen asked, almost goading her brother into action. She could already see where this was going, even if he couldn't quite get his own head around it.

"Carmen, regardless of what you both think, I'm too busy to just go swanning off, on a fool's errand. Valéncia's a huge city and I've absolutely no idea where she lives. So what do you suggest I do - fly there, then simply pound the streets, searching for her? If she's moved on, as the signs clearly indicate, she's unlikely to give me her address, is she?" Antonio waited, unsure whether he needed them to agree or disagree with his logic, but as neither responded he continued. "Anyway, if I did go, and I did manage to find her, which is a big 'if', what would I say to her? She clearly doesn't feel the same way about me, does she?"

Regardless of what the two women believed, Antonio had a defeatist attitude. He simply sighed and sat back, picked up the remains of his sandwich and continued to stare out of the window.

As he had been talking, the two women had exchanged a glance. Sofía started surfing the net for flights to Valéncia, whilst Carmen busily messaged away on her phone.

After a couple of minutes, Sofía looked up from her computer. "Well, I can get you on a direct flight, first thing in the morning. It departs at ten-fifty and arrives at two-forty five, which is doable. You'd probably need a hotel for the night and a car, which I'll need to look at. Alternatively there's an earlier flight, with a later return. So, that gives you the option to get there and back in the day, if you wanted. It would be a long day, though," Sofía pointed out. "Either way, I'll be here in case anything comes up, which means there's nothing at all stopping you going, is there?"

"And by then, I will have Isabella's address for you. One of the teachers owes me a favour, and he's just said he can get it for me without any problem. He believes she left it with Señora Gómez, the headmistress, with the clear instruction that it could be passed on, if anyone needed to contact her. I can't imagine who she might have thought that could apply to, can you Sofía?" she added mischievously.

"So, that's all sorted then. Which flights shall I book for you?" Sofía asked, enjoying the little game they were playing.

Once again Antonio realised he had been backed into a corner, and this time by both his sisters. It was becoming a habit of theirs, although he was not complaining. The more he thought about it, the more uncomfortable he felt about the way things had been left. At least if he spoke to her in person he would understand for himself how the land lay, not left spending the rest of his life wondering, 'what if?'

"Okay, I give in," he said, putting his hands in the air as a sign of submission. "Why don't you book me on the outbound flight, and book a car and a hotel too, just in case. I can sort out the return leg later. As I've no idea what I'm going to find, I wouldn't want to have to rush back to catch a plane, if she's not at home, or out for whatever reason, would I? At least if I have the evening to spare, I've more chance to catch her at home, and more time to have a proper talk," he suggested, weighing up his game plan. "Oh, and Sofía, can you make sure it's a nice hotel, with a bar, just in case I need somewhere to drown my sorrows when it all goes pear-shaped!"

Chapter 40

Around four o'clock the following afternoon, Isabella was in the kitchen preparing the evening meal. The radio was playing in the background and for once she had the house to herself. She was enjoying the peace and the quiet interlude it was providing, in what had otherwise been a hectic few days. Her mother had taken a taxi earlier that morning to the hospital for an appointment. She was hoping the doctor would agree to her having the plaster cast removed, as it was nearly two months since the accident and everything appeared to be healing well. Her father had accompanied her there, reluctantly sidling into the taxi alongside his wife. He had asked if she would prefer to go, but as Isabella could think of a hundred or more better reasons to stay at home, he had not forced the issue.

All being well, if the cast was removed, or even if her mother was given a support boot to wear, she would become more mobile after the appointment. Which in turn meant Isabella would have more time to herself and more freedom to do what she wanted, without having to be at her mother's beck and call all day long. She loved her mother, there was no doubt about that, she just wasn't too sure she liked her very much. Not at the moment at least, with her constant demands and instructions — always telling her daughter what to do, or what not to do, without giving any consideration to the fact she was a grown woman with a mind of her own.

Although, in terms of what she did want to do, Isabella was not entirely sure. The thought of re-planning her wedding to Tomás, which was clearly at the top of her parents' list, did not fill her with the same level of excitement, especially not the second time around. Her white bridal dress was still hanging in the wardrobe, along with the rose-coloured bridesmaids' dresses, including the one her best friend would have worn, had she not slept with Tomás the week before the wedding. She would certainly not be invited to the rematch, and Isabella did not have the heart to approach anyone else to wear it in her stead.

Sadly, she had not been in contact with any of her previous friends since she had returned home, so in terms of who the guests to the wedding might be, she had little idea. It was one of those events she was trying to put to the back of her mind, and even though she and Tomás were going to see the priest the following morning, to formalise a new date for the wedding, it was not an activity she was looking forward to.

She had barely stopped thinking about the phone conversation with Antonio the previous day, annoyed it had been cut short by Tomás' arrival and his insistence on driving her home with her shopping bags. It was considerate of him, especially as he had taken time out of work to do so, and she was sure he meant well. It was just that it was all getting much more intense than she felt comfortable with. He was trying too hard, and coupled with the fact her parents were clearly backing his endeavours, she was feeling claustrophobic. No one had really given her a proper chance to discuss the wedding, or the events that had led up to it being cancelled the first time around, with everyone simply assuming it would go back to how it was. The last few months were clearly a blip that would easily be forgotten, swept under the carpet, along with Tomás' infidelity, never to be spoken of again.

For Isabella, whilst his betrayal had been hard to bear, with the prospect of returning to his bed an eventuality she was not looking forward to, the rest of her time away was not something she chose to forget so easily. Yet, every time she started to talk about her life on the island, she had barely said more than a few words before one of them changed the subject. It was as if none of them had any interest in her as a person, other than as a wife, a mother, a daughter. They had no appreciation of the life she had led, of her independence in running her own home, or the type of responsibility she had assumed teaching at the school. At one stage, she had mentioned she had owned a dog, and enjoyed walking her, even suggesting she might look to get another dog at some stage. To which her parents had just remarked, "Phhh, dogs are hard work," without even enquiring of the dog's name or breed, or questioning whether she was actually missing her, or who was looking after her now. To them her previous life was immaterial.

Equally, whilst she had been away, no one seemed eager to fill her in on what she had missed. How Tomás had spent his time was a mystery to her. The questions of whether there had been other women, what had happened to her 'friend' and why was he suddenly interested in rekindling their relationship were all left unanswered. To Isabella's mind there must be other women who could easily fill that bill, surely? He was a good-looking man after all. She had tried to ask her mother one day and got a blank response. It was irrelevant, she was home now. The past was in the past, that was all that mattered to anyone.

When Isabella heard the knock at the door, she wondered who it could be. She was just about to put the stove on in order to heat through the meal, as she was expecting her parents to arrive home at any time. They liked to have their dinner at a regular time, so it was all prepared and just needed warming through. They would have no need to knock, though and no one else ever called at the house. Unless it was the priest, Father Vincent, her parents' only other regular visitor. Isabella was certainly not in the mood for him today. She wasn't ready for another lecture on the sanctity of marriage, or more platitudes about how lovely it was to see her home again, with that pitying, almost condescending smile. She had that to look forward to in the morning, and that alone was enough.

The table was already set, and as she had received a message earlier advising that Tomás had kindly offered to pick her parents up from the hospital, so would be joining them for dinner too, there were four places. If the priest was here, she would simply have to set an extra place. Father Vincent knew when meal times were in the house, so if it was him he would have come with an appetite as well as an agenda. Isabella felt she had no choice or say in terms of who came into the house.

Wiping her hands on her stained apron, and checking herself in the mirror, she approached the door, pulling it back slowly towards her. It was an old heavy wooden door that didn't hang too well and regularly got stuck. When it opened, she was surprised to see it was not the priest on the pavement.

"Oh, Antonio. What are you doing here?" she asked, unconsciously stroking her hair as she spoke. It was loosely tied in a scarf and having just seen her reflection in the mirror she was well aware how much of a mess she looked, and how tired, with her heavy eyes and drawn complexion. She was also dressed in an old blouse she had found in the back of her wardrobe and a skirt that hung off her. She was not at all presentable.

Isabella looked up and down the street, checking that none of the neighbours were out, conscious her mother would be anxious if they later reported seeing strangers outside her door. Their house was an old three-storey town house, painted a bright shade of pink, situated on a narrow street, barely wide enough to enable cars to pass, let alone park. Antonio's hire car was parked right outside the front door, creating a potential blockage.

Antonio checked her up and down, with a look of concern in his eyes. "I came to see how you were. I didn't like the way we had left it, the night I dropped you off at your house, and I was also worried when we spoke. Something didn't sound right, so I needed to find out if you were okay. Are you?"

"Yes, I'm fine, thank you. There's no need for your concern."

"Well, may I come in? It would be nice to talk, and to perhaps understand why you left in such a hurry," he persisted.

Isabella felt nervous about inviting him inside, apart from which her parents and Tomás would be home shortly, and what would they think? A strange man in their house.

"There's nothing much to say, Antonio. I left because Mama needed me after her accident," she began, barely able to start to explain her feelings. The fact of him being on her doorstep, having flown over to find her, had left her confused. He obviously cared, yet she was unsure how deep those feelings went.

"But once your mother improves, surely you could come home?" he said, his voice almost pleading with her for the truth.

"Antonio, there is nothing for me to come back to. I no longer have a job, or an apartment. My dog I have had to give away, as I had no friends to leave her with. Above all else, I have no money. On what I earned, I simply couldn't afford to live by myself."

"Isabella, those are all excuses, not reasons," he said, beginning to get a little frustrated with her responses. "You could easily get a better job, another apartment and even reclaim your dog, if you really wanted to." He waited for her reply. "Isabella, is there something, or more importantly someone, other than your parents that's keeping you here?" He needed to know whether Tomás was the real reason for her reluctance.

"No, Antonio, that's not really it. And as much as I loved my time in Tenerife, I just don't have a reason for coming back." She put her head down, partly to hide the tears that were starting to form in her eyes.

Leaning over, Antonio lifted her head and looked deep into her eyes. He could almost feel her sorrow. He took her in his arms and kissed her, as passionately as he felt able to, standing on the doorstep. Without meaning to, Isabella found herself responding, with an equal amount of passion. As they eventually broke apart, Antonio smiled at her and saw her smile reflected back at him.

"Is that reason enough for you to come home?" he asked, feeling a little breathless after their embrace. "And in terms of the rest of your so-called excuses, we'll deal with them together. None of them is going to be a problem, I can assure you. You know, Isabella, we really do need to have a proper conversation," he said reassuringly, almost pleading with her for a positive response.

Before she had time to reply, Isabella saw her parents and Tomás walking up the road. Tomás didn't look at all happy and Isabella wasn't sure whether he was most upset at the fact he had been forced to abandon his car further down the road, given Antonio had parked outside the house, or that the woman he believed he had reclaimed appeared to be in a passionate embrace with another man. Either way, she imagined she had some explaining to do.

"You had better go, Antonio. My parents are home and I will need to talk to them." Seeing the look on her mother's face too, as she marched towards the house, now relieved of her plaster cast, Isabella had a sense of how that discussion would play out. And having Antonio there to witness it would not bode well. "You must go, I will call you later, if that's okay?"

"Yes, if you're sure. I'm staying at the Hotel Vincci Lys tonight, in the city centre. So if you can get away later, why don't you join me there? We can have a drink and a proper talk," he just about managed to say, unsure whether she had heard him fully, or whether he had said the hotel's name correctly. It was one Sofía had booked for him, and not one he was at all familiar with.

"Yes, yes, now go……please," she pleaded, almost pushing him towards his car. "I will phone or try to join you later, I promise."

As Antonio drove off, feeling unsure what else he could do, he glanced back to see her parents and Tomás entering the house. Getting into the car he really did not know what the chances were of her being in touch with him later that evening, or ever again for that matter. At least he had given it his best shot, and if he was a gambling man he would have said his odds were fair to even.

That, however, was before he had seen Tomás. Driving off, dejected, Antonio realised he could never compete with those looks, or that physique.

Chapter 41

The following afternoon, Antonio had checked out of the hotel, driven to the airport and boarded the flight home. The hotel had been luxurious and he needed to remember to thank Sofía for her selection. The bar was well-stocked, the restaurant was of a high standard and they had even allowed him a late check out, given the flight he had managed to book onto was not departing until later that evening. Overall, it had been a very pleasant stay, and there had even been the chance for a short stroll around the city before leaving. Valéncia was a city he had never visited before, and unsure whether he would ever return, decided it would be worth seeing the sights whilst he was still here. It had not disappointed.

The flight was delayed, meaning the aircraft would not touch down into Tenerife South airport until after ten o'clock, and with the drive home he would be lucky if he saw his bed before midnight. With all that had been happening, as the pilot prepared for final take off and the cabin crew completed the safety briefing, he began to feel drowsy. It had been an eventful time and as he relaxed into his seat, he reflected on the past forty-eight hours.

One minute he was busily finalising all the details for the cookery school, sitting at his desk and anxiously worrying about getting everything right, in the clear knowledge the clock was ticking before the grand opening in June. It was now only a matter of weeks away and was beginning to feel real.

The next minute he was throwing caution to the wind and boarding an aircraft, in search of a woman; a woman to whom he sensed a connection, without being able to fully articulate what that connection meant to him. His gut feelings were the best he could go by, and that had usually been enough, yet this time it had taken his sisters' intervention to urge him into action.

Why was it that in matters of business he was so clear thinking, so determined and sure of himself that he never thought to question his decisions? He was confident and successful, with whatever he touched turning to gold, understanding that the devil was in the detail and nothing should be left to chance. The restaurants in London, even without his day- to-day involvement, were thriving. The business model he had established long ago was proven to work, and the team he had built around him, with Philippe at its helm, was trusted to deliver on his vision. The end results were rewarding, emotionally as well as financially, and for that Antonio was grateful.

He was certain the cookery school would equally be as successful, having worried the details of that so much it was unlikely to be anything other. He had poured his heart and soul into its planning, and felt assured the execution would be just as smooth-running as the restaurants themselves. There would be the inevitable niggles when it got started, of that he was certain, yet with the team around him largely consisting of his family, there was that added impetus to make it a success.

Even now, weeks before it had even opened, he only needed to look around at his family to see the positive effects it was having on them. Sofía was positively blooming, although that might not just be down to the development, he suspected. Her new man, Lorenzo, obviously had a lot to answer for in that regard. Carmen too had developed new skills and was an entirely different woman these days, without the shackles of Juan around her. She was finally living a life she was proud of, and had gained so much as a consequence, emotionally as well as physically. Her previous temper and frequent bad moods were a distant memory, with the sense of humour and fun that had taken their place making her a joy to be around. He wouldn't be surprised if that teacher who owed her a favour might be the same one who had given her the recent twinkle in her eye. In fact, he was enjoying the company of both his adult sisters, realising how much he had missed out on getting to know them growing up.

In terms of Lucía and Theresa, well it was fair to say they were both now living the good life. Lucía was excited about the future and ready to move on with her life. She would never forget Mateo, and would probably never look to love again, but she now had something positive in her life, a reason to live, without any of the financial pressures she had previously experienced. It had lifted a huge weight off her shoulders, and that in turn had taken years off her. That and the new wardrobe Theresa had insisted she invest in, making her look like the beautiful woman she truly was.

Theresa. What on earth could he say about her? His yaya one moment, his mother the next, and whilst he was still getting his mind around that, he could not fail to recognise she was perhaps the one person who'd had the greatest influence on his adult life. He loved her more than he could say, acknowledging that without her he would be nowhere. So, having her beside him as he returned to Tenerife had been the icing on the cake. The idea of her subsequently returning to London, without him, was something thankfully she had soon closed down, knowing her life was destined to be lived out among her family.

Theresa had provided him with so much. His opportunities for a new life in England, as well as the expensive education she had enabled, would simply have remained pipe dreams if it hadn't been for her intervention. Things his parents could never have contemplated, nor afforded. Whilst her motives had now understandably become questionable, at least she'd had the bravery to enact them. And without moving to England, he would never have met Duncan, or received the surprise inheritance following his death. He would not be the rich man he was today, able to enjoy his life and follow his passions. So much he owed to Duncan. His British father figure, his business role model, his number one supporter, and above all the man who had believed in his dreams of becoming a chef, investing in him wholeheartedly.

He had so much to be grateful for and so many good reasons for returning home. As he accepted his coffee from the stewardess, he looked around at the other passengers, struggling to hide the smug feelings he felt.

"And what about you, madam. Would you like a drink too?"

"How about a glass of wine, Isabella?" he asked, taking her hand. "I know I have to drive at the other end, but you don't. In fact, why not order a bottle of champagne," he laughed.

"No, thank you, but a coffee would be lovely," she replied to the stewardess, smiling sweetly over at Antonio. "I'm feeling tired too, and even though I'm not driving I do need to keep a clear head for tomorrow. Apart from which, I think we had enough champagne last night, don't you?" she added, laughing.

Antonio had checked into his hotel, feeling quite dejected after his visit to see Isabella. He had hoped his kiss would win her over, at least earn him an explanation as to why she had left. He couldn't read the signs at all, though. He knew he felt a connection and sensed she did too, yet Tomás loomed as a huge obstacle between them.

Antonio had witnessed the proprietorial look in his eyes, the way he'd marched up to Isabella and led her into the house, without question, simply leaving her parents to stare at his car as it slowly drove into the distance. He had feared for her, yet at the same time feared there was nothing else he could do. The gods would decide his fate, and for once his gut had failed him.

So, when the reception desk had rung, less than two hours later, advising he had a visitor waiting for him in the lobby, he had been nervous. He feared her parents or Tomás had come to send him packing, and not wanting to have that debate in the lobby asked if the visitor could be shown up. And when Isabella had knocked on his bedroom door, he had been both surprised and delighted. It was clear she had been crying, and equally clear she had left in a hurry as she was still wearing the same clothes he had seen her in earlier. However, there was a smile on her face and a look in her eyes that made him realise she was happy to see him. With the bags she had by her feet, the same ones he had seen her load into a taxi a few weeks earlier, there was enough evidence to suggest she was considering coming home with him.

"Were you sure about what you said earlier? If I came back to Tenerife with you, that you would help me get my life back together?" she had asked, nervously standing in the doorway.

"I'm more sure about that than anything else I have ever said in my life," he'd replied, taking her bags from her and leading her into the room, closing the door behind them. Feeling emboldened, he had then taken her hands. "I think I've fallen in love with you, Isabella, and I couldn't imagine my life without you. It's been torture these last few hours, imagining you with Tomás, believing I couldn't compete with him, and thinking I'd lost you for good this time."

Looking into his eyes Isabella had seen his sincerity, along with the pain he had so obviously been feeling.

"I started to fall in love with you weeks ago, Antonio," she'd sobbed between her smiles. "Perhaps even as early as that first day in the playground, when I believed you were trying to abscond with the girls," she'd laughed, embarrassed by her admission. "I just didn't want to believe it, sensing there was no way you could ever feel the same way about me. Not until you turned up earlier today, that was. That, and your kiss, gave me reason to hope."

He'd smiled. "I did sense you felt something, but I also felt you were holding back a little. Then, when I believed Tomás was back on the scene, I guess I assumed he was the reason behind your reluctance. You hadn't got over him, and wasn't ready to leap into bed for some meaningless night with me. So, I gave you space, then concluded you'd come home to be with him. In my mind your mother was just your excuse. When I saw him earlier today, with his muscles and his obvious good looks, I guess I finally convinced myself you hadn't had feelings for me after all. I accepted there was no way I could compete for your affections."

"We've been doing a lot of guessing and assuming between us, haven't we?" she'd laughed, for the first time starting to relax. "Perhaps it's time for us to stop trying to second-guess each other and for us to have that proper talk you mentioned earlier. Because I for one am still trying to make sense of what's been happening these last few hours. Not least of all where I'm going to sleep tonight, let alone do with the rest of my life."

"Why don't we have that talk later? I have something better in mind," he'd suggested, leading her towards the super king-sized bed that was in his room, grateful once again that Sofía had opted to upgrade his booking. "And in terms of the rest of your worries, I assure you we will work something out."

Now as the plane headed towards Tenerife, all Antonio could think about was if his family would ever be able to love Isabella anywhere near as much as he already did, as well as accept her and recognise the important part she would be playing in his life from this day forward. Because without wanting to pre-empt the future too much, that was important to him. He knew from the very early days, even before their marriage, they had never warmed to Charlotte on any level. That much had been obvious. In turn she had never been enamoured by them either; a fact that had made for a conflicted family dynamic. One that had on too many occasions torn Antonio in two.

He no longer wanted to live that way, no longer wanted to feel he was on a battleground, or forced to act as a referee between his loved ones. No, he needed everyone to get on together. Love second time around had to be different, it had to provide him with the harmony he sought in his life. That wasn't too much to ask for, was it?

Although, looking at Isabella, the beautiful woman sitting beside him, who could fail to love her? She had already won over his nieces and his sisters, so Lucía and Theresa should be a walk in the park. He was worrying unnecessarily, reassuring himself he was indeed a lucky man. What more could he ask for? The love of a good woman, the love of his family all around him and the beginnings of a new and exciting business venture ahead of him; a venture in which they could all play their parts. There was absolutely nothing else he needed in his life.

Chapter 42

Two months later and it was the end of June, the last day of the school term had finally arrived. The day Maya, Anya and all their classmates left primary school, all eager to join high school when school resumed in the autumn.

When the end-of-day bell rang, enabling the children to run out to the playground to greet their parents, there was a mix of feelings among staff, parents and pupils alike. Relief, mainly from the teachers, that they had made it to the end of the term without any real incidents. Excitement, from the children, that the long summer holidays were ahead of them, with all that entailed. All mixed with a tinge of sadness and trepidation from the majority of parents. For them it was the end of an era. The next phase of their children's lives was about to begin. The stage that would see them develop greater independence, as they entered those difficult teenage years, before steadily growing into the adults they would become, unsure what their futures would bring.

It was the time of year Isabella found most difficult too. Having to let go of the children she had nurtured. Whilst she had done her best to prepare them for the changes that lay ahead, she still hoped she had not let them down, or even short-changed them in terms of equipping them with the skills they would need for their journey. This year especially, with all the changes and distractions in her own life, she was more worried than most. Had she taken her eye off the ball, been distracted?

Señora Gómez, the headmistress, approached her. "Señorita Rodriguez, you should be very proud of this year's crop of youngsters. You have done an amazing job with them. You really are an exceptional teacher. I can't tell you how grateful we all are that you came back to us." She smiled over at the young woman. "When you left, I felt your sorrow and prayed for you. I prayed to St Jude that God would return you to us, and my prayers thankfully were answered."

"Thank you, Señora, that is very kind of you to say," replied Isabella, feeling herself blush at the compliment. "It was kind of you to take me back, especially after I'd left at such short notice. When I left, I had no expectation I would ever return to the island, or else I would have perhaps asked you for a short period of leave."

"Yes, sometimes life has surprises in store for us all, doesn't it?" she added wisely, patting Isabella's arm as she walked off to bid goodbye to another parent. She had heard rumours around the staffroom of the reasons for Isabella's departure, and for her subsequent return, but as it was not something that had been discussed with her directly, she chose not to say too much. She was just happy to see the young woman looking so well and contented, almost glowing.

The Return

"Yes, life certainly is full of surprises," Isabella replied, quietly to herself. The last couple of months had been full of revelations, and quite frankly she could not quite believe her luck – or how close she had come to losing everything.

Had Antonio not arrived that day, unexpectedly turning up on her parents' doorstep, she would have gone to see Father Vincent the following morning and rearranged her wedding to Tomás. There would have been no alternative, given the pressure she had felt under to settle for what was in front of her. "He's the best you can expect," her mother had been quick to point out. By now she would be unhappily married to a man, good looking as he was, who she neither trusted nor loved, and most likely pregnant, with a life of servitude mapped out ahead of her.

Antonio's arrival and his kiss had made her see sense. It was a real lightbulb moment, one that made her seriously think about what she wanted from her life.

To a large extent, Tomás was a known commodity, someone she knew in her heart she would be settling for. She had loved him once, and possibly could grow to love him again, although she doubted that. In their early days, sex had been a large part of their relationship, yet her rose-tinted glasses had long since been removed on that score. She feared he would always have a roaming eye, and in the long run, even given his reassurances, she would never be enough for him, or him for her either, for that matter.

Then again, in terms of Antonio, what had she really known about him? They had spent only a handful of hours together, barely amounting to a couple of days if it was all added up. A few hours in a café, an afternoon on the beach, a discussion at the takeaway and a day out touring the island. They had never been intimate, in fact other than exchanging a couple of kisses, that was as far as anything physical had progressed between them.

There was also a lot about him she hadn't known, not least of all what he really did for a living. "I'm a chef, someone who loves to cook," was as much as he had said, but what did that really amount to? Could anyone call themselves a chef, just because they liked cooking? She doubted that. And where did he live? A penthouse apartment, near to her own was all she knew. She had never visited, let alone was even aware of his address. It could be a hovel, something like her own. At least Tomás' apartment was clean and relatively well furnished.

Yet, regardless of all that, with Antonio that feeling of trust was already there, and coupled with feelings of love she was struggling to deny, she believed he offered her a much better alternative. She would certainly be taking a leap of faith, as would he, because in reality what did Antonio know about her either? Other than chatting, their conversations had never gone very deep.

However, weighing it all up, it was a risk Isabella felt willing to take, and if it did not work out, what had she lost? She would have avoided a loveless marriage and a life similar to the one her mother had led, so that by itself was worth the risk. Moreover, at twenty-nine, she was too young to settle. Too young to give up on her search for love, or the independence she so desperately craved.

Over dinner her parents and Tomás had been furious, arguing she was a silly child who didn't know her own mind. They demanded she simply forget about 'that man' and get her head around her wedding, her father telling Tomás it should now be arranged as a matter of urgency. There was no talking to any of them, and certainly no adult discussion, just a one-way dictate that left Isabella physically and mentally exhausted. To placate them, she simply agreed, knowing at least that would put an end to the discussion.

When Tomás had left, reassured everything was settled, she had gone upstairs and packed her bags, before bringing them downstairs. She walked into the kitchen and told her parents she was leaving. Having thought they had convinced her otherwise, they tried to stop her, immediately phoning Tomás to come round. Yet Isabella had finally found the strength within her to defy them and had simply left. If she never returned, or never saw her parents again, then that was a price she was prepared to pay.

So then to receive the welcome she had from Antonio was beyond belief. On the metro over to his hotel she had questioned whether she was being too impetuous. Whilst he had suggested she come over to talk, he would not expect her to arrive and dump all her woes and worldly possessions on his doorstep. Her plan had all the hallmarks of backfiring on her, leaving her with little option, other than to return home with her tail between her legs, once they had spoken. That was something she was unprepared to do, regardless of the reception she received.

As he had led her to his bed, before making the most gentle love to her that she had ever experienced, Isabella instinctively knew it had been the right call. A risk well and truly worth taking.

Then, arriving back into Tenerife, tired and still a little apprehensive about what awaited her, to finally see his apartment and realise that would become her home was truly amazing. Followed by an introduction to his family and the opportunity to learn more about his life, his background. They had all been so welcoming, so warm towards her - not at all like her own parents, who had cut off any communication with her since she had left. A brief message letting her know how embarrassed her actions had made them feel was all she had received in reply to her message to let them know she was safe and well. No suggestion of needing to contact them again.

The biggest surprise had been to eventually understand Antonio's businesses and what being a chef really meant to him. London was somewhere she had dreamt of going one day, so to learn he not only had a home there, but several award-winning restaurants left her dumbstruck, to say nothing about the concept behind the cookery school, which she fully bought into and wanted to play a part in. She had told

Antonio about her own passions in the kitchen, so was eager to see if there was a role she could take on, and having toured the school itself and the accommodation facilities, it did nothing to dampen her excitement.

Great wealth or material possessions had never been high on Isabella's wish list. All she had ever wanted was to be loved and to feel secure in a relationship she could trust. And she had certainly never gone out to trap Antonio, based on his wealth, but to understand it need never be a worry for her again was beyond her wildest dreams.

Humble beginnings he may have had, yet with his humility still intact, he had made a success of his life. Together they could have a good life, she was certain of that.

"Isabella, hi. Are you ready for tomorrow?" Carmen asked, bringing her out of her reverie.

"Oh hello, Carmen. Sorry I was miles away," she admitted. "Yes, I'm looking forward to it. In fact, I'm going home shortly to get myself ready. Apparently Philippe, who I believe is Antonio's friend and business partner, is flying in from London this evening, ahead of the opening tomorrow. We're going out to dinner, to that new Italian restaurant in town. I can't wait to meet him, can you? He sounds like a real character, although I am a little nervous about the rest of the event. I hope it all goes well for Antonio, well for all of you, really. You've certainly put your lives into it these last few months, I understand."

"Yes, it will be amazing – as is everything my brother touches, you included," she added cheekily, smiling over at Isabella. "He's become a different man since he met you, and we're all so pleased about that. You're certainly an upgrade on his previous model, I might add," she laughed. "Right, come on now Maya, Anya, time for home. You'll both see Isabella later."

"'Bye, Carmen, girls. See you later," she replied, waving to them as they left the playground. Considering her last comment, and having seen the occasional photo of Charlotte, Isabella doubted, on pure looks alone, whether most people would agree with Carmen's comment. Charlotte was truly stunning, with her blonde good looks and her model figure. A true English rose, some would say. Although, having spoken at length to Antonio about his ex-wife, looks apart, she knew they were like chalk and cheese on so many levels.

So, yes, she tended to agree with Carmen. In fact, she'd even go as far as to admit they had both traded up this time around, compared to their previous relationships.

Thankfully now Tomás and Charlotte were distant memories, and that was something they all appeared happy with.

Chapter 43

The morning of the cookery school's opening eventually arrived, and with it the first of the speciality events, where a series of VIPs had been invited to come along and sample what was being offered. People who would enjoy the experience, whilst hopefully act as influencers - spreading the good word in terms of attracting fee paying clients – once they returned home, or began uploading photos, or whatever they did to connect with their many followers. Sofía had spent a lot of time convincing Antonio of the importance of social media, and as a consequence their marketing campaign had been developed accordingly.

Their guests would begin arriving mid-afternoon, with taxis already organised to meet and greet from the airport. There was then a launch event planned for early that evening, followed by a special dinner, with a menu that had been designed to showcase some of the best of the local cuisine, as well as a selection of the finest wines.

The course proper would then begin the following morning and run for three days, and as all twelve VIPs had opted to stay on site it would be a real test of the facilities, as well as the course content itself. The programme provided for a two-week interval before the next course would run, which allowed for minor tweaks if necessary, but as so much thought had gone into the overall planning it was hoped these would be kept at a minimum.

A group of local men and women had been employed to come in on a daily basis to clean the bedrooms and generally help with the operational side, as well as cooks and waiting staff. As meals would be provided as part of the course, a vast amount of food would need to be prepared on site, with a host of local suppliers engaged to support with deliveries of their produce, including the wine merchant Antonio had spoken to. Clients would be offered a well-stocked bar to enjoy in the evening, as they sat on the terrace taking in the vistas or watching the sun going down, discussing their days. The finca's grounds had been transformed and looked truly stunning, with the terrace furnished to make a relaxing and inviting space, with a traditional fire pit taking centre stage for those cooler evenings.

Tonight, though, the VIP clients would be joined by a handful of invited guests, including some local dignitaries who would talk about the area and what the business would bring to it. Sofía and Carmen between them had been working hard to cajole local interest and had a few noteworthy speakers lined up.

Philippe had also kindly offered to run one of the seminars, in addition to proposing the toast at the formal dinner. He was fully behind what Antonio and his family were doing and wanted to offer whatever support he could. It was his first time on the island, so as well as reconnecting with Antonio, he was anxious to immerse himself in whatever the island had to offer during the limited time he had available. It was the first time he had taken a holiday for a long time, so had tagged on a couple of days for some well-deserved R&R.

"Well, my friend, you have certainly achieved a massive amount these last few months, and you should be truly proud of yourself," Philippe said, having just received the grand tour from Antonio. "I have to admit, I did have some doubts initially, questioning whether you could pull it off. It looks like I was wrong. You have worked so hard and I wish you nothing but good fortune with it."

"Thank you, Philippe, coming from you that means a lot. I am very proud, though, it's clearly been a team effort. I couldn't have done any of this without my family. Whilst the idea might have come from me, the hard work and enthusiasm definitely came from them. And, at the end of the day, it's Lucía's money that's provided for everything. Without her inheritance, we would never have had the wherewithal to do it. So, it's a family investment, one that will hopefully be good for them all, as well as the community, with the benefits it will bring to the local economy."

"Yes, I can see that," he nodded sagely. "I think it's been good for you too, my friend. You were not in a good place before, if you don't mind me saying. I know how hard you took everything, not just the loss of your father, but also Charlotte and the divorce. Now you have the world at your feet, and you seem happy again. Especially with Isabella, who, I have to admit, I found quite charming yesterday evening. Coming back here was certainly what you needed. I suppose the question now is, will you stay, or will you ever return to England?"

Before Antonio had time to reply, Isabella approached, with Peca lolloping closely by her side. As soon as she saw Antonio, Peca bounded up to him, ready to be showered with attention.

"Ah, who's this beauty?" Philippe asked, bending down to stroke the dog too, noting her interesting markings, a plethora of small dots all down her back and around her nose. He tried to think what it reminded him of.

"Oh, she's Peca, Isabella's dog," Antonio replied, bending down to scratch behind her ears. "She spends most of her time at the finca now, and does a great job catching the odd rat, or other small vermin around the farm. I found it was easier bringing her with me, and much better than leaving her in the apartment all day when Isabella is at school. She loves it."

"Yes, I can see that. What interesting markings she has. It's almost as if she's covered in freckles," Philippe continued, clearly taken with the dog.

"That's where her name comes from. I believe *Peca* roughly translates to freckles, in English," Isabella offered. "When I initially collected her from the dogs' home as a puppy, she was called Bella, almost the same as me. That would have been too confusing, so

I chose to rename her Peca, because of her markings." Her whole face lit up as she spoke.

Philippe watched Antonio as he listened to Isabella speak. It was almost as if his friend was mesmerised by her, and having met Isabella the previous evening he could easily see why. She was a beautifully natured young woman, with none of the airs and graces of Antonio's ex-wife, Charlotte. There was just a simple natural beauty, wrapped in a very attractive package - a very curvaceous figure. Like Antonio, Philippe liked his women to be proper women, with meat on their bones, and detested this fad towards dieting, in which so many women of today engaged. It was becoming a nightmare, particularly in the restaurant industry, keeping abreast of all these food trends and so-called allergies that were in danger of becoming the fashion.

To Philippe it was clear his friend had landed well and truly on his feet with his latest love, and he wondered how serious it actually was between them. He knew it was very much early days, and understood both were recovering from previous relationships. Antonio had told him that neither of them wanted to jump in too quickly, given they had both been hurt before. However, judging from what he had witnessed first-hand, as well as what Antonio had spoken to him about earlier, there was already a level of connection and intimacy that suggested neither saw it as a short-term arrangement, or equally were holding back.

This worried Philippe, who was still keen to get Antonio back to England, and back to running the restaurants again, for as much as he enjoyed the cut and thrust of being his own boss, and appreciated the opportunity it had given him, it was not where he saw his life in the longer term. He wanted to settle down too, and to find someone to share his life with, something that was difficult enough, let alone in the industry in which they worked. That much at least he could see for himself, not only from his friend's own experiences, but the fact his own love life had been barren for some time. Now in his mid-forties, and with nothing on the horizon, Philippe was starting to worry that doors were closing for him.

No, there was a discussion they needed to have, decisions that needed to be taken about the direction the restaurants should take, and whilst today was not the day for those discussions, it was clear these couldn't be put off indefinitely.

Yet, the more he saw of the set-up Antonio had made for himself on the island, and especially the people and family he had wrapped around him, particularly the woman to whom he was currently locked in an embrace, the more Philippe questioned, rather enviously he had to acknowledge, whether Antonio would ever return to England.

Then again, who would judge him if he stayed, as what did he really have to come back for? Businesses and property, surely - both of which made him a substantial income, but neither was currently demanding of his time, nor his presence, and they could easily be managed, or simply sold off if it came to that.

Otherwise, all he needed to make him happy, emotionally at least, appeared to be all around him. Would that be enough for Antonio, Philippe was curious to know. At the same time, he realised longingly, should the shoe be on the other foot, it would be a very easy question for him to answer.

"Theresa has sent me to ask you both to come over to the house. Lucía says lunch is ready, and she wants us all to eat now, so that we can get cleared away before the first guests start to arrive," Isabella implored. "Everyone is so excited, especially the girls, who are both desperate to get their dresses on. They see it all as one big party and don't understand what all the fuss is about. In fact, it's getting quite tense inside, which wasn't helped when Rosa turned up around an hour ago and began trying to organise the waiters and waitresses. They were attempting to do the final set-up for the dinner tonight, and Carmen had already given them their instructions, before Rosa apparently started directing them otherwise. She's desperate to be a part of it all.

"It's quite funny watching Carmen trying to bite her tongue. I think Sofía's the only one at the moment who's maintaining her calm, although once Lorenzo arrives, she's bound to start panicking too, or at least get herself flustered, I'd imagine. Hence why I felt like I needed to come out for some air," she laughed, taking Antonio's hand and leading him back to the kitchen, with Peca still by his side, leaving Philippe to follow in their wake.

"Oh dear, I'm not sure we want to go in, do we Philippe?" Antonio laughed, turning to his friend, "we might be safer eating outside. It sounds to me like there may already be an overload of female hormones inside, perhaps more than we can deal with today."

Philippe wasn't too sure. He quite liked the idea of watching Carmen getting excitable. He had met her the previous evening, along with some of the rest of the family, and had found something very appealing about her, something extremely sexy. She was a very attractive woman, a few years older perhaps than Isabella, but with a much more worldly experience about her, and a mischievous glint in her eyes. He was hoping to get to know her a little better over the coming days, and had even suggested to Antonio that if the chair next to her at dinner was free this evening, that is where he would like to be seated. Antonio had raised a knowing eyebrow, and simply said to leave it with him. Whilst the idea of Philippe and Carmen getting it together was something that amused him, if it gave either of them pleasure, then who was he to judge?

Life was too short to not take your happiness where you can. If nothing else, these last couple of years had taught Antonio that. What value is there in holding on to people or things that don't make you happy, when you can align yourself to those who do? He had learned that the hard way, recalling walking out of his house in London, with barely a second glance for the woman he had once loved, and choosing to take nothing material with him, other than his chef's knives. At the time he had thought little about his choice, simply packed his knives up carefully and boxed them away for a later date.

Now they were at use again, in a place where he was discovering more about happiness than he had ever imagined possible; back among his family and the people he loved. And even though Lucía, Theresa, Carmen and Sofía, now with the addition of Isabella, to say nothing of his nieces, Anya and Maya, ganged up against him, almost on a daily basis, he wouldn't want it any other way. At least with the recent addition of Lorenzo to their numbers, things were starting to rebalance in a small way, so he had to be thankful for small mercies. Those family bonds were simply incredible, and the strength of them was the real testament to how they had all pulled together during some very difficult and testing times.

"I don't know, Antonio," Philippe said, willingly following behind the two of them. "I think we should go inside and see what delights the women have in store for us, and as I don't believe there's anything left for you to do, other than wait around for the cars to start arriving, we might as well eat. In my mind, what better way to spend an afternoon, than eating and drinking in the sunshine?"

Philippe watched as Isabella and Antonio exchanged a knowing glance, one that suggested they could both think of a much better alternative for whiling away their afternoons, if only they didn't have a cookery school to launch. Perhaps that would have to wait, until they were at home together, just the two of them – well, apart from Peca. Their little family of three.

Philippe pondered to himself as he followed them inside, a wry smile on his face as they headed towards the kitchen. He was pleased to see that for now this lifestyle appeared to be more than enough for his friend, although, seeing the glint in Isabella's eyes, and noting the way she had gently rubbed her stomach as she had stood speaking to them, and the way she had passed on the wine the previous evening, it suggested it was unlikely to be just the three of them for too much longer.

Philippe was wise enough to realise that any chances he might have had of tempting his friend to return to England were diminishing right in front of his eyes. Yet, as sad as that made him feel, as he looked around and allowed himself to absorb the feelings of love, there was certainly no way he would question that decision.

It was clear, the beautiful island of Tenerife had certainly worked its magic on Antonio, and with that, and the love he had found for Isabella, his spirits had been well and truly healed. All Philippe could do now, as he accepted the selection of tapas dishes Carmen offered to him, with a mischievous smile on her face, was pray that a touch of that same magic would rub off on him.

The End

Review

If you have enjoyed The Return, I would love it if you could leave a positive review on Amazon, and perhaps recommend it to your family and friends.

And, if you haven't yet discovered any of my other novels, please check these out at Amazon.com or Amazon.co.uk

Thank you, Angela

Printed in Great Britain
by Amazon

61483241R00221